Also by Kat Meads

The Invented Life of Kitty Duncan
Little Pockets of Alarm
Not Waving (Livingston Press)
Senestre on Vacation (as Z.K. Burrus, Livingston Press)
Sleep (Livingston Press)
When the Dust Finally Settles

FOR YOU, MADAM LENIN

Kat Meads

Livingston Press
The University of West Alabama

isbn 13: 978-1-60489-099-0 library binding
isbn 13: 978-1-60489-100-3 trade paper
Library of Congress Control Number 2012938185
Printed on acid-free paper
Printed in the United States of America by
Publishers Graphics

Hardcover binding by: Heckman Bindery
Typesetting and page layout: Joe Taylor
Cover photo: Nadezhda Konstantinovna Krupskaya in 1919
(David King Collection). Used by permission.

For E. Willis Brooks

first edition

6 5 4 3 3 2 1

FOR YOU,

MADAM

LENIN

All art is propaganda (but) not all propaganda is art.
—George Orwell

The Gossip in Russia

It was said that Yelizaveta Vasilevna Krupskaya thought her daughter, Nadya, unmarriageable.

It was said that Fanya Kaplan dreamed primarily of hawks and monkfish.

It was said that Inessa Armand believed behind every man there would always be another, and another.

It was said that Maria Ilyinichna Ulyanova was the first to call her brother's wife "fish," a description further refined to "herring" by elder sister Anna—neither the original remark nor its refinement intended as compliment.

It was said that even before her eyes popped, her stomach pooched, her rear broadened, her ankles swelled, her hair grayed and her chin doubled, Comrade Fish was no fan of mirrors.

It was said that, introduced to her prospective son-in-law, Yelizaveta Vasilevna asked whether the future Bolshevik leader was a better conspirator than his brother, the captured, hanged Alexander.

It was said that the man questioned screwed up his eyes, cocked his head and sized up his inquisitor before answering: "Indubitably."

It was said that Yelizaveta Vasilevna had her doubts about that brag—then, later, doubts on a more or less continuous basis.

Those were the rumors. Now: the fiction.

IN POLAND
AND PITER

Forecasts

When the tsar's government ordered us from Poland in the spring of 1874, my daughter, Nadezhda Konstantinovna Krupskaya, was forced to leave behind her dog.

A mongrel dog with a limp and copious fleas.

Did such defects and disadvantages lessen my Nadya's love for the beast?

Not in the slightest. Very likely such misfortunes made my daughter cherish her pet all the more. When the two were together, it was my Nadya, not the animal, who served as protector, my Nadya who chased away his enemies, who carried him and his injured paw across river stones, who would not consent to eat until her dog had been fed.

Nadya was five years old when we left Poland to return to Piter. A sturdy, healthy, curious, joyous child of five with dark red hair that escaped her braids no matter how tightly I plaited, her chubby knees accustomed to the joys of dirt and grass.

Five is an impressionable age.

To break the news of our leaving, her father, my husband, Konstantin, led her beyond the verandah of our home into the wilder profusions of that Polish spring. From the window, I watched them settle side by side on a yard bench. Greenery twined above them. Branches of blooms crisscrossed behind their backs.

I could not hear their conversation; I could only chart its effects. With his arm around her shoulders, Konstantin spoke. Thrilled by her father's undivided attention, Nadya looked up with eager pleasure. And then, from one heartbeat to the next, pleasure turned to grief. Tears streaming, she ran toward the corner bushes and stopped, back to us, body heaving.

I stepped out onto the porch, but Konstantin motioned for me to remain where I was.

He would attempt the consolation of our daughter.

Consolation?

There would be none of that for any of us, either in our last weeks in Poland or in Piter, where the defamation of my Konstantin's character would accelerate.

Beside the bushes and Nadya, Konstantin once again began to speak. Briefly, briefly, she turned an anguished face toward him, then away. She had been beating her fists against her thighs in protest. That now ceased.

Again I started in their direction; again Konstantin discouraged me. A moment later Nadya wiped her nose on the sleeve of her dress. And then, with the gravity of a seasoned mourner, our daughter squared her shoulders.

Nonsense! you will say. A child of five? Squaring her shoulders? Romantic revisionism!

Do you imagine it pleases me to report the squaring? The necessity of it? To admit my powerlessness in preventing the wrenching that occasioned that squaring?

Konstantin kissed the top of Nadya's head and left her. The dog approached, ears quivering.

"What did you tell her? How did you explain it?"

"I said that a Polish dog that had enjoyed the run of a yard would not be happy in an apartment in Piter. I said that she must think of the dog and the dog's happiness before her own."

In the yard, our child had planted her cheek against what she must abandon. She chewed her lip but there were no more tears.

"May the tsar and his generals dream of vultures! May they toss and turn and cry for mercy in their sleep!"

"Yelizaveta! Your tongue!"

Perhaps you believe that losing a dog is of little consequence in a world of war and slaughter, hunger and neglect, inequity and oppression. In the larger sense, certainly you are correct.

But in the forming of my daughter's character?

A child of five who gives up a pet for the greater good will either grow into an adult determined to make those responsible for her loss pay or become so accustomed to sacrifice she will cease to define her behavior as such.

In my daughter's case, the result was not one or the other; the result was both.

City of Tsars

I would prefer to be thought of as the mother, but preferences count so little in times such as ours. If you recognize my name, Yelizaveta Vasilevna Krupskaya, very likely it is because you worship or detest my son-in-law, Vladimir Ilyich Ulyanov, known to history as Vladimir Ilyich Lenin.

About that relation by marriage, there is more to be said and will be said, but not instantly.

We had a life, my Nadya and I, before the Simbirsk native arrived in Piter and began issuing directives, and I will not slight who we were before by colluding with the legend that our contributions began only after the great Ilyich crossed our threshold. The balding redhead revealed to us no injustice in our city or in Russia about which we were not long aware, nor was he the first male in the household to undertake reforms. That honor belongs to my late husband, Konstantin.

Before you hear more about Vladimir Ilyich, you will hear more about Konstantin Krupsky.

Konstantin and I met in Piter, both of us orphans reliant upon ourselves and only ourselves. After receiving a diploma from the Pavlovsky Institute, I was employable as a governess and as a governess I earned my living. Although by no means content with my situation, I was far from desperate. Compared to the women and girls forced to sell themselves on the streets in the snows of winter, the mud of spring and the endless nights of summer, my exploitation proved quite genteel. Nonetheless, a governess is viewed as a servant and treated as such.

"Yelizaveta, we are shorthanded today. After lessons, you are to help Alena polish the silver."

"I have misplaced my embroidery, Yelizaveta. Search for it in the children's rooms. Perhaps I left it there."

Never was I allowed to forget that the luxuries and comforts of my surroundings—the plump pillows, the plush carpets, the crisp table linens, the lovely lilacs spilling from crystal vases—existed neither for my benefit nor my enjoyment. Never was I allowed to object to the interruption of my pupils' lessons, even when the cause of those interruptions sprung from capricious and fleeting parental whim. I was expected to accept, to accede, to acquiesce and to hold my tongue. Of the various skills I have been forced to acquire, I am least expert at holding my tongue. As a governess, a wife, a mother and the mother-in-law of the founder of the Bolshevik Party, I have been accused of lacking verbal restraint.

Do you imagine such criticism haunts me?

It does not.

My Konstantin possessed a less excitable nature and more charitable heart than his bride. A man who said little but felt deeply, he sheltered his family as best he could from his own escalating despair. I sometimes think our Nadya, through no fault of her own, inherited the unlucky mix of her mother's unbridled temper and her father's silent stoicism.

A painful pairing for a woman.

For a revolutionary? Quite useful.

Konstantin first served his country as an infantry officer in the tsar's army. Unlike the majority sent to Poland to crush the insurrection of 1863, he grew fond of the Polish people and sympathized with their grievances. Appointed military governor, the *nachal'nik*, of the Grojec district of Warsaw, he returned with his wife and child to a country he cherished, eager to institute reform. Immediately he set about regulating labor practices. He oversaw the construction of a hospital and a school. He refused to tolerate the persecution of Jews. A progressive Russian civil servant, my Konstantin, with every reason to feel confident of the future and his family's modest place within it. I shared his optimism, but our happiness and good fortune were of short duration. A general from Piter arrived to conduct a tour of inspection. What he observed displeased him. Our family's camaraderie with the Poles? "Distasteful." Our conduct in public? "Un-Russian." Charged with "exceeding his authority," Konstantin was ordered back to Piter to stand trial. In that travesty of a courtroom, he was mocked and browbeaten. Why did he speak Polish and dance the Mazurka? Why had his wife published a children's book in Polish? Why was his daughter fluent in the language of her new home? With eloquence and great dignity he explained himself. In turn, he was stripped of his rank and status, discarded by the very government that had launched his career, and treated as if he were no more valuable than yesterday's rubbish. When he lost his position, our family lost its livelihood. To put food on the table, Konstantin accepted a series of demoralizing positions. For a time he worked as an insurance agent, then as a clerk. When he came home, discouraged and fatigued, his daughter climbed into his lap and asked for her favorite Polish songs. He never refused the request, my Konstantin, but I could not remain in the room while he sang those ballads with such tenderness. I could not.

Do you think Nadya did not sense her father's misery? Do you imagine that when she grew too old for lap sitting she did not continue to search for remnants of her once strong, decisive father in the ill, defeated man gazing out the window, his face and its melancholy played upon by Piter's shower of lights?

Dead at 45, my Konstantin. He left behind a wife too young to be a widow, a daughter too young to lose a parent. Perhaps our Nadya would have become a somber, single-minded revolutionary whether or not she had seen her father ruined for his liberalism.

Perhaps.

Who now can say?

To support ourselves after Konstantin's death, Nadya and I both gave lessons: I, throughout the day; Nadya, after she had returned from her own schooling at the gymnasium. We taught where we lived, in small but completely adequate apartments on Znamenskaya Ulitsa and later on Staro-Nevsky. Before my Nadya called herself a Marxist she called herself a follower of Tolstoy, the count who preached education and, in her mother's opinion, sanctimonious self-denial. As a novice might pour over her scriptures, my Nadya studied "Luxuries and Labor."

"Mama," she announced one afternoon, the first of the season's icicles growing fatter on our window. "Starting tomorrow, I will take over the household's cooking and cleaning."

"In addition to your studies. In addition to your teaching," I said.

"Yes."

If I had tasted my daughter's cooking previous to that discussion, there would have been further reason to object.

"Come, Nadya. We are not so poor as that."

My daughter's brow, so like her father's, began to furrow.

"It is not a matter of poverty. It is a matter of duty," she said.

"And what of your duty to health? To youth?" I countered.

Nadya's complexion is also like her father's. Upset spots her cheeks, as it did during that hour's wrangling.

When argument fails, I resort to teasing. Sarcasm rarely succeeds where logic falters, but I persist in its practice nevertheless. Familiar with accounts of my son-in-law's penchant for vicious ridicule, you will perhaps conclude that I have, in this life, received my fair reward.

The afternoon of swelling icicles, I responded to my Nadya as was my wont.

"How very fortunate for the count, Nadya! When he tires of writing of duty in 'Luxuries and Labor,' he can write of Anna and Vronsky's more craven appetites. The pleasures and perils of adultery. The temptations and satisfactions of the flesh."

Many have called my Nadya prudish. Never was she prudish. But she was and is a very accomplished pouter. Very accomplished. Following that exchange, as I recall, she pouted throughout the evening and into the next morning.

If a mother cannot outwait a pout, she does not deserve to be a mother.

It was neither my sarcasm nor opinion that caused my daughter to turn her back on the tenets of Tolstoy, of course. It was her introduction to Marx, which led, ultimately, to her introduction to Ilyich.

Nadya met Ilyich went she was 25, he 24. His hair—what little remained of it, even then—was wispier and lighter in hue than my daughter's, but also red. A significant bond, that shared hair color? I and the rest of the world can only speculate. In stocking feet, my Nadya stood taller, although in Ilyich's presence, as time went on, she slouched to diminish the disparity. As soon as I noticed that accommodation, I hotly objected. To end my complaints, she improved her posture, but only for the moment it took to silence me.

As innumerable photographs and films reveal, it was Ilyich's habit to stand and to walk with chest thrust forward. His habit of hooking his thumbs into the sleeves of his vest accentuated the thrust. He did not, as many assume, adopt that stance along with fame. Sneaking about Piter disguised as a shabbily attired Vyborg worker, he could not keep his thumbs from his armpits. When my Nadya grew famous, she was often photographed in hats. I wish they had been prettier ones. Unlike Inessa Armand, my daughter had no interest in appearing stylish. She wore hats primarily to keep the hair out of her eyes. With her hair, ⟨ never showed the least forbearance. The assumption that my daughter learned impatience from the irascible Ilyich? Ridiculous. Impatience she had mastered long before meeting her future husband.

My daughter believed any act of subversion committed against the tsar and his regime, whether perpetrated by a selfless revolutionary or an opportunistic scamp, was an act to be applauded and, if at all possible, funded.

Did I agree?

I did not.

Did ever I believe that Ilyich and his ruthless, impatient kind would finally and fully succeed at what legions of others, including my Konstantin, had struggled and failed to accomplish by methods more diplomatic?

I did not.

But I admired my son-in-law's trying, as I admired and admire my daughter's trying. Whatever else might be said of them, Nadya and Ilyich cannot be accused of giving short shrift to The Revolution. Before considerations of health, comfort and safety, before food, drink or sleep, came The Revolution.

I leave the scholars and pundits to decide on Ilyich's greatest contribution to The Revolution but here disclose my Nadya's greatest asset to her cause: tenacity. In ferocious tenacity, my daughter excels. In that aspect, she is not so unlike the much loathed tsarina.

I think back on a somnolent summer afternoon, mere months before Vladimir Ilyich entered our lives and brought with him round-the-clock intrigue. We had left our close apartment to stroll past peddlers of thread and pencils and shoelaces, bakeries and boot shops, kerosene vendors and card players, simply a mother and daughter walking the Nevsky arm-in-arm without hurry or set destination.

Block after block we ambled, savoring the free pleasures of Piter—the prism of afternoon light, the fragrance of linden trees. Its miseries and turbulence notwithstanding, Piter is a city that captures and recaptures the heart. Built on swamp and marsh by a tsar mad for all things European, populated by Romanovs and agitators, poets and proletarians, soldiers and ballerinas, a restless city on the edge of a vast, vast empire, it is also where my Nadya was conceived and born. As we walked that afternoon, Piter belonged to us, to anyone and everyone around us, until the soon-to-be tsarina's carriage rolled from a side street onto Nevsky proper and with that appearance turned the lindens' creamy petals into a stage set, the citizens of Piter into an aristocrat's captive audience.

Others, many, the majority, rushed in for a closer look at Princess Alix of Hesse, fiancée of the tsarevich, but my Nadya stepped back, rigid with contempt.

The woman inside the carriage glanced neither to the right nor left, impervious to the street, indifferent to and unaffected by the adulation or derision of its denizens. On she went, Princess Alix, passing us and our insignificance. For who were we? Mere scenery that breathed.

"For the price of a single one of her Fabergé baubles, an entire village could be educated," Nadya hissed.

The statistics of inequity, inspiration to my daughter's ears, have always grated on mine. And because I longed to resume our lovely stroll, to lighten the mood, I said: "Come, Nadya. She is only another woman likely to prove stronger than the man she marries."

Do not misunderstand.

As time revealed, there was much to dislike about Alexandra Feodorovna and her regrettable character. Even for a tsarina, her prejudices and pettiness were legendary. She lacked insight. She lacked empathy. She owned too many strands of pearls. She liked too much to be obeyed and in disappointment turned too fanatically to her adopted God. But she was also a woman excessively devoted to a cause: the preservation of the monarchy. And like my Nadya, her enemy, she would, while she breathed, never quit the fight.

Shall I tell you something else my daughter and the haughty tsarina had in common, even if by doing so I risk redirecting Nadya's wrath upon myself?

As the tsarina loved her Nicky, so my Nadya came to love the sturdy fellow with the endless forehead and rasping laugh.

Again, do not misunderstand.

My daughter was devoted to The Revolution. If The Revolution required that she rise at dawn, she rose before dawn. If The Revolution required that she take on the work of two or four, she took on the work of ten. For the sake of The Revolution, she endured prison and exile. For the sake of The Revolution, she battled Mensheviks and forgave the man we knew as Lev Davidovich Bronstein and history calls Trotsky for his temporary lapse in loyalty. For the sake of The Revolution she submitted to the tyranny of Comrade Stalin, that treacherous, inferior Georgian. But I tell you this as the woman in whose womb she started: of all my Nadya's hardships, none proved harder than the struggle to hold in check the *meshchanstvo* attraction, the petite-bourgeois tingling, she felt for the man who was her husband.

When Ilyich came into the room, my stern, unyielding daughter softened and warmed to the *man*—not to the leader, not to the strategist, to the man.

And Vladimir Ilyich? His feelings for my Nadya?

He admired her fierce commitment to the cause—he would have been a despicable hypocrite had he not. He relied on her; he confided in her. Never did he doubt her allegiance. He was immensely fond of her and of her company. Had he lived longer, he would have destroyed the crude usurper who dared treat her so vilely. He valued her; he trusted her—with his life and, more importantly to his way of thinking, with his revolution. But he did not love my Nadya as a woman, as a wife. He esteemed her as a comrade. And this my Nadya accepted. With this arrangement, she made do.

If They Cannot Learn, How Will They Win?

"Nadya, please! At least finish your tea. The wind will make your walk to Nevskaya Zastava no shorter, only colder."

"I will be late!" she told her mother. "I cannot be late!"

"The workers will wait."

"*They* wait on *me*? After fourteen hours on their feet?"

The very idea made her bristle.

She had misplaced her gloves. *Where* were her gloves?

"And if," her mother persisted, "the Evening School teacher faints from hunger, will that help the workers learn their sums? Counting off the moments she lies before them, lifeless?"

"I do not intend to faint!" she said.

"Such *krasne* cheeks!"

"Enough, Mama!"

Once again she had allowed herself to be provoked by her mother's rough teasing. She, who was teased constantly by Yelizaveta Vasilevna: *Too much reading! Too little exercise! Too many hours devoted to Pushkin and Nekrasov! Too many frowns! Too few smiles!*

"Reformers as well as teachers need their strength," her mother chided.

"And have it!"

"Drink your tea, Nadya. As a favor to me. Spoil your mama if not yourself."

"I cannot drink and dress at the same time!"

Together they searched the dining room that doubled as a sitting room and tripled as Yelizaveta Vasilevna's bedroom for the mislaid gloves, her mother at her heels.

"Tread any closer and I will feel as if I live with an Okhrana agent!" she complained.

In her own bedroom, she at last found the gloves, perched on the corner of the worktable where an hour before she had sat, tutoring her newest pupil. Head swiveling, he had demanded the identity of the man whose photograph hung where an icon "ought."

She had not said "my father"; she had said "Konstantin Krupsky" because her father had been a man concerned with the welfare of more than his family.

"And the tsar? Where is your picture of the tsar?"

If they had not so badly needed that impertinent student's money, she would have answered his insolence with some of her own: *You are referring to the Romanov who plays dominoes while his people starve? His picture has vanished, as will the man himself.*

"Now that you have found the gloves, finish your tea," her mother ordered.

And this from the woman who accused *her* of stubbornness!

"I must *go*, Mama! If I arrive before seven, I will be able to speak with Ivan Babushkin about something other than sums and vowels and consonants."

"Ivan Babushkin," her mother repeated.

"You have heard me speak of him. A worker in the porcelain factory."

"A conversation in the hallway with Ivan Babushkin. That is your plan," her mother said.

"A plan unfulfilled unless I *hurry.*"

"At least let me re-plait your hair. Sit."

With the hairbrush her mother tapped the chair.

"Be *quick*, Mama!"

"But the day has freed so many strands from their servitude."

"Stop this slyness or I will remove every hairpin and deed the mess to wind!"

On a daily basis her mother prodded: "Who would it hurt, Nadya? To wear a dress less severe? A jumper with more color? Shoes that once upon a time had been polished?" The better question: who would such vanities help? It did not matter that she looked like a woman unconcerned with hair or boots or jumpers. It only mattered that she arrived at the factory on time and taught with a zeal that made tired workers eager to listen and learn.

"If you jiggle your feet, you jiggle the chair and if you jiggle the chair, you jiggle what sits in it."

"Surely I am improved!"

Her mother sighed.

"You will be careful?"

"I will be careful."

"You will not wait, Nadya, until the last seat is empty, the last light extinguished?"

"I will leave with the others."

"And you will take a biscuit. To eat before starting back."

"I will take a biscuit."

"And if detained, you will send word."

"I will send word, Mama."

Her mother sighed again and kissed her cheek. "Off with you."

The wind on the street was sharp but not yet icy. She would not arrive this evening with frosted eyebrows. She sped up, almost to a trot, gleeful to think that if she broke into a run the true Okhrana agent shadowing her in his pea-green overcoat might break a leg if not his neck, trying to keep up. Broken limbs, chilblains, frostbite, she wished those blights and worse on the tsar's spies. The colleagues of the street-patrol agents were even now methodically sifting through the mail of Piter's citizens, reading their fill, carelessly re-stuffing envelopes. The Okhrana no longer bothered to refold the pages in proper fashion. Another means of threat, that wanton disregard, that arrogant refusal to cover their tracks.

Dearest Nadinka, her mother archly responded to a letter she had written over the summer. *Thank you for your letter, which arrived the worse for wear. Divots in several paragraphs, pages torn.*

She understood her mother's warning but ignored it. Let the Okhrana read her descriptions of village life, of trying to teach peasants exhaust-ed from ceaseless labor, of peasants sharing unventilated huts with their work animals, of drunk and abusive peasant men, of bruised and battered peasant woman, of peasant babies howling from neglect and hunger. One in 15 of those babies would not reach a second birthday. The household's adults would be lucky to live past 35. Such were the conditions in which 85 percent of Russians lived—attempted to live. Her summer in the coun-tryside had been more instructive for her than for her supposed students. The *narodniki* had been mistaken. Despite their revolutionary promise, the peasants would not lead The Revolution. That force must come from the workers of the Putilov, the Maxwell, the Laferme, from Thornton Mills, from all the gunpowder and carriage and tar factories in Piter. The industrial proletariat. The Ivan Babushkins.

At this street corner, always, she spat. It was a patch of Piter forever spoiled by association with Nicholas Romanov's insufferable bride-to-be.

She, her mother, the entire Nevsky, had been made to stand idle for the imperious passing of that pearl-wrapped neck, those ruffles of silk and voile.

"Enjoy yourself while you can, princess," she had muttered. "The people have splintered the carriages of tsars and tsarinas before and will again."

"Hush, Nadya, hush," her mother cautioned. "Even the breeze has ears."

Once beyond the Narva Gate, she would have known she neared her destination even as a blind woman. The Vyborg stank of feces. In every alleyway, piles of human waste. The men with their carts and shovels made fewer trips to the poorer districts. Come the spring, the runoff from such piles would collect in rancid cesspools.

And yet: not without service, those rancid cesspools.

Last spring she had seen angry workers fling their foreman into a fetid puddle. When he tried to escape, they had rolled him repeatedly in the filth. The surrounding cluster of spectators had raucously cheered. She also had cheered. To advance The Revolution, there could never be enough factory bosses writhing in cesspools. There could never be too many acts of retaliation against exploiters by the exploited.

Her heel slipped; she stumbled, recovered, rushed on. The Okhrana would report her clumsiness but could not report that she had dawdled getting to her classroom.

In the narrow brick building, down the corridor, she glanced about for Ivan Babushkin, standing alone or huddled with other worker students in the hallway. Without exception those worker students behaved cordially toward the "school mistress" from Nevsky Prospekt but not, she was pleased to note, deferentially. When she spoke with them, they met her eye. When she asked whether their wives and children also worked at the factory, they answered straightforwardly. When she asked if they had been encouraged to attend the Evening School, they did not lie.

Evening School instructors were allowed to teach the alphabet, basic reading and the first four rules of arithmetic: addition, subtraction, multiplication and division. Anything more the authorities regarded as excess.

Admirably, one of her colleagues had ignored the restrictions and taught as she pleased. When an inspector visited her classroom, one of her students proudly volunteered to demonstrate his knowledge of decimals. The inspector smiled sourly and departed. The following day the teacher was dismissed. In the moment, however, all was not lost. Behind the unappreciative inspector's back, one of the workers had made a rude gesture. Many laughed; others repeated the insult. Small acts of defiance, but not inconsequential.

She began the hour with a writing lesson. Their chalk squeaked on the slate. They formed their letters slowly, with great difficulty. Even at a distance she sensed their struggle. They came to the classroom weary and likely hungry. The barracks-like room in which they gathered was underlit. Shadows did not help men who needed spectacles to see more clearly. Stuffiness did not help tired men to stay awake and alert.

My name is_____.
My children's names are_____.
My family comes from_____.

They blinked and twisted in their seats. They squinted and they yawned. And when they yawned, like her peasant pupils, they exhaled essence of vodka. Her mother constantly worried about her safety in the company of drunken men. She worried that minds dulled by drink would not, could not, learn fast or well enough. And if the workers did not learn, how were they to triumph?

Ivan Babushkin entered, cap in hand.

"I am late. I apologize for the lateness."

"We have just started. You will have no trouble catching up."

"I have brought along someone I would like you to meet."

While her other students finished the assignment, she followed Ivan Babushkin into the hallway.

"How do you do?" she asked the one-legged man with the jagged scar on his cheek, then flushed.

He had but one leg! Of course he did not do well!

"Would you like to join the class? It will require some paperwork but that is easily arranged."

"Perhaps he will join the class, but that is not why he came tonight," Ivan Babushkin said. "Yakov and I work together in the factory."

She nodded, waited. Ivan Babushkin would not call her out of the classroom on a frivolous matter.

"Today he told me he had had a revelation. Speak freely, Yakov. The teacher will be interested in what you have to say."

The smaller man raised his chin.

"I have given up religion for revolution."

"And why is that?" she asked, pulse quickening.

Again he looked to Ivan Babushkin, who encouraged him to continue.

"Because a slave to God can do nothing about his slavery. A slave to the tsar can fight."

Progress indeed.

INTERVIEW WITH HISTORY
Tsarina Alexandra Feodorovna

"But you're also known as 'Sunny,' correct? At least by Nicky, your one true love?"

"Who are you? Who allowed you inside the royal apartments?"

"Oh. Sorry. Would you rather we follow the lead of your favorite monk and call you 'Little Mother'?"

"I favor no monk."

"But you will, Tsarina. You will. Another possibility: *pechvogel*, bird of ill omen. The name you gave yourself. Shall we go with that?"

"Your presence, your *impertinence*, is intolerable. *Where* are my attendants?! How did you elude the guards?"

"We ask the questions, Sunny. You answer."

"I am the tsarina, the Empress Consort. Address me as such!"

"A tsarina who expects history to treat her kindly?"

"Tsarinas act according to God's will. They do not concern themselves with history."

"A very regal answer."

"I *demand* to know who permitted you to enter."

"History is equally demanding, Tsarina. Shall we sit? To ease your sciatic pain? On the usual chaise lounge? With the usual embroidery on your lap? This room is *indeed* a shade of mauve. Seeing is believing, yes? That's why you trusted your special 'Friend,' the *starets*? Because you saw with your own eyes the relief he provided the tsarevich?"

"God in his wisdom will send who is needed."

"And Prince Yusupov and gang will snatch him away. True or false: you grew up eating baked apples and rice pudding. You fished for crabs on an English beach while visiting your grandmother, Victoria the queen. At your father's hunting lodge, Wolfsgarten, you dressed up in your mother's castoff finery and demanded infinite curtsies."

"My life before Russia, before I married the Emperor and Autocrat of All the Russias, the absolute monarch imbued with divine authority, is without significance."

"Even so, you weren't terribly keen on relocating. Grandma Victoria had to insist."

"God's will brought me to Russia."

"But it was Grandma who told you to lighten up: Lutheranism, Orthodoxy. Six of one, half dozen of the other."

"I embraced my new faith."

"Your *faith* but not your fellow believers. Grandma also had to remind you of your duty to cultivate the love and respect of the Russian people."

"Russia is not England. Here we do not need to earn the love of the people. The Russian people revere their tsars as divine beings from whom all charity and fortune derive. As for the opinion of St. Petersburg society, it is of no importance whatsoever."

"All the same, some early complaints once you and your hemophiliac gene came to stay: *Alix of Hesse is clumsy. She towers over her husband-to-be. She dances poorly. Her French is badly accented. She is cold, arrogant.* Later, these refinements: *Rasputin's whore, Germany's spy.*"

"I do not answer to peasants, to rumors, or to lesser members of the Imperial Family. I answer to God and to the Emperor and Autocrat of All the Russias. And I *will not* be cross-examined."

"Trust us, Tsarina. We know the future. Cross-examination is the least of your worries."

"Leave my sight!"

"Heads up! The Emperor Autocrat will one day exclaim: 'Better one Rasputin than ten fits of hysteria a day.'"

"You reek of insolence."

"And the *starets* will smell of goat."

"The holy on earth often smell of earth."

"Holiness—a tried and true tsarina excuse."

"Tsarinas do not offer excuses."

"But suffer their consequences all the same. World crumbling, you'll instruct Nicky: 'Act more like Ivan the Terrible, less like a wet noodle!'"

"What passes between tsar and tsarina is known only to them and God."

"And the maids. And the clerks. And the Duma. And the revolutionaries."

"Do not presume to sit in my presence. Unless otherwise ordered, you are required to stand."

"History's requirements seem to be in conflict with yours."

"It is time for my prayers."

"Your penchant for pearls, long and multiple strands. At every ball, in every photo, Alexandra and her pearls. Do you also pray in pearls?"

(Silence.)

"Another word to the wise, Alexandra Feodorovna: the charlatan Dr. Philippe, French practitioner of 'astral medicine,' will announce that, after four daughters, you carry a son. Your tummy will swell—but only with air."

"God will provide Russia with a tsarevich when God is ready."

"Under Red guard in Ekaterinburg, your husband will browse *War and Peace* to while away the hours. And you? Any predictions?"

"My Bible is always with me."

"And when you and your Nicky and the grand duchesses and the tsarevich, destined to die a tsarevich, are being herded into the basement of Ipatiev House and lined up, supposedly for a photograph…?"

"If told we are to be photographed, I will be thinking of the photograph."

"And wearing pearls?"

"If given the opportunity to dress properly."

"Dying, you will attempt the sign of the cross."

"In my heart I will complete it."

"Two comforts: you will die with your husband and children. Dead already, you will not see the family lapdog slaughtered as well."

"I will be aware. I will see."

"History doubts that prophecy, Tsarina. History gives no credence to visions and miracles."

"Then history is to be pitied."

The Pampered Son

Does it not make a pretty picture?

Vladimir Ulyanov creating a workroom of the family garden in Samara, spreading his books and papers on a table shaded by lime trees, a jug of cool milk at his elbow, studying in depth the plight of the proletariat while surrounded by 225 acres of Ulyanov land. And when his eyes grow tired of reading, there are the ready diversions of hunting partridges or picking mushrooms or swimming in the pond or practicing gymnastic stunts until another farm-fresh meal prepared by female hands is delivered to his garden table.

All his life, Ilyich was catered to, consoled and coddled by devoted and solicitous women. He was used to being waited on. He expected a clean bed and a tidy house. When he wanted his tea and kasha, he wanted them, and for many years I was the woman who brought him both.

Ilyich's mother, Maria Alexandrovna, spent her inheritance on those acres in Samara. She moved her family from Simbirsk, a town she loved, to try to make a farmer of her second son and thereby save him from sharing the fate of Alexander, her first. Of course Ilyich became no farmer. It was Maria Alexandrovna who oversaw the mill and the planting and the harvest.

But before Ilyich studied Marx in the shade in Samara, he came of age in a *gubernia* that contained four million forested acres, more than half of that land owned by the tsar and his family, as Nadya and her statistics will tell you.

"In Simbirsk, Vladimir Ilyich learned to despise feudal barbarity," Nadya has often declared—incensed as always by the injustice but equally proud that in such a milieu Vladimir Ilyich succeeded in honing his hatred of oppressors of every stripe.

Though a failure at farming, Ilyich was a gifted hater. In that area of competency, my son-in-law excelled.

Along with lessons in feudal barbarity, it should be noted, Vladimir Ilyich's birthplace offered a view of the Volga, queen of Russian rivers, mountains to the west, and the beauties of endless steppe to the east. The citizens of Simbirsk also had at their disposal exquisite apple, plum and cherry orchards, raspberry and currant bushes, an unending supply of fresh fish, bushels of wild mushrooms to mix with onions and dill, merry-go-rounds in the square on holidays and wave after wave of itinerant, strolling musicians to entertain them.

Ilyich was quite a singer. Indeed he was. One of his favorites, "You Have Charming Little Eyes," he used to sing incessantly. At the chorus line: "I perish for the love of them," he liked to make his voice break with mock passion. Then he would fall back in his seat, laughing at the absurdity of the lyrics, waving his arms, and sputtering: "They are the death of me already!" He knew this song before my Nadya suffered Basedow's disease and its effects. Ilyich did not continue to sing it with the objective of hurting my Nadya, but I could see that his sisters, particularly Maria, enjoyed the humiliation the tune caused my daughter because of her poor bulging eyes.

There are those who claim Nadya was by nature immune to snubs. As her mother I can tell you she grew practiced in the art of seeming so.

Ilyich's maternal grandmother was a prosperous German; his maternal grandfather, a Jewish physician. Maria Alexandrovna came from a more cultivated, affluent family than did her husband, Ilya Nikolayevich Ulyanov, who worked as an inspector of public schools. It was from his father that Ilyich inherited his fleshy nose and a countenance that revealed both intellect and cunning, with cunning winning out.

Young Ilyich began his life's adventure in a two-story wooden house on Streletskaya Street in Simbirsk. A noisy, boisterous child with a large head, he learned to walk late, fell frequently and when he fell screamed at a volume that shook the walls. Even as a child, Ilyich liked to win and resorted to slyness in order to triumph. In physical contests, he used his elbows. If events did not go his way, he threw tantrums, shattered dishes, broke toys—his own and those belonging to others. Old enough to read and appreciate Bakunin's remark: "The passion for destruction is a creative passion." If I know Ilyich—and I did—he slapped his thigh in merriment. One always likes to have at the ready a pithy justification for one's behavior.

Maria Alexandrovna deserves much credit. She has my deepest and most sincere respect. Her daughters—none. But Maria Alexandrovna I hold in high esteem, a mother who suffered much on her children's behalf and suffered it nobly, without complaint. As a young wife and mother in Simbirsk she could not have imagined what lay ahead for her eldest, Alexander, or for the son who followed.

Sasha and Volodya, they were within the family.

"Delight us with your absence!" the brothers supposedly crooned when interrupted at their chess game.

Sasha took after his mother in looks and temperament. An excellent student, he went off to Piter to study chemistry and the visual capacities of annelid worms.

You are of course familiar with Alexander Ulyanov's activities in Piter?

Drawn into student revolutionary circles, Sasha used his chemistry skills to fashion nitroglycerine grenades and dynamite bombs. Along with his comrades, he plotted to assassinate Alexander III as the tsar rode in his carriage from the Winter Palace to St. Isaac's Cathedral to attend a memorial service for his slain father, Alexander II. Letters, recklessly exchanged, had been duly opened and read by the Okhrana, resulting in the arrests of Alexander Ulyanov and three others. In the police station, one of Sasha's comrades launched the last of Sasha's handiwork. The fuse was defective. The bomb failed to explode.

Who could not feel for Maria Alexandrovna, newly widowed, the single parent of six?

By horse and cart, Maria Alexandrovna made her frantic trip to Piter to plead for the life of her eldest. And while she went door to door pleading, the tsarist henchmen, as my Nadya calls them, executed Alexander Ulyanov in the yard of Schlüsselburg Prison and buried his remains in a common prison grave. His mother learned the bitter, bitter news from a leaflet handed to her on the street by a stranger.

Ilyich's sister, the younger Maria, Maria Ilyinichna Ulyanova, is the family member responsible for the myth that Ilyich declared upon receiving news of Sasha's execution: "No, we will not follow that road. That is not the road to take."

Maria Ilyinichna was eight at the time she supposedly overheard this vow; Vladimir Ilyich, 17. At 17, Ilyich was not a revolutionary; he had not read a word of Marx. The Ulyanovs produced two sons remembered by history. More than enough achievement for any family, but Ilyich's sisters did not shy from further embellishing the Ulyanov legend at the expense of truth. On many occasions, over many issues, Vladimir Ilyich and I have quarreled but on no occasion have my reprimands involved grandiosity. Personal vanity was not one of my son-in-law's shortcomings. Consistently and vehemently he opposed efforts to enshrine him as The Revolution's deity. When urged to accept individual honors, he seethed with impatience. "I am just like everybody else!" he would shout as beside him my Nadya approvingly beamed.

Such modesty cannot be said to characterize his sister, Maria Ilyinichna.

No, I have no affection for Maria Ilyinichna. Neither she nor Anna treated my Nadya as she deserved, either as a sister-in-law or as a comrade.

Following the execution of her eldest son, Maria Alexandrovna succeeded in gaining permission for Ilyich to take the examinations necessary for a law degree. It was another foolish hope on the part of Maria Alexandrovna. Ilyich was no more cut out to be a provincial lawyer than he was a farmer. She did her best, Maria Alexandrovna, to keep Ilyich away from turbulent Piter, but once Ilyich declared himself a revolutionary she did not try to dissuade him from his chosen course. As I supported my Nadya, she supported her now eldest son and his convictions. Thereafter Ilyich lived and breathed for one purpose: to destroy the tsarist government and, with a pampered son's confidence, assumed his cause would be victorious simply because he desired it.

When Ilyich arrived from the provinces, he shared the streets of Piter with flagrantly unkempt nihilists, scruffy fellows with gnarled walking sticks and untamed hair. The nihilist costume suited neither Ilyich's politics nor his personality. Aside from lacking the hair for such a style, he made a conscious choice to dress properly but unpretentiously in Piter and elsewhere. Always careful to avoid calling attention to himself among strangers, he did nothing to cultivate the eye of passersby. Before he took to wearing the cap and shabby coat of a Vyborg worker, he wore a vest, a tie and carefully brushed trousers, his beard and mustache neatly and regularly trimmed.

To say that he did not attract attention on the street is not to imply that those he met failed to find him attractive—quite the contrary. In Piter he quickly established himself as the rising star of Marxist circles.

Acerbic, brash, a man of action, as my Nadya would say, impatient with study groups, the distribution of leaflets and the gentler tactics of persuasion.

More than a few men and women fell under his spell, my Nadya but one of them.

Shrovetide

"Nadya, you will cook the blinis?"

She? Assigned cook?

"Do you hope to eat the blinis?" she tartly replied. "Because mine will come scorched and soggy."

"Regardless, if the Okhrana burst in, we must be holding plates of pancakes in our laps."

They were not actually celebrating Shrovetide; they were taking advantage of the fact that tsarist spies were less vigilant during the holiday, perhaps off celebrating winter's end themselves. "Pancake Week" provided an excellent cover for their Marxist study group to gather at the apartment of the engineer Klasson.

Scarcely had she begun to beat the batter when the discussion began. Indignant, she turned up the heat, dumped the whole of the bowl's contents into the skillet and left it to burn. Taking her seat, she noticed her skirt. It looked as if she had been pelted by street urchins. The splatter did nothing to improve her mood but hers was not the only anger on display. The usually placid Klasson glared steadily at the newcomer who glared back. She had joined less a discussion than an acrimonious debate.

"Are you denying the terrible suffering inflicted by the Volga famine of '92?"

The newcomer shrugged. He was not quite burly but displayed the broad chest of a wrestler. When arguing, he jabbed the air. His eyes were very shrewd.

"Our guest comes from the Volga," Radchenko clarified in a whisper.

"And still you state with pride that you took no part in the relief efforts, in the soup kitchens? How can you call yourself a friend of the people?"

Klasson's challenge was met with scorn and answered with sarcasm.

"I am first and foremost a friend of The Revolution. Every calamity that befalls Russia brings us closer to revolution. Anyone who refuses to see and make use of that fundamental is a cretin and deserves to waste his days ladling soup."

No member of their study group, no matter the dispute, had ever insinuated that another was a cretin.

They had seen nothing like it, like him.

"Your rudeness is not appreciated, comrade. We do not trade insults here. We treat each other and ideas with respect."

"Then let us take care to be polite! Revolutions have always benefited from manners!"

He was not wrong. None of their exceedingly polite discussions and prettily-formed arguments had helped the workers. None of their broad tolerance for any and every idea expressed had resulted in a clear plan for overthrowing the tsar.

"We must put more of our efforts into the work of the Committee for Illiteracy."

Again the newcomer roared with contempt.

"By all means! If anyone believes he can save Russia through the Committee for Illiteracy, we will not hinder him!"

"So now you are against educating the workers?" Klasson baited.

"I am against *committees*. No advance can be made until the workers themselves are thoroughly saturated with revolutionary ideas and the theoreticians are thoroughly saturated with the habits and tastes and modes of thought of the working classes." He made a pretense of scanning the room. "And who among you answers to the factory's whistle? In which of these chairs sits a worker? We need to hear from workers' mouths the grievances of the masses. Study circles are a bourgeois indulgence. Insipid and useless to the masses."

With that remark he disparaged everyone in the room. And yet, she noticed, he did not care. The Volga native did not care.

Apparently she was expected to clean the blini skillet as well!

"Nadezhda Krupskaya?"

When she turned from scrubbing, to meet his gaze, she had to look slightly down. He gave no indication of minding that he had to look up.

"Yes. I am Nadezhda Krupskaya. And you? I did not catch your name."

"The Okhrana know me as Nicholas Petrovich."

If he expected her to defend or apologize for their circle, she disappointed him. They could do better. Always they could do better. What remained to be seen was whether their critic would contribute to their improvement or be satisfied with simply castigating their weaknesses and failures.

"I am told you teach the workers beyond the Narva Gate."

Wiping her hands on the back of her skirts, she could think of no reason to deny the fact.

"At the Smolensky Evening School, thrice weekly."

"Then you are not like the others here," he said and she flushed—from his casual dismissal of the others and the individual praise. "You are capable of convincing the workers of the necessity of political struggle."

She neither inflated nor minimized what she knew.

"I have a certain familiarity with life on Schlüsselburg Post Road. As an Evening School instructor there is ample opportunity for studying labor conditions and the temper of the masses."

He nodded quickly and leaned forward. Her first instinct was to step back but this she did not do.

"There are how many at the school?"

"Six hundred at the Smolensky School, but that does not count the pupils in the technical classes and the Obukhov School."

"And you speak of anything—in these classes?"

"Every class contains at least one police spy. But if a teacher avoids the words 'tsar' and 'strike,' if she frames her comments with care, she can make herself understood without interference."

He nodded once more, seemingly in approval. His eyes were hazel. His fingers quite thick. Nicholas Petrovich had somehow avoided taking on the scent of burnt blinis. Instead he smelled quite…she could think of no better word…*clean*. It was not easy to smell clean in Piter.

"Perhaps I could also speak to some of your students?"

"I believe that can be arranged."

The last members of the circle were leaving. At the door, Radchenko waited for her. They had agreed beforehand to discuss portions of *Anti-Dühring* on the walk home. After devoting more than a month to the study of section two, she continued to have trouble understanding several passages.

"I must go."

"I would like to hear more of what you have learned from the workers," Nicholas Petrovich persisted. "When can we discuss it further?"

She gave him her home address, which he copied on a crumpled slip of paper already crowded with notes and numbers.

"My true name is Ulyanov," he suddenly revealed. "Vladimir Ulyanov."

She strove to maintain a neutral expression, to react in no manner detectable by those shrewd eyes.

"We will see each other soon," he declared and did not wait for her to agree or disagree.

The sun had already begun to set by the time she and Radchenko left the Okhta District.

"And darkness again conquers light," Radchenko forlornly observed—a Marxist but also something of a poet.

Fighting, contention. It was a legacy of their city. In the sky and on the ground.

For several moments they walked alongside the Neva's ripples in silence. As yet they had discussed neither *Anti-Dühring* nor the newcomer. But it was as if the latter walked with them, between them.

She had shared with Radchenko the newcomer's true identity. Reason enough for silence.

"I daresay the brother of Alexander Ulyanov will have no patience for political stupidities," Radchenko ventured.

"He showed none today."

"To do so would make him a fool."

"Yes," she agreed.

"The brother of Alexander Ulyanov will reveal himself to be many things, I suspect. But a fool? That I cannot see happening," said Radchenko.

Nor could she.

The Presentiment of Scaffolds

"I am still awake, Nadinka," I called, propped on my pillows, hearing the creak of the apartment door. "Come! Entertain your mother with your night's adventures. She is in need of a bedtime story."

On that evening, the book in my hands had proved a disappointment. I had not lost myself within its pages. I had remained far too aware of the clock and my Nadya's continued absence. For bedtime reading in those years I often chose accounts of kings and their castles. Generally speaking, the exploits of the entitled can be relied upon to provide both entertainment and instruction. Russia, as it happens, is not alone in producing vain and shortsighted sovereigns. Any number of countries—Germany, England, France—have also contributed their fair share.

During a previous protracted winter, the Neva hard as marble, snow falling so continuously it turned air to scrim, I had filled many a frigid hour reading about England's much-married Henry. It should surprise no one when I say that those bearing the brunt of the monarch's whims were by and large members of the opposite sex.

"Did you know? Did you realize?" I quizzed my Nadya. "The 69-year-old Countess of Salisbury was also beheaded by her monarch and she not even a wife, merely kin."

My daughter objects first with silence. That has always been her way.

"The Countess gave her executioner quite the run around the scaffold, dashing to this corner and that, dodging his ax, skirts hiked, ankles exposed. Is such resistance not inspiring?"

Nadya brought her scowl to my doorway.

"In the end the Countess was caught, of course. Head hacked off and, for good measure, that rebellious body deprived of every limb."

"Why read such nonsense?"

"History nonsense, Nadya?"

"Gossip, not history. The foibles and caprices of kings."

"*Ruler* kings."

"This is not sixteenth-century Britain, Mama."

Certainly not.

We were then still in Russia, in Piter, ensconced in the final decade of the nineteenth century.

The night she met Ilyich, I noticed at once the difference. She did not look or act as she usually looked and acted after a long day and longer night's work and meetings. Weary stoicism had been replaced by a curiously focused distraction. Taking a seat on the bed, she sat on me, indifferent to the lump.

"Nadya, please! My foot is no cushion!"

Although she shifted her position, she did not speak.

Always before when I had labeled her outings "adventures," she vehemently protested. This evening the remark stood uncorrected. She smelled of burnt pancakes, strongly suggesting that she had been drafted to serve as the evening's cook.

"And what is the cause of this rampant gaiety?" I taunted, tired of waiting for an explanation. "Has the tsar abdicated his throne? Has Alexandra Feodorovna packed up her jewels and returned to Germany? Nadya! Indulge your mother! Mine has been a boring night."

"A new comrade has joined us."

Such an answer hardly revived my interest, but I preferred talk to silence.

"And this new comrade? Is he young? Old? Where has he come from?"

"He is young but does not seem young. Originally he comes from Simbirsk."

"And has moved to Piter to take advantage of our conferences and study groups?"

That tease did penetrate. She turned sharply in my direction.

"He is the brother of Alexander Ulyanov."

At once my back left the pillows, my teasing finished. It was all very well for Nadya to teach at the Smolensky Evening School, to tempt fate and the Okhrana with pilgrimages to the industrial district, to spend her evenings discussing ideology while drinking tea and eating blinis, but this newcomer to her circle…his very name imposed a challenge, perhaps an *obligation*, to undertake more dangerous and defiant acts of resistance.

"He is a terrorist? He has declared himself so?"

"He has not declared it, no," Nadya hedged. "But he will do what is necessary for the people."

Apprehension had turned me as grave as my daughter. We were no longer speaking lightly.

"That much he has said? That he will do what is necessary for the people?"

"He has studied the forces of reaction."

"Many have studied the forces of reaction."

"But Vladimir Ulyanov has studied for a specific purpose: to learn why we failed in the past and where our opportunities now lie."

How often have I recalled that conversation, the instant favoritism accorded the native of Simbirsk by my Nadya. A mere evening's acquaintance had convinced her Vladimir Ulyanov could correct the mistakes of the past and retrain the soldiers of revolution.

"Before there was an Alexander Ulyanov, Nadya, there was a Sophia Perovskaya. Do not forget Sophia Perovskaya."

"I shall never forget a comrade's sacrifice!"

We were talking at cross-purposes, my daughter and I. I mentioned Sophia Perovskaya as someone whose end I wished my Nadya to avoid. Since the tsarist government had now executed a revolutionary woman, who or what would prevent it from executing a second, a third, a fourth?

In 1881, it was Sophia Perovskaya's reconnaissance that verified Alexander II's Saturday visits to the Grand Duchess Ekaterina. It was Sophia who skillfully positioned her comrades along the Catherine Canal embankment. It was at her signal that bombs flew and mortally wounded the tsar. Along with three other members of *Narodnaya Volya*, she was executed in Semenovskaya Square. Her executioner wore scarlet; she wore black. A placard on her bosom read "The Regicide." Before dying along with him, she kissed her lover/comrade Andrei Zhelyabov. And then she swung.

If not Russian history, Sophia Perovskaya's story would be a Russian fairytale. The black, the scarlet, the final kiss. A young woman's passion for revolution entwined with the passions of romantic love.

"Beware the suggestive power of fairytales," I used to tell my Nadya when she was a little girl. "Real life is not so simple. Goodness is never so pure. True evil is not so easily unmasked."

Neither as a child nor as a young woman did my Nadya heed such cautionary advice. She believed with the whole of her being in the fairytale of revolution. And in that fairytale, Ilyich played the prince.

INTERVIEW WITH HISTORY
Sophia Perovskaya

"We will not take up too much of your time because your time has passed. First question: are you satisfied?"

"If you are asking whether I am satisfied that Alexander II is dead, my answer is of course yes."

"Dead—but replaced. By Tsar Alexander III."

"You've come to ridicule me?"

"Actually, no. We bring good news from the future! The final tsar is doomed. Nicholas II will soon breathe his last. And with his last breath goes the dynasty."

"The Romanovs' end will mark Russia's true beginning."

"And no doubt you're keen to celebrate. But why not clear up the niggling details first?"

"I am not averse to details."

"In addition to your regicide label, history remembers you as the first female executed for a political crime. The first *aristocratic* woman, as so many have noted. The granddaughter of a governor. The daughter of a governor."

"Do not speak to me about my father."

"No love lost?"

"He was a despot among despots. He insulted my mother. He forced my brother to insult her as well. To remain under his roof would have been morally unendurable."

"But to commit murder, morally endurable? Perhaps you should have killed your father instead?"

"Do you imagine the idea never crossed my mind?"

"You left your father's house to bunk with the Kornilov sisters. To work as a physician's assistant in the village."

"I left to begin my life as a radical, yes."

"A grand rebellion that at the onset conspired to save, not snuff out, lives."

"Would you be badgering me in this way if I were a man? Would you be skeptical of the worthiness of my dedication to change the course of Russia if I were not a Sophia?"

"History always badgers. Otherwise it would not be history. To continue: you abandoned both the village and the healing profession to become a terrorist."

"I left the village for Piter. When my comrades decided the only recourse to repression was violence, I stood with my comrades."

"A delicately featured girl with a flaxen braid and childishly round cheeks."

(Silence.)

"From all reports you took to your new life like a duck to the Neva. A conspirator among conspirators. Ruthless, methodical, precise. Do you know this quote? From your good friend Vera Figner? 'Tender toward the working people, exacting and severe toward her comrades. And toward her political enemies, the government—merciless.'"

"How would I know it?"

"Sophia Perovskaya, legendary ascetic. *The* will behind The People's Will."

"What had to be done was done."

"That 'done' in summary: along the embankment of the Catherine Canal, you and four armed comrades took up your positions. At the appearance of Alexander II's bomb-proof carriage, a gift from Napoleon III, you signaled with your handkerchief. The first bomb reverberated citywide, slew two Cossacks, three horses, and lured the tsar from his safe-haven carriage onto the street."

"I have no quarrel with that summary."

"Wait. We haven't finished. When a guard exclaimed to his sovereign: 'Thank God, you are unhurt!' one of your more ironic comrades delivered this riposte: 'A bit early to be thanking God!' The second bomb ripped open the emperor's stomach, shattered his legs and drenched the snow with royal blood."

"I continue to have no quarrel with the summary."

"In the House of Preliminary Detention, your mother came to sit with you, bringing along a silk *sortie de bal*, an evening wrap, to drape around your condemned shoulders."

"My mother possessed an unassuming spiritual beauty and gentleness, but she did not understand the needs of the people."

"Or her daughter's needs at that particular juncture."

"It was over, my contribution. It did not matter what my mother brought or did not bring."

"Like a sick, tired child, you reclined on your mother's knee, awaiting execution."

"Not sick. Not tired."

"We have to agree with Yelizaveta Vasilevna's interpretation: all very fairytale-ish. Your life. Its play-out."

"The aristocracy is the fairytale, a story nearing its end."

"Any advice for Comrade Krupskaya, soon headed for prison?"

"If she is dedicated, if she is strong in her beliefs, she will emerge stronger and more dedicated."

"The prisoner's obligation, is it? To remain strong? To remain supremely dedicated? You *are* exacting and severe."

(Silence.)

"Knowing what you know now, is there anything, anything at all, you would have done differently?"

"I would have taken possession of one of the bombs earlier."

"And?"

"Before stationing myself along the Catherine Canal, I would have returned to my father's house."

"And?"

"And placed that explosive beneath his bed."

"And detonated it while he slept?"

"Or while he watched."

"One last question. Which adjective do you prefer: 'merciless' or 'ruthless'?"

"Neither. I prefer the phrase: 'The tsar is dead.'"

She Did Not Say

In the immediate aftermath of the pancake meeting, sitting on her mother's bed, she had indiscriminately answered whatever she was asked, too preoccupied to censor.

Since then she had grown more circumspect.

What she subsequently learned about Vladimir Ilyich Ulyanov she did not always share with Yelizaveta Vasilevna.

She did not say to her mother: "He is practiced at dodging tsarist spies. He is familiar with the through courtyards of Piter. He is very well suited for conspiratorial work."

Because her mother would have said, in turn: "A man adept at conspiratorial work is a man adept at lying."

She did not say: "He has already invented and used all manner of aliases. He is expert at clandestine communication. He is equally skilled at packing trunks with double-liners and illegal literature."

Because her mother would have said: "So he plans to leave Piter? When?"

She did not say: "Vladimir Ulyanov knows all about cowardice. When the tsarist thugs imprisoned his brother, he could find no one in all of Simbirsk to accompany his mother to Piter. No neighbor, none of the so-called liberals, no one wanted to be seen with the mother of an arrested man. Spineless cowards, the lot."

Because her mother would have said: "Even the brave pick their fights, Nadya."

She did not describe the mounting excitement with which she read his *Friends of the People*, how adroitly he exposed the errors of the *narodniki*.

Because her mother would have said: "To despise what we once believed is to despise part of ourselves."

She did not quote Vladimir Ulyanov's contention that Marxism required opposition to all liberals and their minor reforms.

Because her mother would have said: "So now, before we fight the tsar, we must fight the liberals?"

She did not repeat Vladimir Ulyanov's belief that the most urgent task before them was the organization of a revolutionary proletarian party.

Because her mother would have said: "Eluding a tsarist jail cell? That is not your most urgent task?"

She did not share Vladimir Ulyanov's prediction that the overthrow of absolutism in Russia would spearhead victorious revolutions across the globe.

Because her mother would have said: "Russia is not enough to take on? We must now lead the world?"

She did not say: "There are no, there can no longer be, morals in politics, only expedience. If a scoundrel is of use to The Revolution, he will be used for The Revolution."

Because her mother would pretend to hear nothing of that speech except the word "scoundrel" and inquire whether Vladimir Ulyanov knew intimately of whom he spoke.

She did not say to her mother: "Stop waiting up for me. It is not good for your own health. If I am caught, I am caught. I can survive a tsarist prison, if it comes to that. And if not, nothing you can do will save me."

Because her mother would have said: "You are all I have left, Nadya. A parent does not easily give up her only child."

As Agreed, He Came to Tea

He did not come by way of Nevsky Prospekt; he used the through courtyard. From the rear window of our apartment, I saw his approach.

"Look, Nadya. Here comes our skulking company now."

My daughter, chewing her lip, joined me at the window.

"And look at you! Your hair combed and neatly pinned. Our visitor will be pleased, I'm sure."

"Whether or not I comb my hair matters not in the least to Vladimir Ulyanov!"

Those were her *words,* but she could not keep her hand from flying to her forehead to re-tuck an errant strand.

The door opened, and my daughter's favorite agitator graced us with his presence.

"I thought it was the window's perspective. But no. You are indeed a short fellow."

"Mama!"

We settled together in a cordial group, in my room, drinking tea. I noticed that our guest took in the sweep as well as the details of our home. I noticed that he seemed to approve of the orderliness that met his eye.

"Nadezhda tells me you both give lessons."

"If we are to eat, we must."

"And how would you characterize the youth of Piter?"

When Ilyich desired information, he did not waste time on pre-ambles.

"Like youth everywhere, I suppose. Headstrong and quarrelsome."

"The headstrong are often valuable," Nadya interjected—her way of warning her mother to watch her tongue.

"And what do you teach these headstrong youth?" Ilyich persisted.

"What history teaches."

"That the people are exploited?"

"That when one fool dies another takes his place."

"Mama!"

I heard then, for the first time but certainly not for the last, the laugh so many would remark on and try to characterize. In truth, it sounded as much like a bellow as a laugh, a quick short burst of racket, powerful, infectious. I liked Ilyich's laugh. And I appreciated that, for the most part, he laughed when genuinely amused—not to intimidate.

"You are so right, Yelizaveta Vasilevna. There are many idiots in Russia. But what can we do? We must work with what we have."

Ambitious but practical. So much more practical than my Nadya.

What other personality traits and quirks defined Vladimir Ilyich? He was peevish, short-tempered, and without exception astounded when "idiots" failed to agree with his theories. He preferred books to people. He relished his privacy. He required absolute silence when he worked. He abhorred landladies. And when he took a break from promoting revolution, he loved nothing better than to gossip.

Do you imagine I counted myself spared in that regard?

I have no doubt that Ilyich spoke of me with more sarcasm than respect on multiple occasions. For myself, I cared not in the least, but I did not like to think of my Nadya caught between husband and mama. That situation I did not like.

Certainly he could be charming—when he chose to be, when it suited his purpose. About those calculated charms, he and I came to an understanding early on. If I am not mistaken, we arrived at that understanding when he invited himself to a second tea.

"Vladimir Ilyich," I said. "Do not waste your flattery on me. The effort will exhaust you and even then you will not be sure of the outcome."

I saw the twinkle in his eyes if my Nadya did not.

"Then I am grateful to be spared the exertion, Yelizaveta Vasilevna. I thank you and the people thank you."

"As far as the people are concerned," I said, "I have it on good authority they as yet reserve judgment."

He cocked his head at that. The remark gave him pause. No more than a moment's pause, but during that moment it was delicious to watch him wonder. Had an old woman's mockery trumped his own? Did the mockery merely mock or deliver a truth wrapped in jest?

During his second visit to the apartment of the Krupskayas, as during the first, I watched Vladimir Ilyich minutely inspect his surroundings.

When he had finished, he helped himself to another glass of tea, another sweet.

He pulled at his beard.

Calculating.

From the pancake breakfast, he must have realized he would get no cook in Nadezhda Krupskaya.

But in her mother?

Perhaps.

Agitations

When Nadya began consorting with Ilyich, the Okhrana's interest in her sharply increased.

The alliance frightened me—why deny it?

Any mother would have felt uneasy.

Because she taught workers at the Evening School, Nadya had long been known to the Okhrana and followed. Half of Piter shared that fate. The city's prisons could not hold all who were suspected of revolutionary activity. But what previously had been suspected of my Nadya her association with Ilyich confirmed.

From the beginning, Ilyich made no attempt to disguise either his purpose or his determination. He was not the kind to play at revolution for a few months, then retire to the countryside to lick his wounds. He would not lose interest in The Revolution; he would not stop scheming to topple the Romanov dynasty. I, as well as my Nadya, realized that when she threw in her lot with Ilyich, she threw in for life.

You will remember the first structure of Piter, built by imperial order of Peter Romanov, warrior prince and first tsar?

Standing on Hare Island, His Majesty reduced his great height by half to touch sod and thereby indicate where his minion should erect the prison fortress of St. Peter and St. Paul. As ordered, so it was done by thousands upon thousands of conscripted Cossacks, Tartars, soldiers and peasants, toiling round the clock to solidify swamp and marsh.

You will also perhaps recall the prison's earliest inmate? Convicted of conspiring against his father and fomenting rebellion, heir to the throne Alexis died from the father-approved torture of forty lashes of the knout. In the years since, the Peter and Paul Fortress has housed many revolutionary luminaries: the Decembrists, Bakunin, Chernyshevsky, Nechaev. Call it a mother's selfishness: I simply did not want my Nadya to join that list.

Did I care more for my daughter than for The Revolution?

Yes, always I cared more for my daughter than for The Revolution.

In the fall of 1895, Ilyich lived on Kazachy Street, near the Fontanka Canal, a quarter-hour walk from the heart of the city. He ate his main meal with family friends, the Chebotarevs, who routinely helped him out-fox the Okhrana. Disguised as the dockworker Nicholas Petrovich, he spent his days in the Vyborg district, conducting his own interrogations. "What is happening in the factories?" he demanded of the workers. "Tell me everything, but in proper order!"

To gather similar information, Nadya and her friend and comrade Lydia Knipovich disguised themselves as factory women.

"And what is this new style of headdress?" I asked when I came upon my daughter tying—ineptly—a kerchief around her hair.

"I am not wearing a kerchief for *style*," she objected. "This is not a matter of *frivolity*."

As if I had ever accused her of frivolity!

"Lydia and I have arranged to visit the Thornton Mills barracks."

"As potential residents?"

"Yes."

"Is that wise, Nadya? To deceive in so brazen a fashion?"

"It is *necessary*," she thundered but did not forget to kiss me goodbye.

Until she returned I could not sit. I could not read. I could not eat. Again and again I went to the window without seeing the kerchief I strained to see.

When I heard her running, half stumbling, up the stairs, I opened the door. She tore off the kerchief with such force its knot took bits of her hair.

"You are hurt? You have been assaulted? What has happened? Tell your mother!"

My hysteria only heightened hers.

She sank, weeping, into the chair.

"Nadya, you are frightening me! Please! Do I need to send for a doctor?"

"It is horrible, horrible, what they must endure. No water to wash. If a wife has a bed to sleep on, the husband must sleep on the floor. Filth and sickness are inescapable. And yet this is how they must *live*, Mama! Stray dogs on the streets are better treated."

I too sank into a chair. Relief had made me hiccup.

I do not mean to discredit or undermine Nadya's report. I have no doubt that conditions in the barracks were as deplorable as she described and likely worse. But in truth one did not have to cross to the Vyborg to witness tremendous want and suffering. Adolescent girls sprawled near the doors of taverns, too drunk to sit. Child beggars carrying dead siblings wrapped in rags to increase their chances in the begging pool. Adult beggars at every corner of the Nevsky, hollow-eyed, shoeless, talking to wind and spirits. The aristocrats did themselves no good flaunting their indulgences: caviar and champagne, imported roses and gold plate, costume balls that started at dusk and lasted through dawn, the hour hungry workers set off for the factories. They did themselves no favors, travelling the streets in their sleighs and troikas, wrapped in mink and ermine, returning to their mansions on the Fontanka and the Moika exhausted by nothing more strenuous than amusement. Ever wider and more pronounced grew the divisions of privilege and poverty in Piter.

During that period, I developed a series of peculiar ailments. Repeatedly, in one or another of my extremities, I experienced a complete loss of feeling, the numbness coming and going of its own volition. At other times my hands would burn or tremble uncontrollably. While instructing my pupils, I would forget what I had the moment before emphasized. My thoughts were not on lessons; they were on my Nadya.

And yet, the daughter I worried so continuously over had never looked lovelier. Her beauty regimen? For weeks on end, she returned home only to rest and then but briefly. She completely ignored her hair and her dress. Always she forgot to eat. Nevertheless, the escalating pace of working for The Revolution brought a bloom to her cheeks. Conspiring, my daughter thrived.

The same could not be said of Ilyich. In identical circumstances, he fell ill with pneumonia, lost weight, grew sallow. Such was to be a pattern with Ilyich: frenzy followed by collapse. When not pushing full force ahead, he became angry, then despondent. The headaches would begin; the sleeplessness would set in. In Piter, in Paris, in London, in Cracow, when Ilyich turned despondent, it was my Nadya who took on, in addition to her work for The Revolution, the work of tending to Ilyich and raising his spirits.

Because of the disease that has distorted her once lovely gray eyes, famously and cruelly, my daughter has been physically likened to a fish. In her labors on behalf of The Revolution, she would be described more aptly as the tortoise to Ilyich's hare. And who was not a tortoise to Ilyich's hare in terms of work speed? Perhaps Lev Davidovich could match his tempo, but The Revolution did not produce multiples of Lenin and Trotsky. Moreover, speed is not the only virtue. When Ilyich collapsed, my Nadya kept going.

During the summer of 1895, Nadya had taken work as a copyist with the accounts section of the state railroad administration. She did so for The Revolution. Because so much of her job involved issuing complaint forms, she could easily arrange to meet comrades under false pretenses.

"Do not grow too confident, Nadya," I pled constantly. "The Okhrana's incompetence ebbs and flows."

Ilyich and his band of Marxists renamed themselves. Henceforth they agitated at the Thornton and other factories of the Vyborg as Social Democrats. Their success, and the strikes that followed, moved them to the top of the police watch list.

The Okhrana put the brag out on the streets that Ilyich was as good as caught. This I heard from a pupil, a dim child whose attention could not long be held by paragraphs.

"Madam Krupskaya, are you not excited? The police have announced they will soon arrest an important state criminal named Ulyanov. The police say he is trapped and this time will not get away from them. They promise he will be hanged like his brother!"

Imagine hearing this from a child.

Yet the information was not altogether invalid. The Okhrana indeed possessed Ilyich's address. He had been betrayed by a dentist, posing as a socialist.

When Ilyich failed to appear as usual for dinner with the Chebotarevs on the ninth of December, they, my Nadya and I feared the worst. In a matter of hours, our fears were confirmed. Ilyich had been caught and arrested. And not only Vladimir Ilyich. The Okhrana had also ambushed Lydia Knipovich on her way to Valdaika.

In the Forest of Valdaika

She must hurry, hurry, Comrade Krupskaya must hurry.

But in her hurry she must make no mistakes, arouse no suspicions.

She must look as if she is an ordinary citizen of Piter, taking a holiday, travelling to a country fair.

But on the train Comrade Krupskaya keeps forgetting to smile, to behave with light-hearted giddiness, to project the sham of carefree festivity, because Comrade Krupskaya is brooding on the failure of comrades.

There are several, many, who could have reached Lydia Knipovich's cottage sooner and more quickly destroyed the incriminating leaflets signed by Vladimir Ilyich.

But those nearer refused to enter a cottage presumably watched.

Refused and thereby jeopardized all.

On the train, Comrade Krupskaya refuses an apple. Curtly.

She has brought nothing to eat. Another passenger takes pity.

Very likely the offer to share provisions will not be repeated on the traveller's next journey. And she will be the reason behind that cessation, the cause of one less instance of cordiality in Russia.

But she cannot dwell on apples or hurt feelings or friendliness. She must remain focused. Plan ahead. Concentrate on outwitting obstacles before they arise. Above all, she must not, *must not*, be caught in Lydia Knipovich's cottage.

Off the train, to get her bearings, she pauses briefly. Once more she reads the directions to her destination. If she consults those directions too often, she will look lost, confused; she will stand out and be remembered. Remembered well enough, she will be described.

Along the roadway, she encounters batches of men who study her with frank suspicion. Her mission depends on a peasant's hatred of police trumping his distrust of a frowning stranger hurrying past, of a female who smells of the city.

The cottage gate rattles as she enters. A peasant appears from the side yard.

"Lydia Knipovich sends regards. She is permitting me, her friend, the use of her cottage this morning to rest before attending the fair," she bluffs.

He does not say: "You come from Piter for a country fair?"

He does not say: "You have been speaking with Lydia Knipovich, who sits in a tsarist prison?"

He returns to picking apples.

Inside, leaflets lie in bundles and teeter in stacks. To burn them in the fireplace will take hours. There will be a constant curlicue of smoke rising from the chimney, announcing her presence and activity.

But she cannot swallow hundreds of pages of paper!

Hunkering close, she builds the necessary fire hotter than hot. Her neck runs, her nose drips, her blouse darkens from sweat. Before they burn, she fans herself with Vladimir Ilyich's words, then tosses.

Again the rattling gate. The peasant is departing, laden with apples.

And whom will he tell that the city woman who came to rest has spent her afternoon burning? And whom will he tell that she did not go to the fair? And how soon will he tell and tell again?

As ash smolders, she undertakes one last search: under the mattress, behind the pots, beneath the floorboards, which is where she finds a box of typefaces the fire cannot consume.

There is give to her waistband, room for expansion.

From a closet, she snatches a coat to camouflage her new odd shape.

Swaddled, thicker than she arrived, she leaves the cottage. In the nearby woods, she waits for dusk and then, in deepening shadow, drops to her hands and knees.

A good and forceful digger, Comrade Krupskaya.

Unafraid of worms. Untroubled by dirt. With spirit and conviction she shovels with her fingers, blackening skin and skirts. And when she leaves the forest of Valdaika, she leaves behind, buried deep, a relic of The Revolution.

On the forest floor of Valdaika, a patch of hallowed ground.

House of Preliminary Detention

In Piter, Vladimir Ilyich sat in cell 193. In Moscow, newlyweds Nicholas and Alexandra were crowned the new tsar and tsarina. In celebration, half a million Russians gathered at Khodynka Field, military training grounds located on the outskirts of the city, to receive the new tsar's gifts of free beer, a bit of sausage, a slice of gingerbread. When the tsar's bounty ran short, a stampede ensued. Hundreds fell into the military trenches where they died, crushed and suffocated.

The terrible and senseless tragedy of Khodynka Field represented the opening act of the reign of Nicholas and Alexandra.

And the imperial response to that tragedy?

While the mangled corpses of their countrymen and women were being carted away, Nicholas and Alexandra, attired in golden military braids and pearls, attended the French ambassador's ball.

"Dancing on the peoples' graves," my Nadya said.

Or perhaps it was precisely then that the tsar and tsarina began dancing on their own.

From cell 193 in the House of Preliminary Detention, Ilyich sent forth a steady stream of directives. The Chebotarevs served as a mail drop. Nadya picked up Ilyich's letters from the couple and distributed them, according to the correspondent's instructions. Between the lines of innocuous letters describing everything and nothing, Ilyich wrote messages of importance in milk. Heat revealed his true letter.

Trying to rush the appearance of Ilyich's covert words to her, Nadya leaned too close to the candle's flame and singed her wrist.

In rushing to treat the burn, to Nadya's fury, I damaged the letter. But in that instance her anger did not exceed my own.

"My daughter's flesh is far more precious than anything Vladimir Ilyich has to say!" I raved.

Nadya pursed her lips. She did not share my view.

Since prison provided Ilyich the opportunity to study and write without interruption, initially he was quite pleased with his stay there. Other prisoners experienced difficulty falling asleep on straw mattresses reeking of disinfectant; Ilyich devised his own solution. Before retiring, he exercised vigorously. Exertion brought fatigue and fatigue sleep. Alas, Ilyich's inventive adjustments could not completely overshadow the privations of prison life. As the months dragged on, again he turned morose.

"And how is Ilyich?" I habitually inquired of Nadya, primarily as a means of gauging my daughter's mood.

"Vladimir Ilyich despairs that his work is being disrupted."

"But he is working nonstop."

"To test and shape his ideas, he needs the back and forth of debate."

"He cannot debate himself?"

"Isolation does not suit his temperament."

"Your nerves are stronger than Ilyich's."

"Mama!"

"I state the obvious."

The comparison mightily displeased her.

"He is suffering a bout of prison melancholy," she excused. "It will pass."

Perhaps it would, perhaps it would not. But Vladimir Ilyich's melancholy did not give him the right to risk my own Nadya's health.

When my daughter prepared to leave the apartment wearing two coats and multiple scarves, I asked if she intended to sled the Neva on her belly.

"I plan no sledding," she evaded.

"The truth, Nadya, or I will knock aside the Okhrana and follow you myself."

"Ilyich has asked me to stand on a certain spot of the Shpalernaya pavement."

"Whatever for?"

She hesitated.

"Do not lie to your mama!"

"If I stand at a certain spot, when the guards walk him back to his cell from the prison yard he will be able to see me."

Imagine my reaction! That Ilyich would ask more of my Nadya, already risking so much for him and his revolution!

"You are telling me that Ilyich has asked you to shiver in Baltic winds merely so that he will catch sight of your vigil?"

"I will not shiver in two coats."

Ignoring my protests, Nadya did as she and Ilyich wanted. Perhaps I was wrong to object. The request I considered supremely selfish history has labeled a rare romantic impulse on Vladimir Ilyich's part. Imprisoned, he yearned for a glimpse of his future bride.

Regardless of how many prisoners the government of Russia detained, the year 1896 scrolled forward. The white nights of June came and went. The record temperatures of July carried over into August. Now when my Nadya stood on the Shpalernaya pavement at the appointed hour, she wore her lightest cotton. And I, in the sticky air of our close apartment, wore the same, fighting the effects of vertigo. Whenever Nadya left my sight, fear set the room spinning. We could no longer discern who counted as friend or enemy and possessed no sure, uncorrupted means of finding out.

On the tenth of August Nadya returned even later than her usual hour. She had noticed a new police agent following her, she said, and to make his job more tedious had crisscrossed the city before coming home.

"Have you eaten?"

"I am too tired to eat."

Never before had my indomitable daughter admitted to fatigue.

"It is the heat. And your longer walk home. You will feel better once you sleep."

She stretched across the bed fully clothed.

I removed her shoes and rubbed her feet.

"This one calls himself Larionich," she said without inflection. "He pretends to be an artisan in a metalwork shop."

"Is he aware you suspect him?"

She shrugged; I did not press.

We both realized Nadya's suspicions were immaterial; at issue was how much this Larionich had gleaned of her recent activities and would subsequently report.

Two days passed—the most ordinary of days, hours seemingly without distinction or particularized peril. And yet, in retrospect, how precisely one remembers and cherishes their ordinariness.

On the morning of August 12, I insisted Nadya sit down to breakfast. I even threatened, as I recall, to follow her around with a full spoon, if she refused to obey. On the table I laid out bread and berries. I had already put cheese on her plate. I was in the very act of pouring tea when the knock I had so long dreaded shook our door.

In the moment, I confess, I felt a very stupid woman, absurdly out of touch with the new ways of an old regime.

I had always expected, you understand, that summons to come in the middle of some black night.

I had always assumed that once the sun rose on us and Piter, at least until another darkness fell, my Nadya remained safe.

While I shook with fear, Nadya went very still. She did not cower from the intruders. She did not deny or explain. She prepared to go with them.

"Let go, Mama," she said. "You must let go of my hand."

But to release her hand was to speed her toward a jail cell.

"I will be fine," she announced—as much to her captors as to me.

And then, only for me, because only I would understand and appreciate the vicious contempt implied, she asked her captors to wait.

"I need a moment to tidy my hair."

Prison Dialectics

They had not dragged her through the streets by the hair as they had dragged others. They had not chained her hands. But two additional Okhrana agents waited at the bottom of the stairs. On the street they formed a close rectangle around her. If, at any time, she had twisted or shoved within that box of four, she would have been grabbed: by the hair or neck—by any body part conducive to grabbing.

She was not naïve.

The Okhrana were rewarded for capture, not gentlemanly behavior.

Market basket in hand, the downstairs tenant had been nonchalantly stepping across her threshold at the precise moment "one of the Krup-skayas" was being escorted down the stairs into the street. Nonchalance did not survive the woman's first glimpse of uniforms. With the nervousness of a ferret, she had leapt backward and slammed the door.

As if a division of wood would save her from arrest by tsarist thugs if arrest were in the offing!

Not even their staunchest adversaries accused the Okhrana of dereliction of duty. Until they caught their intended quarry, they did not give up the pursuit.

Coming up alongside the entourage of which she was now part, a few citizens on the street averted their gaze, pretending to be neither concerned nor curious. But others stared boldly, in challenge.

"Oh, she is a dangerous one, is she?" an old man muttered as they passed. "And that one? And that one?" He pointed randomly at others who lacked, for the moment, Okhrana escort.

She must remember to write about that citizen to Ilyich, to describe in detail his blatant derision, how he categorically refused to bow and scrape in the presence of tsarist police. Ilyich would take heart at that defiance. On the streets of Piter, fear and submission were no longer the only attitudes in evidence. There was also anger, seething resentment. Emotions of value to The Revolution.

Inside the House of Preliminary Detention, she was lead into a room of calculated filth and left there, alone.

Perhaps the excrement in the corner came from vermin, perhaps not. She did not pull up her skirts in disgust. What did the cleanliness of hems matter in this context? Where ordered to sit, she sat. She did not request a more comfortable chair. She neither pled nor argued. In no form or fashion did she attempt to interact with her captors. She picked out a spot of wall and fixed her gaze upon it. She folded her arms and settled in, prepared for a lengthy wait.

Before her stamina for waiting had barely been tested, they returned. She had only time between visits to twice recite to herself Nekrasov's "Who Can Be Happy and Free in Russia":

Thou art so pitiful,
Poor, and so sorrowful,
Yet of great treasure full,
Mighty, all-powerful,
Russia, my Mother!

"What is the reason for your arrest?"

"You know it better than I," she replied.

"Indeed! Is that so?"

She maintained her wooden expression. Her jaw, her face, she could readily set and keep set.

"Only criminals are incarcerated here."

What a pleasure it would have been to counter that claim with: "Indeed! Is that so?"

"Criminals! And we keep them here to squeeze the hidden truth out of them!"

They hinted at repercussions: never would she leave whatever cell they planned to lock her in. No brisk walks in the fresh air of a prison yard for prisoner Nadezhda Konstantinovna Krupskaya.

And this they considered leverage?

She cared nothing for walks in the prison yard. Undoubtedly they would occur at a most inconvenient hour and disrupt her reading.

"You were a teacher. You consorted with the workers."

"My students were workers."

"And you introduced them to intellectuals, the *raznochintsy*."

"One or two," she said.

And then they began to shout.

"What else are you guilty of?"

"I do not consider myself guilty."

"You have a willful nose," they taunted. "A contemptuous mouth."

The strategy of insult, badly managed.

Her fondest wish, confined in a tsarist interrogation room, was to appear willful and contemptuous.

"You are no beauty now, Nadezhda Krupskaya. Before you leave here, you will be worn and wide."

And what of it? Ugliness was of no consequence. Ugliness did not compromise her ability to work for The Revolution.

They did not formally charge her; they led her to a solitary cell with a Judas aperture through which every gendarme in passing could peep.

So let them. They would see a woman indifferent to the surveillance.

Even in August, the cell she stepped into felt chilly.

Chilliness would not kill her.

The walls ran with moisture, slimy to the touch.

But she need not rub up against walls.

The air stank of sweat, fear—and she would add to that collective stench.

So she could not wash.

So she was allowed no tooth powder.

So she could not rest except on the lice-ridden pallet of boards that was to be her bed.

So she could walk but five paces before a wall blocked her progress.

So she would speak to no one for hours and days on end.

She would adapt.

One blackened lantern hung from the ceiling and fogged the room with smoke. To read she would have to stand directly below it.

She would learn to read standing, squinting.

The chill, the stench, the isolation, the vile food, the eye at the Judas—all could be surmounted. She would train herself to ignore the shuffle and stomp of the gendarmes, the moans and cries of prisoners incapable of holding in their anguish. She would reconcile herself to the inevitability of sleeping and waking in discomfort, the constant seepage of unsettled bowels. And during the next interrogation and the next and the next she would take care not to implicate by random comment or awkward pause any comrade still at large. At their own hectoring game, she would best the conceited gendarmes.

Before the lock-in, a parting admonition.

"No singing! Singing is forbidden!"

Her "contemptuous mouth" curled in amusement. For her to refrain from singing was no loss—to her or anyone within hearing range. She had never been able to carry a tune. Long ago as a child at a Polish fair, mesmerized by a native folk singer, she had listened breathlessly to each note of the ballad, determined to memorize every flourish. At home, standing before a mirror, she had done her best to replicate the performance, mimicking the singer's voice, miming the grand, melodramatic gestures.

Her mother had come up from behind and gently placed a palm across her mouth.

"I have no doubt you will grow up to accomplish many wonderful things, my Nadya. But singing is not one of your talents."

She must remember to say when next she saw her mother: "You will be happy to know the Okhrana have no use for your daughter's singing either."

Because the sheer ridiculousness of the injunction might make her mother forget, if only for the moment, the rest of what an imprisoned daughter could not do.

Do Not Give Them the Satisfaction

They could not prevent me from seeing my Nadya, a mere political detainee.

Even murderers were allowed visits from their mothers.

At the House of Preliminary Detention, I took my place in line, a lengthy one that spiraled. An abundance of prisoners and therefore an abundance of relatives, desperate to see loved ones who had been snatched from them by the tsarist police. One had to wait one's turn for a vacant seat in the visiting hall.

Throughout the visit, Nadya and I would be closely observed. In the abstract, the restriction did not terribly upset me. In practice, yes, very much so, but I did not anticipate that reaction in advance. Waiting for admittance, I felt wholly confident of my interpretive abilities. I had witnessed my daughter's first laugh and first tumble. Long had I studied her countenance and its fluctuations. I had schooled myself to detect her evasions and half-truths and when she lied to spare her mother heartache. The moment I saw her again, I believed I would be able to judge the extent of her suffering.

Brought into the visiting room, she walked as if she were the tsarina on parade—shoulders back, chin elevated—far more upright than she ever walked the Nevsky, the exalted posture and carriage meant to convey a message: *they have not broken me.*

Wearing my blackest dress, I also indulged in pantomime, my spine as straight as any arrow.

During my Nadya's arrest, I had not behaved becomingly. With much shame, I admit this. Although I had not groveled, I had wept in front of her captors and for that blatant display of emotion, that regrettable lack of strength, I will never forgive myself. With all that she faced, I should not have made her leave behind a distraught mother. By showing weakness, I failed her. I had promised myself I would not fail her again in the House of Preliminary Detention.

In the visitors' hall, as my daughter approached, to counteract a resurgence of tears, I pinched my wrist.

As well as I read my Nadya, she reads her mother.

"No tears, Mama!" she whispered fiercely as we embraced. "Do not give the tsarist swine the satisfaction!"

"No whispering! Whispering is not permitted!" the gendarme within inches of us rebuked.

From my Nadya, I tried to take courage, to match her haughtiness and disdain. Although she seemed defiant and unscathed, even stronger than last I had seen her, in that odious room, surrounded by men who possessed both the authority and opportunity to do her grievous harm, faith in a mother's intuition faltered.

Men and women flogged, pregnant women beat about the belly. One could not live in Piter and escape such prison tales.

"You have not been hurt?" I asked as soon as we were seated.

Because of the whispering reprimand, Nadya shouted her answer. As intended, every gendarme, visitor and prisoner who shared the space heard her scathing response.

"No, Mama. I have not been subjected to the whip. The Okhrana do not own a slice of my tongue. As yet, I am no more harmed than the workers of Piter."

My daughter's vehemence seemed to call forth my own. I twisted in my chair. I bared my teeth. With wild abandon, I assailed one gendarme after another after another.

"What evidence do you have against my daughter? What evidence do you pretend to possess against Nadezhda Konstantinovna Krupskaya?"

Unlike my daughter's insolence, mine did not reflect control. It reflected fury, helplessness, nerves that had once more given way.

Again I had failed my daughter.

"Mama, do not upset yourself. Do not waste breath petitioning the rotten—"

"Do not tell your mother what to do!"

"Mama, Mama! Look at me. Look only at me."

She took my hands, shook them playfully. "Who do you guess I saw yesterday? At me, Mama, not the gendarme. Look at your daughter."

I looked as directed and saw, behind her, a sea of sneers.

"Mama! Pay attention! On the way to the prison yard, I passed Lydia Knipovich. She had a cold but was no less her splendid self."

She swung my hands in hers, the better to disguise their shaking.

"Mama, Mama! Do you remember what you used to tell me? That imagination does not always count as a gift?"

I did not remember. Or could not remember in the visiting room of the House of Preliminary Detention. What had I meant when I said it? In what circumstance, for what reason, would I make such an observation to my daughter?

In a tsarist prison, imagination would count as a liability; it could not count otherwise. The horrific needs no enhancement.

"Prepare to be amused, Mama! Prepare!"

If my expression altered in response to that admonition, I could not feel it.

"Your daughter's recent experiences"—and here she arched an eyebrow—"have revealed that she possesses no such gift in any measure."

I believe it was then that I brought a fist to my lips.

"Mama, Mama," she said. "Listen to me. I am healthy. I am strong. I have my studies to occupy me. Time will not pass swiftly, but it will pass."

I shook my head. To speak was to blubber.

"Ilyich and I have not killed a tsar. We will not swing like Sophia Perovskaya. Our work and lives have been interrupted, not ruined. Like others, we will be exiled."

By predicting exile, she meant to console her mother.

In the year 1896, death still seemed a revolutionary's worst destiny. European exile would soon challenge that assumption, but at the time, yes, death seemed the harsher and more dreaded fate.

In the Cell Next to Comrade Krupskaya

Another young woman imprisoned.

This one: frightened, troubled, lacking the fortitude and resilience of Nadezhda Konstantinovna Krupskaya.

Once upon a time?

Perfectly sane.

Now?

She sees faces in bricks, believes the walls around her undulate before they wail.

A Marxist?

No.

A revolutionary?

No.

Only a university student in the wrong hallway at the wrong hour, caught in the latest Okhrana sweep.

While Comrade Krupskaya stands below her kerosene lamp and ruins her eyes squinting at shadowed text, the young woman in the adjoining cell chatters and spins like a top.

Too fragile for the House of Preliminary Detention.

Too *imaginative*.

If she does not chatter, if she does not spin, the walls will accuse louder than they wail.

She is not stupid. She is a medical assistant in training. She realizes, pity this girl!, that she is going mad.

"You must find my brother Mikhail! He will explain my innocence. He will tell you I am only a university student."

"As if we have not heard that excuse before!" scoff the gendarmes. "If you must plead, find a more original defense."

"I am an innocent mermaid," she tries.

"I am an innocent particle of dust," she tries.

"Mikhail! Mikhail! Save me! Save your sister who has done no wrong!"

And then she whispers: "What did you suggest, Mikhail? Again?"

Comrade Krupskaya looks up from her book, used to hearing frenzied feet, piteous shrieks, squeals, moans—not silence coming from the next cell.

Prying apart the seams of a tin kettle takes concentration, determination, time, but it is a relatively quiet pursuit.

The prisoner is crouching.

She often crouches.

The prisoner is bleeding.

Women often bleed.

What do you expect of gendarmes?

That they would distinguish, bother to distinguish, the variation through a Judas hole?

A sawed wrist, a punctured artery.

A young mad girl fatally damaging her young mad self.

And who is this self, this she, this prisoner, this Russian?

History forgets.

Call her the nameless and the dead.

The Proposal

When visiting the House of Preliminary Detention, her mother no longer wore black. Nor did she weep or tremble. Her glaring, however, had substantially increased. Arriving, departing, and at any opportunity in between, Yelizaveta Vasilevna used her pointed chin to great effect. Vehemence wrapped in the tiniest of packages, but virulent nonetheless. Even the gendarmes had begun to give Yelizaveta Vasilevna a wide berth.

Clearly, on this visit, her mother had something of importance to confide—otherwise she would not be slighting her glaring ritual.

"I have news, Daughter."

"So I have guessed."

"Ilyich has been released."

"Yes, I have heard."

"And you are not jealous?"

"Why would I be?"

"Because he is free and you remain here."

"They imprisoned Ilyich before me."

Her mother's eyes glittered—perhaps in malice at the gendarme who had, at the mention of Ilyich, given them more of his unwanted attention than usual.

Empty tables surrounded them. The downturn in visitors did not reflect jails less full, only the inconstancy of relatives. Not every mother or uncle or sister proved as conscientious and stalwart as Yelizaveta Vasilevna.

"And that is all, Nadya, you have to say about the matter?"

"Ilyich will be happy to be on the streets of Piter again," she said.

"But his time in Piter will be brief."

She withstood gendarme scrutiny far better than her mother's. And now she understood: neither gendarmes nor malice accounted for the glittering eyes.

"Yes. As expected, he has been ordered to Siberia."

"I must tell you, Nadya—"

"What must you tell me, Mama?" she challenged.

"I do not look forward to Siberia."

She had braced for such a comment and still a wave of heat swept from her neck to her cheeks. Infuriating to have no control of one's cheeks!

"Then he has told you."

"That he has petitioned for you to follow? You are surprised he informed your mama of such intentions?"

"Ilyich will need a secretary."

"But a 'secretary' is not what you are to be called. You are to call yourself his fiancée."

"That is the term I must use in order to join him."

"And in order to stay in Siberia with Ilyich, you must become his wife."

The otherwise featureless visiting hall contained two long mirrors—for the gendarmes to watch behind their backs or perhaps to observe their own preening. Neither mirror was fogged; neither was mottled. She could not blame her current appearance on the distortion of glass. Her cheeks had begun to sag—the beginning of jowls. There were fleshy loops around her neck, as if she had acquired extra skin.

To anyone and everyone, including herself, she did not look remotely bridal.

"*Nu, chto zh, zhenoi tak zhenoi.*" Well, so what? If as a wife, then as a wife.

Her mother reached across the table and sharply rapped her wrist.

"Reserve such foolishness for others. Do not repeat such things to a mother who knows her daughter's heart."

Release

Banged upon, her cell door shook.

No gendarme knocked before entering.

Knocking constituted a courtesy.

Also unprecedented: the overt—and excessive—uneasiness.

Why would a gendarme be nervous?

"Gather your belongings."

"Which belongings?"

"All of them! At once!"

While ordering her about, she noticed, he carefully kept half his body, one leg, one arm, one shoulder, outside her cell, visible to anyone passing.

She rose from the bed, the extent of her compliance.

"Am I to be transferred?"

"Gather your belongings, I say!"

"For what purpose?" she persisted.

"Released! You are being released!"

A lie, she thought. Who believed a gendarme? But what sort of interrogation required a prisoner to pack?

"Hurry!" the gendarme demanded.

She did not hurry. Why oblige the police by rushing? With the speed of an indolent aristocrat, she began to circle her cell.

"I am to take my books?"

"Yes, yes! Everything! Leave nothing behind."

While collecting her books, she listened. A cacophony of cell doors swinging open.

How was that possible?

And yet it was.

All women prisoners turned out of the House of Preliminary

Detention and ordered to leave the surrounding premises immediately.

At the apartment, she had to knock. Carted off to prison, she had not taken a key. She might have hidden one in a pocket during the transit, but it would not have stayed in her possession. Gendarmes routinely confiscated keys.

"Nadya?" her shocked mother repeated. "You are home? To stay?"

The length of her return was as unpredictable as the return itself. An hour earlier she had not expected to spend this night on a lice-free bed.

"Why?" her mother asked, then retracted. "It does not matter; it does not matter. You are here now. You are here."

Her liberty, they soon learned, had been gained at another's expense.

To escape the men who entered her cell and repeatedly, brutally, violated her, prisoner Marie Vetrova had drenched her skirts with kerosene oil and struck a match.

Although the gendarmes "valiantly tried" to save the prisoner's life, the burns went "too deep."

Despicable, despicable swine.

Because "excitable" women were "prone to extreme behaviors," because the authorities feared "copycat" immolations, the tsar's ministers had ordered the release of all women inmates—for now.

"A young woman, senselessly dead," her mother moaned.

Yelizaveta Vasilevna had not recovered her equilibrium. At every footfall on the stairway, her mother blanched. Any knock on the door might herald a uniformed rapist come to escort Nadezhda Konstantinovna Krupskaya to another locked cell patrolled by other brutes with keys.

And so she did not further upset her mother by expounding on Marie Vetrova's gift to The Revolution.

The workers were outraged.

There was rioting in the streets.

Everyone knew of Marie Vetrova's vile treatment.

The flames that killed a tsarist prisoner had also seared the tsar and his corrupt regime.

Marie Vetrova's suffering had ended, but her contribution to The Revolution had just begun.

INTERVIEW WITH HISTORY
Marie Vetrova

"Are the rumors correct? Your only crime was to read clandestine literature? Otherwise you took no part in *Narodnaya Volya* schemes?"

(Silence.)

"The Director of Police entered your cell. Gendarmes entered your cell. Assistant *Prokuror* Kichin of the Court of Appeal entered your cell. You understand why there might be confusion? So many men coming and going?"

(Silence.)

"Will you assist history, Marie Vetrova? Will you now disclose, for once and all time, the identity of the man or men who raped you and continued raping you while you futilely screamed?"

(Silence.)

"After reading Count Tolstoy's essay, 'What is Happiness?'—do you remember?—in your diary you thanked the Count for revealing the truth."

(Silence.)

"We are not in the business of defining happiness, Marie Vetrova, but with your help we will reveal the truth."

(Silence.)

"When you doused your flesh and skirts with kerosene, when you struck the match, when you chose to die, how many watched and refused to save you? Name them. Please. Name them."

(Silence.)

"Marie Vetrova, we apologize for the intrusion. We apologize for man."

SIBERIA

The Honeymoon

It is a peculiar sort of punishment, Siberian exile. The tsarist government sends radicals off into the wilds of Russia where they have abundant time and leisure to regroup and hatch new schemes to overthrow the autocracy.

When Ilyich learned he would spend his three-year exile in Shushenskoye, a village bordering the Yenisei River, he burst into song. Quite appropriate, that gleeful response. There were so many more uncomfortable places to which to be banished. Shusha is considered the Italy of Siberia. The climate there is tolerable, if not temperate; the police presence understated. For the political exile, there is also honor by association. Once Ilyich set foot in the village, he joined the revolutionary elite. The Decembrists preceded him to Shusha.

The distance between Piter and Shusha is some 2,500 *versts,* a journey undertaken by the Krupskayas at their own expense. Neither Nadya nor I begrudged the outlay of rubles. We were seeing parts of Russia new to us both. Nizhny-Novgorod, Perm, the majestic Urals. The West-Siberian express took us as far as Krasnoyarsk, where we waited for the Yenisei to thaw. On the first northbound ship of the season, we sailed for Sorokino. For the remaining 55 *versts* overland to Shusha, we tested our rumps and balance on a rickety sleigh, carrying with us the "necessities" Ilyich had demanded: his green-shaded study lamp and two crates of books, exceedingly heavy volumes on railroad economics and coal production.

"Mind your noses," our driver warned as we entered the village.

Heaps of manure lined the roadway. The wheels of our transport reinvigorated the odor. Even so, Nadya and I liked Shusha instantly, a fondness that prevailed.

When we arrived, Ilyich was nowhere to be found.

"A fine way to start a marriage," I observed.

"A marriage that does not yet exist," my Nadya shot back.

Quibbles.

I was quite put out, quite put out, that my future son-in-law was not on hand to greet us.

"I cannot find him or his dog," our driver apologized.

"His dog!"

That my Nadya would again fall in love with a dog! That she would again have to leave what she loved!

"Stop fussing, Mama. Ilyich will show up eventually."

And why was Vladimir Ilyich not there to welcome his prospective bride and mother-in-law? Because he was hunting—or his version of hunting.

Let me here discuss Ilyich the hunter.

He was hopelessly inept. Nonetheless, he took it upon himself to stalk woodcock, rabbits and ducks. Toward that end, he had acquired leather breeches, the bird dog Zhenya, and a secondhand Barden rifle for which he paid eight rubles, an entire month's stipend.

"And the leather breeches? Their purpose?" Nadya was soon to bait.

"For those occasions when I find myself in the bogs," Ilyich admitted.

"And you find yourself in the bogs because…?" Nadya ribbed.

"The game is there, of course!" blustered Ilyich.

Once we settled in, Nadya went hunting with Ilyich and Zhenya and never failed to return merrier than she had departed. Back at the cottage, she set about involving me in the mischief.

"Ask Volodya about this day's hunting vow."

"A huntsman's vow, Ilyich? One would have thought there were enough vows to uphold already," I remarked.

In Shusha, Ilyich felt relaxed enough to play the clown. While raising an eyebrow, he pulled comically at his beard.

"Your vow, Volodya! Own it!" Nadya insisted.

"If we met any hares, I vowed not to fire because I had forgotten to bring along straps."

"And?" Nadya nudged.

"And carrying the hares would be inconvenient."

"Yet immediately a hare darted out…," Nadya clapped her hands, "Volodya fired."

"So where are these hares?" I asked.

Nadya tittered. "Exactly where they were before Volodya fired. Safe and sound."

History has recorded that upon seeing my soon to be son-in-law, I exclaimed: "Vladimir Ilyich, you have grown positively fat!"

Those were not my first words. My first words were: "Where the devil have you been, Vladimir Ilyich? To leave us here without escort!"

Before Nadya and I joined him, Ilyich had spent 18 months in Shusha. His exile pension covered room, board, and laundry in the log hut of the peasant Apollon Zyrianov. A second room had been prepared for Nadya and me. Unlike the peasant huts my Nadya had seen during her summer of teaching, the Siberian log hut of Apollon Zyrianov was quite presentable. The walls had been whitewashed; brightly colored mats covered the floor. On several ledges fir branches stood in decorative pots.

Our first hour in Shusha, Zyrianov followed us following Ilyich inside.

"These bookshelves?" he boasted. "I made them myself for Vladimir Ilyich."

Instead of complimenting the handiwork, I noticed that my daughter turned aside, stony-faced.

She did not, from the first moment, warm to Zyrianov. And the antagonism intensified.

"You must find us other lodgings," she demanded of Ilyich on the eve of their wedding.

"He is harmless," Ilyich said.

"Because he can build a splendid bookcase? He is too much in our business. And when he drinks, he talks."

"Not yet a wife and already demanding!" I thought to tease. But in that particular argument, I did not interfere. Nadya had set her jaw.

Since history slights the wedding ceremony, I will do my best to expand upon the event. If Nadya were to stay in Shusha, she could not long keep her fiancée status. The law demanded a wedding, an Orthodox ceremony, the only kind of matrimonial ceremony Imperial Russia recognized. The official permit to marry was received in early July and the ceremony took place in the parish church on the tenth of the month. Besides myself, three other witnesses attended, all peasants from the village. Nadya allowed me to dress her hair with a sprig of lilac, although not before we had argued and I had wept in frustration.

"If you expect a second wedding day, remove the lilac," I said. "If not, grant your mother this indulgence."

In accordance with Orthodox wedding custom, the priest held a crown over Nadya's head and then over Ilyich's head, infuriating them both. Also required: an exchange of rings. Neither Nadya nor Ilyich ever wore those copper bands but my daughter saved hers. Perhaps she thought she had hidden it where no one would notice. But I saw it in Shusha, in London, in Paris, in Piter, in Moscow. Where Nadya went, her wedding ring went with her.

We hosted a small reception afterwards, also as custom demanded. Although we served nothing stronger than tea, Zyrianov became quite drunk and fell off the table while raising his tea glass to the bride and groom.

Nadya glanced meaningfully at her new husband.

The next day Ilyich engaged another cottage.

But first came the wedding night. I retired early, as was only proper, so I cannot reveal precisely how they came to an understanding regarding their conjugal relationship. It was to be a real marriage. I have no doubt that it was Ilyich who proposed such intimacy. Whatever my Nadya secretly hoped, she would not have risked undermining their working relationship for reasons of personal desire. If Ilyich had wanted them to continue occupying separate beds, separate beds they would have occupied.

Our new cottage of notched wood had carved panels above each double-framed window and three commodious rooms. The yard included a kitchen garden where we were able to grow cucumbers, carrots, beets and pumpkins. In time I learned to manage the square brick oven and, more importantly, the oven hook, but not before many instances of scattering soup and dumplings across the hearth. Nadya also assisted in the kitchen, although—and I say this with a mother's love—she often did more harm than good. She could not properly season soup for the life of her. Nor was she an able housekeeper.

But why should my daughter have strived for excellence in either of those domestic realms? Women aplenty have excelled at housewifery and accomplished little else.

After our final meal of the day, Ilyich washed dishes. Doubt me if you dare. One of the reasons Ilyich and Lev Davidovich got along when they did get along as Lenin and Trotsky is that both were meticulous men. The papers on their desks arranged just so. Correspondence catalogued by date received. The tie straight, the coat brushed. In Shusha,

Ilyich sang while he scrubbed and also while he dried. If a government spy had passed by at such moments, he might have concluded that rendering the radical Vladimir Ilyich Ulyanov harmless would be a relatively easy operation: simply provide him with a sink of dirty dishes.

In the evenings, both Nadya and Ilyich studied German, the predominant language of Marxism. Just prior to bedtime, they shared a little Pushkin, a little Nekrasov. In the mornings they worked side by side translating into Russian Sidney and Beatrice Webb's *Theory and Practice of English Trade Unionism*. Since neither was fluent in English, each word had to be checked and rechecked in the English dictionary. They persevered because they had been promised 400 rubles for the completed project and they, we, needed the fee. In the afternoons, Ilyich concentrated on his *Development of Capitalism in Russia*, polishing the prose style that would ever after define him and sycophants would imitate. Hectoring rather than elegant, it was a style that very nearly matched the way Ilyich argued in person. A strident tone, an almost military rhythm. Serial demands and serial abuse, his opponents lumped together.

Nadya spent her afternoons writing her pamphlet, "The Woman Worker," in truth the more subversive text.

And I? How did I keep busy? I battled the peasant oven; I made nightshirts for my son-in-law; I mended Nadya's stockings; I smoked and I played cards.

My daughter's husband stank at cards.

"How can such an intelligent man play so badly against such a weak old woman?"

"Yelizaveta Vasilevna, if you are a weak old woman, the Russian army is a field nest of rabbits."

To be fair, Ilyich did not apply himself to cards, perhaps because he feared the reward of competence would be spending more time with me.

I once asked Nadya whether Ilyich objected to my presence. Toward his mother, Maria Alexandrovna, throughout his life he was unfailingly solicitous and respectful. But I was the mother-in-law and I would not have blamed him for feeling resentful.

"Nonsense!" my Nadya snorted. "Ilyich sees the justice of your joining us."

The justice of it, perhaps. But what of the feelings?

Chess was Ilyich's game and had been since childhood when he played his father and brother Alexander. At Shusha, he played other exiles "by correspondence." Sometimes, from bed, not looking at the boards, he played three games simultaneously. He even dreamed of playing chess. "If he puts his knight here, I'll stick my rook there!" he cried out in his sleep. He woke because Nadya grabbed his jabbing finger and pinched it.

Twice a week the much anticipated mail arrived. Ilyich, a dutiful son, wrote weekly to his mother and to that letter Nadya added a postscript. Over her shoulder I read her description of the onset of the Siberian winter, a white world of white hares and white skies. *There are hours, days, when I forget which week it is, which month. Time simply stands still.*

"What a pretty picture you paint, Nadya," I said. "What a pretty life."

If Maria Alexandrovna hoped with each letter that Nadya would announce the conception of the heir the Ulyanovs so wanted, she met with disappointment. I too was disappointed, and Nadya also, I believe, though she would not dare confess it, even to her mother.

Despite the preoccupations of revolution, Ilyich would have made a good father.

I know this how?

I watched him with little Minya, the sole survivor of 14 children born to the peasant couple across the street. As regularly as the cock crowed, Minya came to visit and when he did, Ilyich stopped whatever he was doing to share a joke or play a game. He devised a contest involving sticks and the dog Zhenya. I cannot remember the rules, or perhaps the rules changed with each playing, but the sport of it turned little Minya delirious with excitement, and in the end Ilyich always allowed the child to win.

"You are strong but sometimes wobbly," Minya would say to Ilyich who did quite often end up on the seat of his pants.

Using a broom, Ilyich coached Minya in the proper method of weightlifting. Hoisting the broom as if it were a boulder, he grunted for good measure. His turn with the broom, Minya made sure to out-grunt his instructor.

"Yelizaveta Vasilevna, do not bother us! Minya and I are occupied with very important matters!"

"So I see. You are becoming quite the weightlifter, little Minya. Very soon you will be able to raise up Vladimir Ilyich."

"If I am to lift Vladimir Ilyich, I must eat more and he must eat less."

"So I am fat, am I?" Ilyich asked.

"I would not say fat, but I would not say thin."

A shrewd little charmer, little Minya. In personality, he could have been Ilyich's natural child.

In Shusha's Soft Air

In October, once the Yenisei had frozen solid, Ilyich and the schoolmaster cleared off a circle of snow to form a rink for the village children—at least they pretended the rink was for the children.

"Come, Volodya, you are aching to skate as much as little Minya," she teased.

"But little Minya does not need to know that," Ilyich replied, winking.

Often the villagers came to watch, cracking nuts and tossing the shells onto the ice. Around those potential hazards Ilyich dodged and swerved with aplomb, skating quite fast.

But his form?

Less than beauteous.

"Volodya, entertain us with your giant steps and Spanish leaps!" she would shout, encouraging him to perform tricks for the village audience. "Again! Again!" For in such moments the world reduced to the mark of blades, Ilyich laughing, their responsibilities no more serious than entertaining the villagers with skating antics.

The children, of course, learned to skate in a heartbeat and when they fell leapt up almost in the same motion to start again.

Skating for her required more concentration than cooking.

For her first skating lesson, Ilyich had brought along a chair.

"Keep it in front of you. Use it for balance."

Ilyich must have appeared quite stern and serious, giving those instructions.

"What is he advising, Nadya?" her fretful mother had called from the riverbank. "Remember, you are no acrobat!"

And yet, despite her awkwardness, the lurching and flailing, she loved sharing the frozen river with Ilyich. If she ignored her ineptness, her wobbly ankles, she could picture the two of them skating throughout

Russia, river to river to river.

For today's lesson they had dispensed with the chair. Supported by Ilyich, she waved shakily at her mother.

Even in late December, at 20 degrees below, the Shusha air felt wonderful, what the natives called "soft air."

"Look, Yelizaveta Vasilevna, look!" Ilyich called over his shoulder. "Your daughter will be a speed skater by spring."

Impossible! Even to master standing upright before April's thaw would count as a major achievement.

As Ilyich led her slowly around the rink, Zhenya barked and pawed the snow beside her anxious mother. Her skating lessons, they had learned, could not proceed alongside the dog. In her eagerness to join the fun, Zhenya knocked humans flat on their backs and left them spinning.

"Keep hold of Nadya, Volodya!" her mother called. "Do not let her slip!"

She thought to shout: *This is only skating, Mama. Not prison, not torture. If I fall, what is the consequence? A cold rump and stocking tear.*

But apparently she could not talk, hold tight and watch her feet all at once.

"Come onto the ice, Yelizaveta Vasilevna," Ilyich invited, "and I will teach you too."

"I am sending the dog instead," her mother said, releasing Zhenya.

And then down she and Ilyich went, down they went, laughing.

A Police-Supervised Idyll Concludes

During our last month of residence, the tsar hatched a scheme so harebrained news of it reached even Siberia. He wanted to ring his vast empire with an electric fence and announced as much to his ministers.

"And who does Nicky imagine an electric fence will keep out and keep in?" my Nadya snorted.

"With enemies like Nicky, The Revolution needs fewer friends," Ilyich mused.

It was an idyll, a police-supervised idyll, as Lev Davidovich would later describe it. Fresh fish from the Yenisei, pine nuts from the forest, a view of the lovely Sayan Mountains beyond a rim of birch. At Christmas, we decorated a tree for the children of the village. We served a bit of sweet and Ilyich led them in song. If I could have kept our family of three there by force of will, I would have done so. We knew true happiness in Shusha, all of us. How much better it would have been if Ilyich and Nadya could have run their revolution from that outpost.

When spring comes to Siberia, it intoxicates—the mind and the senses. The Yenisei's ice fissures, then drifts away. The sap rises. Wild swans return; woodcock commence their clucking. One day there is white and winter stillness, the next birdsong and bursting green. Who is not seduced by the exhilaration and optimism of springtime? Who can resist feeling, at least for a few heady weeks, that the world is indeed a glorious, glorious place?

For two enchanting springs, we had Shusha. Nadya and Ilyich's Siberian honeymoon lasted altogether a year and a half. While we finished off Nadya's term of exile in Ufa, Ilyich planned to rendezvous in Switzerland with the dean of Russian Marxism, Gregory Plekhanov. Forced to leave Russia more than a decade before, Plekhanov had settled in a villa overlooking a Swiss lake and from that tranquil retreat declaimed on the workers' cause. Never less than impeccably dressed, the tall, elegant noble-man had cut a dashing figure even while leading protests on the foulest streets of Piter. Scarcely could I imagine such a man warming to Vladimir Ilyich and his raw vehemence, shared ideology notwithstanding.

In that doubt, I was proved correct. Plekhanov and Ilyich were not to see eye to eye.

In Shusha, the green world once again turned white. With a heavy heart, I helped prepare for departure. An arduous task, simply to pack up Nadya's and Ilyich's books. Fifteen *poods* of books, roughly 550 pounds, were sent ahead by transport. The more precious titles were to travel with us in the open sleigh.

Both Nadya and Ilyich had tried to hire a covered sleigh but none could be found in the village.

"It will be too cold for Mama, Ilyich. It will aggravate her cough."

"Have I not *tried* to hire a covered sleigh *repeatedly*?" Ilyich snapped.

For the previous year and a half, we had seen little of Ilyich's temper. It had lain dormant in Siberia. During our preparations for departure, it returned.

"Only 28 below, Nadya," I intervened. "Surely your mother is tough enough to endure 28 below."

Neither Nadya nor Ilyich acknowledged the comment. Frowning, they continued to pack books.

Bundled up, we left in moonlight. I had baked huge quantities of frost-proof *pelmeny* to sustain us during the ride. Ilyich and Nadya faced resolutely forward, but I made the mistake of turning to look at what and whom we left behind: Minya, who had crept out his window to say goodbye and beside that tiny being, Zhenya. A waving hand, a wagging tail. When Nadya made a gift of the dog to Minya, the child had sworn a solemn oath to "keep Zhenya safe from briars."

My Nadya's voice had caught in replying. She could not finish her list of requests and instructions for Zhenya's safekeeping, and so I finished for her.

"And Zhenya will sleep at the foot of your bed. Promise us, little Minya. Because that is where she is used to sleeping."

"We will eat and sleep together!" Minya promised and saluted like a soldier.

In the moon-streaked darkness, Nadya squatted to hug the dog goodbye. Held with such ferocity, Zhenya squirmed and freed herself.

"We must go, Nadya," I said. "Ilyich and the driver are waiting."

In the sleigh, leaving the village, my daughter said not a word.

I must have shivered—although to me it felt a shudder.

"Are you cold already, Yelizaveta Vasilevna?" Ilyich inquired. "Here. Have my blanket."

"I am not cold. Keep your blanket."

"Did you forget something? There is still time to retrieve it."

"What I have left cannot be retrieved."

"Have you grown superstitious, Yelizaveta Vasilevna? Influenced by the peasants of Shusha?"

"I am an old woman, Volodya. The old are never fond of leave-taking."

"It is all right, Mama," my daughter insisted, meaning: *Do not worry. I am not a child of five. I am capable of parting with another pet for the sake of The Revolution. To lose another dog will not cripple me.*

My Nadya had to insist on, believe in, such a verdict, you understand. The same was not required of me.

In my opinion, after Shusha, nothing was ever right again.

INTERVIEW WITH HISTORY
Maria Alexandrovna Ulyanova

"You are the mother of not one but two famous sons."

"I am the mother of three sons."

"Our interests lie with the elder two: Alexander and Vladimir, Sasha and Volodya."

"Your interests are your interests, beyond my influence."

"A fatalistic response. Previous records reveal no proclivity toward fatalism in your character."

"I have no control over what is written or claimed."

"But you were a mother who encouraged 'intellectual ambition' in her children. A mother who coupled ambition with a 'sense of obligation.'"

"Did any mother of my time and place encourage less?"

"Allow us to pose the questions, please. Your father, Alexander Blank, was a medical doctor—also a crank. At bedtime, true or false, he ordered his daughters to wrap themselves in damp sheets to quote/unquote strengthen their nerves."

"We suffered no ill effects."

"No?"

"No."

"Once more: no?"

"No."

"Perhaps you would feel freer discussing your daughter-in-law, Nadezhda Krupskaya? The woman who compared herself to the Russian countryside: 'no bright colors.'"

"Nadya was exactly the wife Volodya needed."

"Plain enough to avert jealousy? Impoverished enough to endure exile and misfortune without complaint?"

"Many women dedicate themselves to The Revolution but choose the wrong man. Nadya chose the right one."

"You declined to visit the honeymooners in Shushenskoye."

"There was no need to make the journey. Nadya kept us informed."

"A model correspondent, your daughter-in-law. Cheerful letters—from Nadya."

"Unfailingly."

"But from your son?"

"If a son cannot express discouragement to his mother, then to whom?"

"Obvious answer? His comrade wife. But let's skip past that quagmire. From London, for your eyes only, Volodya wrote: 'My life goes on as usual, and unfortunately pretty senseless.'"

"He did not lie to his mother."

"You wanted an heir. Comrade Krupskaya failed to provide one."

"I would have welcomed a grandchild—of course."

"Even if the mother had been Inessa Armand?"

"Marriage is no longer what it was. I have accepted the revision."

"As you accepted the death and/or imprisonment of each and every one of your children?"

"If you are asking whether I expect miracles or justice, the answer is no. I no longer expect justice or miracles."

"In parting, would you care to correct other wrongheaded assumptions? To convey, for the record, other truths?"

"I have left history more than my share. I leave nothing else."

EUROPE

The Richters

In the spring of 1901, Nadya and I left Russia for Europe. We thought we would find Ilyich in Prague, but Ilyich we did not find.

"This is the address? You are sure?"

We stood, my Nadya and I, with our suitcases, two travel-weary women on a narrow street in the workers' quarters before an enormous house with mattresses hanging from every window.

"At least Ilyich sleeps on a thoroughly aired mattress," I remarked.

Nadya did not respond to such a flippant observation. She flicked hair out of her eyes, the better to study the paper in her hands.

"His apartment is on the fourth floor."

"The fourth floor! I will wait where I stand. Leave the suitcases with me."

"I cannot leave you alone on a strange street in a strange city!"

"Unless you plan to carry me on your back up the stairs, I will remain here alone."

The soles of my feet felt as if I had walked from Russia.

"If anyone tries to snatch your purse, you must yell as though your lungs were exploding."

I nodded assent. My daughter had enough on her mind.

"Do not try to *fight* any assailant. Yell."

"Your mother will take care of herself, Nadya. Go."

When next I saw my daughter she was scowling as if bitten by a spider. A blonde Czech woman trailed her.

"There are no more rooms?" I asked.

"There is no Modraczek living here."

The blonde woman nodded in sorrowful agreement.

Modraczek was the alias Ilyich was supposedly using. But using it where? Although Ilyich and Nadya both held legitimate passports that reflected their true identities, in Europe, to carry on work for The Revolution, they lived and travelled under assumed names. Keeping straight the various aliases was a wearisome business.

Exceedingly weary in Prague, I insisted the hunt for "Modraczek" be put on hold until we had located our own lodgings, eaten and refortified ourselves with a good night's sleep.

Quite possibly because she did not want us in her own house, the Czech woman directed us to an establishment two streets over. Our room there, the first of many mean, roughly furnished way stations in Europe, had but one bed. I climbed in at once.

"Nadya, rest. Staring at wrong directions will not turn them any truer."

"I have missed something."

"And why do you blame yourself when it is far more likely someone else has made a mistake?"

Every message we had received in Ufa had been encoded twice. It was a wonder anyone understood what he or she wrote or read.

I cannot claim either of us woke refreshed. The bed pitched to one side and so even in dream one had to adjust for the slanting. Since I slept next to the wall, I rolled into Nadya. If my daughter had rolled, she would have ended up on a bare floor with no rug to cushion her fall.

We paid what we owed for a single night's roof over our heads and again, with our suitcases, took to the streets. We had not gone far when a man, a worker, stopped us to inquire whether we had found the relative for whom we searched.

In such situations my Nadya does not lose her head. She is circumspect and, if circumstances demand, can turn quite cagey. Where there is useful information to be gleaned, she gleans it. But she and her utterly impassive face give away nothing. Years of exile would only improve her ability to size up strangers quickly and efficiently.

"And if we have not found our relative?" she tested.

"Then you might continue on to Munich where Herr Rittmeyer awaits."

"Rittmeyer!" I exclaimed. "Who decides these preposterous names?"

In Munich, I insisted we check our bags at the station. An unplanned expense, but I would not hear of either of us traipsing the streets of another city dragging suitcases.

We had been advised to seek Herr Rittmeyer at a neighborhood beer hall, and there we found him.

"Herr Rittmeyer, yes," declared the short fat German behind the bar. "That is me."

"A 'me' that has gained several inches of height and stomach," I said.

By then I had become convinced that Nadya and I were destined to crisscross Europe in fruitless search of the phantom Ilyich.

It took more than a fat, dull-witted German to discourage my daughter.

Staring down the man before us, she said through clenched teeth: "You are mistaken. Herr Rittmeyer is my husband."

At last a woman appeared.

"Ask her," I urged. "She will have more sense. She could scarcely have less."

"I have come to see Herr Rittmeyer," Nadya repeated. "As I have explained to this gentleman, I am his wife."

"Ah," exclaimed the woman. "You have come to see your husband, Herr *Meyer*, at Herr Rittmeyer's. Herr Meyer has been expecting his wife from Siberia. Follow me. I will take you to him."

And there he was. In a back room, at a desk, preoccupied as usual with the sheets of paper before him. But when Ilyich looked up at the commotion of our entry, his mouth flew open like a gate.

"Where have you sprung from?"

"Damn it! You could not write and say where you were?"

At this, I burst out laughing. I could not help myself. "Now I know why I have roamed every street in Munich! To hear that rebuke!"

"Did not write? Did not *write*? I have written *repeatedly*!" Ilyich sputtered. "I have been three times a day to the station to meet you!"

Eventually they sorted out the confusion. Ilyich had judged it safer to notify us of his changed whereabouts not by letter but in the pages of a book. Unfortunately for us, the comrade assigned the task of forwarding the book began reading it instead.

"Still," my daughter objected, holding to her pout.

"Come, Nadya! Do you imagine I can control the actions of every idiot from here to Ufa!"

Which is not to say my son-in-law did not expend enormous energy trying to accomplish precisely that.

On those few occasions when Ilyich held back from saying what he wished, the effort set the vein in his wide forehead pulsing. In this instance, in my opinion, it did not pulse long enough.

"You brought my English pen points, Nadya? The box of them?"

"This is what you say to us after the journey we have endured, Vladimir Ilyich?" I flared. "You ask for your presents?"

Nadya, however, had already begun rummaging in her bag.

"Ilyich must be able to write, Mama."

"And what has he been writing with before our arrival? Sticks?"

"The Czech and German pen points are good for nothing!" Ilyich whined. "Sticks would be as efficient."

"I have them with me, Volodya," Nadya assured. "They are here somewhere. Two boxes. Enough to write many pamphlets."

Ilyich cleared a chair of papers for me to sit. Nadya continued unpacking. It was another ugly room with a window streaked with grime, a window that by preventing one's looking out, forced one to look time and again at peeling wallpaper.

In retrospect I am thankful that I did not know in 1901 how often I would attempt to brighten the windows and walls of a series of temporary lodgings in London, Zurich, Geneva, Paris, Berne, Cracow and more cities in between. I could, I suppose, compose an inclusive list of our every address after Shusha and before 1917, but I would take no pleasure in the exercise. Why work to be reminded what memory has elected to obscure? There were so many dank and dreary apartments smelling of the strangers who slept there before us. Countless communal kitchens in rooming houses where we drank tea in glasses and cups that our neighbors had drunk from the morning before, where we ate dinner off plates still crusted with egg yolks. In our years of wandering, I was to cook meals grand and piddling for Bolsheviks, Mensheviks turned Bolsheviks, and Bolsheviks turned Mensheviks turned back again. I was to sew revolvers into waistcoats, to stuff and overstuff suitcases with illegal literature, to write superficial letters about nothing so that Nadya might write over my words directions for revolt. I was to watch Ilyich fight and scrap with his supposed comrades, to witness my Nadya's health endangered, then ruined. As much as I ached for Russia, I would have foregone ever returning to spare my daughter the torments of Basedow's disease. Even more gladly I would have suffered the disease in her stead. But such tradeoffs cannot be negotiated by mothers young or old.

In April 1902, as a threesome, we left Munich for London.

I did not warm to London.

As soon as we stepped out into the cavernous darkness that was Charing Cross station, the smoke from the engines made my eyes water. Against a continuous assault of screeching noise, I covered my ears. A busy city with loud machines and loud weather. The plonk and splatter of endless rain was to play on all our nerves. The Russian stomach does not easily adapt to oxtails and fish fried in fat. In London, we were to feel acutely what we were: aliens in a foreign land.

"How I long to glimpse the nose of a *muzhik*!" I would say with a sigh to Nadya. I should not have said it. To express such homesickness caused my daughter to chew her lip.

I quite agree with Vladimir Ilyich. Mrs. Yeo, our London landlady, was the worst of her kind: nosy, utterly conventional and vengeful. Since Ilyich had wrangled a pass to work in the reading room of the British Museum, he was spared her overbearing presence during the day, but my Nadya, posing as an unemployed house frau, enjoyed no such outlet. Working on an uneven table covered in black oilcloth in the room where she also slept, she handled all correspondence to and from Russia—the most frustrating of jobs. Any illegal material had to be sent via circuitous routes, a necessary precaution that delayed arrival by weeks. Since neither Nadya nor Ilyich could be absolutely certain what arrived when and where, much of my daughter's time was spent on redundancies. If the same instructions and communications were sent to a dozen different addresses, the likelihood of success improved. And so she copied and sent to a dozen.

Whatever our personal feelings toward our landlady, it was imperative to keep her snooping in check. To read correspondence from Russia required burning many candles. If Mrs. Yeo began skulking about our door, she might catch a whiff of singed paper; she might demand to know why Mrs. Richter burned so many candles during daylight.

"The devil take her!" Nadya said. "We pay our rent on time!"

But no devil whisked Mrs. Yeo away. Again and again the landlady intruded in our business.

First she complained that we had hung no curtains on our windows. "Everyone" in London covered the windows with lace curtains.

"I am to be blamed for the absence of curtains," I placated. "My cough is exacerbated by dust and by any material to which dust clings."

"But your windows are naked!" protested Mrs. Yeo.

"On the contrary, our windows are free," I countered. "Are they not, my daughter?"

A mistake to take that tone. The very next morning Mrs. Yeo cornered Nadya as she returned from mailing a shopping bag full of letters to Russia.

Mrs. Yeo resembled a bird. When pleased with herself, she tweeted.

Very pleased with herself this day, she tweeted: "I notice, Mrs. Richter, that, like your windows, your hand is also free: of a wedding band."

This remark I overheard from the landing, where I had been waiting for Nadya's return.

"Is that you, Daughter?"

"Yes, Mama. I am speaking with Mrs. Yeo, who is concerned that I wear no wedding band."

I did not say: "There is a copper ring wrapped in her clothes drawer. Would you like to see her copper ring?" I did say: "Allergic to gold. A pity, isn't it, Mrs. Yeo? My son-in-law will permit no less precious metal to encircle my daughter's finger. And so she wears no ring."

When Ilyich returned that damp afternoon, Nadya said: "What a scene you missed this morning, Volodya." And pointed at me.

In his dripping overcoat, Ilyich began to shimmy. The mere prospect of landlady gossip delighted him.

"What mischief have you gotten into, Yelizaveta Vasilevna?"

Because Nadya smiled, he knew it was not mischief of a compromising sort.

"Mischief, Volodya?" I asked. "When has your mother-in-law indulged in mischief?"

As Nadya described my standoff with Mrs. Yeo, Ilyich clapped and spun, showering us as well as the floor.

"And did Mrs. Yeo imagine she could outmaneuver Yelizaveta Vasilevna? Sheer folly! We shall make your mother our guard dog, Nadya. The Mrs. Yeos will soon learn not to trifle with her bite."

It was but one moment's merriment among hour after hour of endless work.

While I rested or read, Nadya set about reestablishing contact with the workers in Russia and their sympathizers elsewhere. It was her responsibility to keep track of comrades and their families—who had been arrested or killed, who had buckled under the strain of underground life, who had become unreliable, who had abandoned the cause altogether. It was also her job to hunt down additional mail drops for *Iskra* and worker pamphlets, to organize the transport of revolutionary propaganda across borders, to request, cajole, nag and needle her correspondents as necessary. *How soon can the literature be delivered? Is this a suitable distribution center for central Russia? We must decide whether this route is suitable for* Iskra *or only for pamphlets.* For exiles, she arranged lodging and summarized their reports on the latest developments in Russia for Ilyich. For those revolutionaries returning secretly to Russia, she provided contacts and false-bottomed trunks. She coded and decoded messages, the language disguise so thin, the meaning so transparent—handkerchiefs for passports, fur for illegal literature—it seemed extraordinary that the Okhrana did not find and confiscate every dispatch.

My daughter's already weakened eyes grew weaker trying to read overlapping lines, trying to decipher unintelligible gibberish.

At her table she swore—repeatedly, if not creatively.

"My darling Nadya," I complained. "If you must be profane, please strive for variety."

But the frustrations revealed to her mama she strove to hide from Ilyich. At night, she worked with her back to him. Whatever irritation her shoulders conveyed, her face broadcast many times over. In the best of moods, Ilyich had no tolerance for incompetence, far less for carelessness. Whenever it became obvious that she could not singlehandedly solve a problem or settle a dispute, when it became absolutely necessary to involve him, he exploded with impatience and insisted on conducting the rest of the correspondence himself. *Once more we categorically beseech and demand that you write us more often and in greater detail—in particular, do it at once, without fail, the very same day you receive this letter!* But it was a bit like trying to drive a herd of cattle from London to Russia and back again without being in sight or voice range of that herd.

"You at your desk fussing, while Ilyich fusses in his dreams," I said.

It was true: even in sleep, Volodya lunged at and argued with opponents.

"Go to bed, Nadya," I urged. "Ilyich has stopped for the night. You must also."

"I cannot go to bed! There is too much to be done and apparently it must be done not once or twice but three times before there is any hope of it being done anything but backwards!"

There were tea stains on her jumper, candle soot on her wrists. With a dampened cloth I sponged off the soot. The jumper would have to wait for tomorrow's wash.

"Nadya, listen to your mother. Do not lose all patience with the human race. Do not turn completely into Ilyich."

In the other room, we heard Ilyich shout Plekhanov's name, followed by a curse.

Nadya turned despondently toward that tossing and turning.

"Tell me, Mama. Will we look back on Munich and count those the bright days of exile?"

The question put me instantly on alert. My daughter does not wax nostalgic. She does not air regrets. That is not my Nadya's way.

"It is exhaustion talking. Now. I insist. To bed."

She obeyed me that night, allowing herself to be mildly coddled. But she was not wrong, my daughter. In London, the dissension escalated; the acrimony increased; the breach between Ilyich and the others widened; the attacks grew more personal, more wounding, harder to forget and forgive. We were all Russian exiles but we were not one happy collective. Nor would we be, in the months and years to come.

For You, Madam Lenin

In the City of Marx

Ilyich had already retired for the night and she very nearly. They expected no company. It must be a comrade, lost or desperate. Who else would arrive at such a late hour, unannounced?

"Mrs. Richter?"

A melodious voice from a figure in shadow.

"And you are?"

It was the visitor's responsibility to identify himself in a way that earned welcome.

The stranger stepped more directly into the light—impossibly young, a cascade of wavy hair, a pince-nez perched rather jauntily on his nose.

As if Yelizaveta Vasilevna had trailed her to the door, her mother's likely commentary reverberated: *Too much hair. Ilyich will not care to compete with such abundant hair.*

"Forgive me for coming at such an inconvenient hour." A quick half bow. "I am a fugitive from Irkutsk."

"A fugitive."

"A fugitive."

On second pronunciation, he showed a bit of teeth, a bit of pride.

"There are many fugitives from Irkutsk," she said.

Quick, this one. He not only perceived the barb within that flat reply, he put it to use.

"But only one known as 'The Pen.'"

If not for the semi-public nature of the hall and stairs, she would have crushed Lev Davidovich Bronstein in a hug then and there. Both she and Ilyich had long admired his rapier prose in service to The Revolution. Lev Davidovich, a.k.a. The Pen, a.k.a. Comrade Trotsky, was precisely the kind of revolutionary who belonged in the small, highly trained cadre Ilyich had described in *What Is to Be Done?*

"A clever dozen," Ilyich maintained, "will be harder to catch than a hundred fools."

The closing of the street door prompted the opening of another. The perpetually meddlesome Mrs. Yeo stuck her head into the hallway.

"Quite late for visitors, Mrs. Richter."

"A relative from Germany, Mrs. Yeo. A traveller at the mercy of transportation not always on schedule."

Mrs. Yeo's cat ran toward her and she picked up the escapee. If nosiness deprived Mrs. Yeo of the warmth of a cat in bed, so much the better.

"Goodnight, Mrs. Yeo."

"You have paid for three lodgers, not four, Mrs. Richter."

Rubbing the cat, she gave its owner the insult of her back.

"Our cousin will not be staying with us. He has just come to say hello and have some tea."

"A charming example of the English bourgeoisie!" Lev Davidovich sneered as they climbed the stairs.

"Stay in London and those charms will sicken you on a daily basis, comrade."

Ilyich, in his nightshirt, sat on the bed. Deliberately she blocked his view of the visitor as they entered, but Volodya must have seen her smile.

"And which comrade has arrived to bother us this night?"

"Guess," she said.

"Come, come," Ilyich huffed. "I am tired and the hour is late."

But like a schoolboy enjoying the game of secrets, he swung his legs.

Lev Davidovich darted forward to shake Ilyich's hand.

"An honor," he exclaimed, and with no additional fanfare, Trotsky and Lenin settled side by side on bed sheets.

She placed the cat in Ilyich's lap and went to pay the cab fare. Lev Davidovich had arrived without a kopek or sixpence in his pocket.

"What is this uproar?" her mother called from her pillows.

"A visitor from Russia, Mama," she said and closed the door between the two rooms. When excited, Volodya shouted. She expected the shouting to begin very soon.

While she made tea, Lev Davidovich regaled them with his escape from Siberia under a bale of hay.

"They are quite stupid, the police of Irkutsk," Lev Davidovich said with disdain. "I sneezed continually. The hay above me bounced."

"Perhaps they took you for a rat," Ilyich said and the two of them chortled together.

"You have read my *Development of Capitalism*?"

"It is read everywhere in Russia," Lev Davidovich reported. "I read it first in a transit prison in Moscow."

"British Marxism? Your opinion?"

"Less than interesting," Lev Davidovich dismissed.

"A hash of socialism and religion," Ilyich expounded.

"So it would seem," Lev Davidovich agreed.

"And Comrade Plekhanov? Your views on Comrade Plekhanov?"

She realized she was holding her breath. The new arrival's opinion of Plekhanov was of far greater importance than his opinion of British Marxism.

"Certainly Comrade Plekhanov has provided brilliant insights in the past."

"And now?" Ilyich persisted.

"He has become too remote from the struggle."

Good, she thought. An ally against Plekhanov.

"And England? What does she offer us?" Lev Davidovich quizzed.

"The grave of Karl Marx," Ilyich replied, not altogether facetiously.

They were each on their third glass of tea, talking themselves hoarse.

"The economism faction denies the necessity of an independent proletarian party," Ilyich criticized.

"It is more than a fight for higher pay."

"An autonomous Bund would be suicidal for the Jewish proletariat."

"First Russia, then the world," Lev Davidovich affirmed.

Wonderful, their accord—although the unity would likely double her workload. Lev Davidovich gave every indication of being able to keep up with Ilyich. To keep up with the two of them, she would need to give up sleep altogether.

"Nadya will take care of the details," Ilyich was too apt to say—and believe. Besides serving as secretary of *Iskra*, she was still trying to improve the reliability of communications London to Russia to Zurich to Paris. There were nights she dreamed those cities were yoked by strings, and she a giantess struggling to yank the ties tauter.

"We had heard rumors that The Pen—back me up, Nadya—was something of a Tolstoyan."

"That is nonsense! Nonsense!"

Lev Davidovich had assumed the pose of a defendant on trial, chin raised, pince-nez clasped, neck muscles taut as rope.

"He is teasing, Lev Davidovich," she said.

"I am. I am teasing," Ilyich allowed. "And what if you were, once, a Tolstoyan? People are not born Marxists."

The curtainless windows brightened and still they talked.

She put on a fourth kettle for tea, and still they talked.

"He is still *here?*" her mother groused when she joined them. "Young man, have you no manners?"

"This is Lev Davidovich, Mama. Also known as Comrade Trotsky."

"I do not care what he calls himself. He has been the cause of no sleep in this household."

"My apologies, Madam. I am to blame."

"As I have already said."

Ilyich laughed. "And this is Nadya's mother, Yelizaveta Vasilevna, who will tell you exactly what she thinks even when you have not disturbed her sleep."

With exaggerated chivalry, Lev Davidovich bowed, kissed her mother's hand and begged profusely for forgiveness.

She and Ilyich exchanged wry glances. Her mother's sourness sweetened. She even inquired whether it were true, as they had been told, that the temperatures in Irkutsk in winter plunged to sixty below.

Lev Davidovich confirmed it.

"Ah, then. You should have been with us in Shusha."

If Lev Davidovich could charm Yelizaveta Vasilevna, what might he accomplish on behalf of the Social Democrats?

"Nadya will take you to Sidmouth Street," Ilyich said. "Vera Zasulich will have a bed for you."

And so the two of them started out in the morning mist. Like Ilyich, Lev Davidovich seemed incapable of walking directly down a London street. Repeatedly he stopped to observe and examine. He craned his neck; he twirled on his heels. Like Ilyich, he seemed determined to miss nothing that defined this bastion of capitalism.

"And the English Social Democrats, Comrade Krupskaya? Have they impressed you?"

As idiots. A few months before, Ilyich had been invited to address a meeting of so-called English Social Democrats, and she had accompanied him. At the conclusion of Ilyich's remarks, a very well dressed and very astonished man had approached her. "This is true? What your husband says? You have also been in prison? If my wife were put in prison, I don't know what I would do! To think! My wife in prison!"

She shared the anecdote with her walking companion.

"They expect to conduct a revolution without sacrifice?"

"Apparently so."

"Idiots," Lev Davidovich agreed.

It was easy, perhaps too easy, to confide in young, exuberant Lev Davidovich. On critical issues, he seemed already to side with Ilyich. Their rapport had been instant—but was it too instant? To rush intimacy was not in character for Ilyich; never before had he shown such immediate, unguarded trust in another comrade. His behavior tonight made her realize how deeply the *Iskra* board's constant bickering and the endless rows with Plekhanov had affected him. Ilyich was feeling beleaguered, isolated—which made him particularly vulnerable to apparently sympathetic associates. Lev Davidovich had criticized Plekhanov, yes, but if Ilyich came to depend on Lev Davidovich, and Lev Davidovich betrayed his trust? What then?

She knocked three times, the signal. Vera Zasulich opened the door in slippers, hair a wren's nest, samovar boiling. Very likely she had not spent the night in bed either. Vera Zasulich preferred to compose her *Iskra* articles "while capitalists slept" and during those compositions walked the floor and smoked. Ashes covered her chest, as well as the tables, as well as the floor. One could not visit Vera Zasulich's apartment and come away ash free.

The hand not holding a cigarette held a strip of nibbled meat.

"There is more on the stove, if you are hungry."

Lev Davidovich demurred.

Vera Zasulich turned in her direction, eyebrows raised. Another fastidious male, was it?

During his time in London, Ivan Babushkin had also stayed with Vera Zasulich. The great strides Ivan Babushkin had made in his revolutionary thinking since attending the Smolensky classes had not lessened his passion for neatness. He swept cigarette ash, stacked newspapers, straightened bedspreads, washed pots and pans and scoured the stove.

For almost a week following his return to Russia, Vera Zasulich's flat remained presentable. It had now returned to its pre-Ivan Babushkin state.

Daintily Lev Davidovich picked his way around the debris to the cot behind the screen. In mere moments he had begun to snore, also daintily.

"And this new one?" Vera Zasulich shrugged in the direction of the screen. "He has impressed Ilyich?"

"They have talked for hours."

"While you waited to walk him here."

"Ilyich must work this morning."

"And you? Your work? Its fate while you escort the latest émigré around London?"

"If I agree to stay for tea, you must refrain from criticizing Ilyich."

Vera Zasulich held up her hands. "All right, all right. I will restrain myself. I will not criticize your precious Ilyich."

Hardly known for restraint, Vera Zasulich.

In Russia, she had killed a general. In Russia and in London, she spoke her mind bluntly, without flourishes. She prettied up nothing: herself, her flat, The Revolution. A true and excellent comrade, Vera Zasulich, but not everyone shared her capacity for frankness, chaos or living surrounded by mounds of mess.

If her mother had not travelled with them, if Yelizaveta Vasilevna had not managed the cooking and cleaning and tidying, she would have had to add domestic chores to her daily task list because Volodya, like Ivan Babushkin, like Lev Davidovich, disliked a disorderly household. He could not think amid clutter.

"You leave for Switzerland soon?" Vera Zasulich asked.

She nodded.

"And already you are dreading the move?" Vera Zasulich pried.

"I am not looking forward to it," she said.

Vera Zasulich shrugged. "It is not as if you love London."

"No," she admitted. "I will not miss London."

"The printers are in Switzerland. Plekhanov is in Switzerland."

"Yes," she said. "I know where Plekhanov is."

"But?"

"Ilyich is against it."

"Ilyich is against many things. He would be wise to be against a few less."

Now it was she who held up her hands. Vera Zasulich supported Plekhanov. For as long as it took to drink her tea, she would not criticize Plekhanov.

The fine mist she and Lev Davidovich had walked through earlier was transforming itself into a dense, impenetrable fog. Outside Vera Zasulich's window, rooftop after rooftop disappeared. She and Ilyich and her mother had arrived in London in fog so thick it had blocked the light of the street lamps. Leaving the train station, they had clung together like waifs afraid of losing one another, afraid of what lay ahead, afraid of what they could not see.

No, she would not miss London, but the move to Geneva would be a setback for Ilyich.

"Nobody has the courage to stand up to Plekhanov!" he seethed.

"That is not true, Volodya," she had countered. "You have challenged him before and will again."

But at what price?

INTERVIEW WITH HISTORY
Vera Ivanovna Zasulich

"In retrospect, not much of a Lenin fan, eh?"

"Vladimir Ilyich was like a bulldog. He grabbed and would not let go."

"Unlike Plekhanov."

"Plekhanov grabbed, then released."

"On the subject of preferences: we hear from Comrade Trotsky that nothing made you happier than a ham sandwich dripping mustard."

"The prissiest man you ever saw, that one. You'd never catch mustard on his shirt."

"Your revolutionary service on *Iskra*'s editorial board. A pleasure?"

"What does it matter? Vladimir Ilyich won in the end. He came to London. He went against Plekhanov. He refused to accept the majority opinion of the Second Congress. He wanted a party run by a cadre of professionals and he got his wish."

"Hard to swallow for a Land and Libertarian turned Social Democrat turned Menshevik turned political dropout?"

"In my lifetime, much has been hard to swallow."

"And with that cue, we return to the youth and revolutionary passions of Vera Ivanovna Zasulich."

"Must we?"

"We must. Your 'unable to cope' mother sent you to live with relatives who arranged for your impressive and thereby 'dangerous' education. In St. Petersburg, you gravitated toward radical circles. Like Nadezhda Krupskaya, you spent your evenings teaching the workers to read."

"In a place far away, in a time long ago."

"With your Land and Liberty comrades, you dreamed of dissolving the Russian Empire, of transferring its land to the peasantry."

"Discouraging, to remember one's dreams."

"The Okhrana infiltrated your ranks. Arrests were made."

"They were savage, the Piter police. Savage brutes, looking for an excuse."

"And when they beat your comrade Bogoliubov for refusing to tip his hat to Chief of Police General Trepov, you decided to…? In your own words, please."

"I shot General Trepov."

"Sorry. History requires a few more stinging details."

"I approached Trepov. 'What do you want?' he asked. 'A Certificate of Conduct,' I answered. As he jotted down the request, I pointed my revolver, pressed the trigger. Everybody around me began moving. I was seized from all sides."

"In a nutshell: you wrote the playbook for Fanny Kaplan."

"I wrote the book for many. Six times The People's Will tried to kill Alexander II. On the seventh try, they succeeded."

"And their success depressed *you*, the trendsetter?"

"I was 25 when I shot Trepov. Do you know, can you remember, can any of us remember, how young 25 is? By 50, I was old and fat, living apart from my country, émigrés for comrades, émigrés for company. Day and night I walked London floorboards, starting articles never finished, debating men who never listened. Condescended to by Vladimir Ilyich as a woman who put morality before Marxist principles. Mocked by Lev Davidovich for my 'subjectivity,' my feverish 'turbulence.' *Poor Vera Ivanovna! Look what a mess she is, what a mess she lives in! See how messily she thinks!*"

"Vladimir Ilyich never shot a Chief of Police."

"Physically, Ilyich was a coward. Nadya, I believe, would stand at the gallows unblinking, but Ilyich would piss himself."

"Nadezhda Krupskaya considered you the epitome of absolute devotion to the cause, despite your lack of support in 1903."

"Nadya was equally devoted. Diligent and devoted."

"To the cause or to her husband?"

"To both, with the edge going to Ilyich."

"Unlike you, Nadezhda Krupskaya never lost faith in the revolution."

"Who can say in the end what Nadya lost or gained?"

"History can say this: that she survived Lenin, continued to survive under his successor."

"Ah, the successor. One of Ilyich's 'professional revolutionaries.' Is this where we are meant to applaud?"

1905

Where They Were Not

A couple on the streets of Geneva, making their way to the Société de Lecture.

Together for a change.

Vladimir Lenin has turned up the bottoms of his trousers to avoid street mud. Nadezhda Krupskaya's boots seep mud and moisture continuously.

In Geneva, they think of Russia. Always of Russia. The ridiculous war with Japan. The striking Putilov workers. Peasants in the central provinces burning manor houses, shitting on oriental rugs. Even news of Nicky's order to paint his Winter Palace red has reached them in Geneva. But what Anna Lunacharskaya, rushing toward them on a Geneva street, short of breath, flailing her muff, will tell them they have not heard.

Three hundred dead, many more hundreds wounded.

In January's fierce winds, Vyborg workers crossed the Palace Bridge to petition the tsar for education and bread. As the workers and their families marched toward Palace Square, the tsar's Cossacks raised their weapons and fired into the crowd.

Men, women and children massacred by the tsar's men.

"You are sure? There can be no mistake of the march, of the dead, of the reason?" Vladimir Lenin asks and asks again.

Nadezhda Krupskaya pulls at her husband's arm.

"Can it have begun, Ilyich? Without us?"

Marx wrote: "Revolution is an art."

The man on the street in Geneva beside Nadezhda Krupskaya wrote: "Revolution is impossible to predict. Revolution is governed by its own more or less mysterious laws."

In Geneva, fighting Mensheviks, caught in an émigré slough,

Vladimir Lenin and Nadezhda Krupskaya, while workers march and die in Piter.

Revolution in Russia.

And they not there. They not there.

Praskovaya Eugenevna Onegina

In late January 1905, a famous American dancer made the journey to Piter to perform her ethereal art. Delayed by a blizzard, her train from Berlin did not arrive until the early hours of morning.

This is how I picture the sequence.

Off that tedious transport, the lithe dancer steps, wrapped in furs against the frigid air. Her immediate destination is the Hotel Europa, where she will rest briefly before appearing at the Salle des Nobles in a performance long awaited by the aristocracy. To get to the comforts and fineries of the Hotel Europa, however, the famous dancer must travel Piter streets.

Although dark, the hour is not quite dark enough. Although swift, her sleigh is not quite swift enough to prevent her from seeing who else travels Nevsky Prospekt, row upon row of the silent and the somber.

What the famous dancer witnesses in Piter has none of the invention or beauty of art, only the emotion. Walking the night streets of Piter are grieving men, women and children. They walk behind makeshift coffins. And in those coffins lie the Bloody Sunday dead.

In Geneva, when I grew tired and my thoughts strayed, they inexorably strayed to Piter. I would remember a Nevsky corner, a shop, the Neva iced or rushing. The tea glass in my hand would remind me of a tea glass I had left behind or I would remember the sensation of settling into my chair to teach lessons, or I would recall my Konstantin, resurrected from an even more distant past.

Heart and soul I missed Piter, but in 1905 I could not describe myself as eager to return. I did not share Nadya and Ilyich's belief, their hope, that the insurrection they both so wanted was actually in play. I suspected the outbreaks of violence represented a more random kind of mutiny and impatience, a distracting diversion, a dangerous, addictive entertainment. I feared being caught among a mob of either persuasion, Cossack or worker.

Such sentiments I kept to myself. To have expressed them would have made Nadya very angry with her mama. Very angry. Because if you believe in revolution as my Nadya believes in it, quite naturally you look for that same conviction in others.

What about a failed revolution bears reporting?

The Revolution of 1905 failed at the cost of many lives and much blood. It dashed many hopes. It mixed idealists and cynics, martyrs and profiteers. It brought widespread suffering and sorrow and despair. But it did not bring down the tsar.

In January 1905, when Isadora Duncan was in Piter, we were not.

While the Admiralty's searchlight swept the Nevsky and demonstrators with revolvers and rifles and Finnish knives roamed the streets, while student marchers sang "Boldly friends, boldly, never lose courage in the unequal fight," while the royal family canoed and shot crows at Tsarskoye Selo and lamented "disturbances" in the capital, Ilyich and Nadya and I remained in Geneva, Ilyich at loggerheads not only with Plekhanov but now, also, with Lev Davidovich.

"Shall I begin packing?" I inquired of my daughter. "I can see to the pots and pans, but I cannot disassemble a printing press."

"Hush, Mama," my daughter cautioned.

Ilyich circled his desk and struck out at impassive air. He had not fully recovered from a case of shingles. The skin on his face sagged. His color was not good.

To return to Piter, we would need new, forged passports. Even with such documents, we would be entering the country in secret through Finland.

All this had to be arranged and by some means funded.

Lev Davidovich returned to Piter.

And still we remained in Geneva.

The tsar's government signed over Port Arthur to the Japanese.

And still we remained in Geneva.

Nicholas Romanov crossed his chest, wrote a note of apology to his mother and signed a document permitting the formation of the Duma.

And still we remained in Geneva.

When we did arrive, the reaction had already set in.

In Piter, my Nadya called herself Praskovaya Eugenevna Onegina.

I continued to call her Nadya.

"Mama! You know that I am Praskovaya! You know that is my name!"

"Nadya" is a far more common Russian name. A name shared by many draws less attention. Is that not the point of an alias? Praskovaya Eugenevna Onegina would have been the unmarried daughter of Eugene Onegin, if Pushkin had provided his hero with a daughter, which he had not.

Even tsarist police know their Pushkin.

The Duma was dissolved.

In protest the city's poets wore radishes in their buttonholes and wrote verses of betrayal. The tsar remained on the throne; Stolypin ruled and cleared the streets. As a protection against the Black Hundreds, my Nadya learned to shoot a revolver. I learned to shoot a revolver. The gutters brimmed with corpses; madmen of every persuasion roamed the city. Ilyich and Nadya conspired and hid and dodged arrest while trying to reignite a revolution that would not oblige.

In that same year, while attending the Bolshevik conference in Finland, Nadya was formally introduced to Josif Vissarionovich Dzhugashvili, Comrade Stalin. She knew of him previously, of course, but in 1905 met him face-to-face for the first time. I regret to say that my Nadya's nose, usually so adept at detecting enemies, current and future, did not pick up that particular scent on Josif Vissarionovich Dzhugashvili.

Another mistake in a year of errors, but for the Krupskayas, personally, perhaps the most grievous.

AGAIN,
EUROPE

The Loss of Ivan Babushkin

We did not return to Europe to escape danger and the tsarist police. We left Piter because, by 1907, both Nadya and Ilyich recognized the futility of remaining. The bosses had regained control of the factories; in the tsar's name, the streets had been "tamed." Although there continued to be pockets of revolt, scattered acts of protest, in number and effect those demonstrations proved too small and weak to reinvigorate the masses. The Revolution of 1905 had effectively come and gone.

To recognize is not to embrace.

Nadya and Ilyich reviewed the situation in Piter and accepted the wisdom of departure. But the decision carried with it much anguish, much bitterness and a festering resentment. Two years of organizing, agitating—and now, again, retreat.

We were already on our way to a second European exile when news reached us of Ivan Babushkin's death. Caught transporting arms for The Revolution in Siberia, Nadya's Smolensky pupil, Vera Zasulich's pristine housemate in London, had been shot in the neck, dumped in an open grave and left for carrion.

Reading the message, Nadya broke down completely. I did not love Ivan Babushkin as much as my Nadya did, but when a daughter's heart is touched so is her mother's. The sound of two women weeping is louder than one.

"Stop, stop, we must stop. We will disturb Ilyich's rest," Nadya sobbed—too late.

Haggard and grim, he joined us.

"What is it? What has happened?"

"We have lost Ivan Babushkin," I said.

Nadya handed him the message.

In that mournful moment, I believe the three of us were united by a single hope: that Ivan Babushkin, and workers like him, had not died in vain.

But hope is a wish, not a comfort.

We moved on.

In Berlin we dined on bad meat with the usual consequences. A pale and queasy trio, we arrived in Geneva, cheerless Geneva, where one could buy avalanche postcards and feed on cheese and eggs and where none of us wanted to be.

To save on funds, we had decided to walk from the train station to our night's lodgings. Almost immediately, Ilyich stumbled. Had he dropped dead to the ground then and there, only one of us would have been surprised and possibly not even the one, my Nadya.

Before he fell, my daughter caught and held him.

"I feel I have come here simply to die," Ilyich admitted in a whisper I was not meant to hear.

Always it was my Nadya who countered Ilyich's morbid outbursts with stalwart assurances, always. But on this day, no. Fear had made dungeons of her cheeks. In response to that cry of despair, she leaned harder against him, eyes pinched shut.

And so it was left to me to intercede.

"Come, come, Volodya! What kind of talk is this? A month of omelets will fatten your thighs and restore your strength. When we again return to Russia, you will be so fit and muscled you will be able to join the Vyborg workers fighting in the streets."

I knew we had weathered that particular bad moment when Nadya twisted in my direction to chastise her mother for suggesting Vladimir Ilyich Lenin waste his skills and talents on a street fight.

But that was only one bad moment surmounted, and there were, awaiting us, so many others. So very many others.

During our first exile I had often dreamed the three of us were bobbing corks at the mercy of currents and tides. The river we bobbed upon was never the Neva. It was the Thames or some more unearthly waterway. During the second exile, I ceased dreaming of rivers. My new nightmares chose for their settings more desiccated environments. A nameless street. A dusty hallway. Or a room in a boarding house that looked like every featureless room we had occupied, would occupy. In that barren, impersonal place, the three of us sat, stranded, waiting, each dream moment feeling as if it took the length of a lifetime to pass. And I and Nadya and

Ilyich locked in its passage, unable to move forward, unable to go back. Stuck there for dream's eternity.

Cycling

You know about Ilyich and his bicycles, yes?

Very proud of his bicycles, very proprietary.

By 1909 we had moved again—to Paris, city of revolutions, City of Light, once terrain of the monkey-faced Marat and the sanguinary Puritan Robespierre, the setting for the two-month socialist experiment so inspiring to the Bolsheviks: *La Commune de Paris.*

Inspiring, also instructive.

The Communards, Ilyich maintained, had shown themselves too "soft." "Excessive magnanimity" prevented them from "destroying" the enemy when they had chance.

And my Nadya?

Had she been in Paris in the spring of 1871, would she have joined the mob surrounding the executioners' scaffold to jeer at the condemned?

"Tant pis pour eux! Tant pis pour eux!" Too bad for them.

I cannot doubt it. For my daughter, for Ilyich, those not for The Revolution stand against it.

In Paris, Ilyich purchased a bicycle to ride from our apartment on the Rue Beaunier across the city to the Bibiliothèque Nationale. The Bibiliothèque Nationale did not measure up to the reading room of the British Museum, in Ilyich's opinion. Constantly he complained of its inferiority and limitations.

"The closing hours change with the season, the rooms are drafty and the chairs not fit for firewood."

It wore out my patience, Ilyich's grousing.

"Volodya! Have you not seen where Nadya conducts The Revolution's business?"

"Mama!"

"I invite you to reacquaint yourself."

My daughter's makeshift desk was once again a rickety table, that table located in an apartment surveilled by yet another disapproving landlady.

When interfering in our business, the proprietor of our initial Parisian lodgings did so with a nose so elevated we responded to nostrils. When a Parisian elevates her nose, there is no mistaking the snub intended. Snubs did not bother us in the least; her intrusions bothered us. And again, it was Nadya, not Ilyich, who had to deal with the nuisance and maintain the subterfuge. The details of such annoyances Nadya spared her husband. Vladimir Lenin's mother-in-law felt less inclined to shield the third member of our household.

"I have heard about hours of operation. I have heard about temperatures. I have heard about chairs, but I have heard not a word about books, the reason you bicycle across the city, Vladimir Ilyich."

Ilyich looked up suspiciously from his soup. He had lived with me long enough to recognize a reprimand in the making. But his fit of pique took precedent.

"The catalogues are in deplorable condition. And the librarians? You would guess they are being paid to scramble books, not find them."

"But they are found, eventually. And brought to your desk."

"I did not say otherwise," he bristled, dabbing his beard.

"A desk that only holds books."

"What is your point, Yelizaveta Vasilevna?"

"Again, I invite you to reacquaint yourself with Nadya's working conditions. Her desk not only holds mail and books and papers. It holds the overflow of pamphlets and drafts of your speeches. She must pinch in her elbows simply to write!"

"Mama!"

Ilyich tucked his chin. Since he could not dispute what I said, he sulked.

Ilyich paid a fee to the concierge of an apartment house near the library for the privilege of leaving his bicycle parked in her hallway during the day. Having taken that expensive precaution, he assumed his bicycle safe from thieves. But thieves found it nonetheless.

The day of the theft, when Ilyich did not return at the usual punctual hour, Nadya began to pick at her pen and drip ink on her skirts. If I took away the pen, I feared she would pick at skin. And so Nadya picked and I scrubbed a pan already clean. If suddenly, unexpectedly, we were to find ourselves two women alone in Paris, ink tattoos and scraped knuckles would neither help nor harm us further.

"Volodya! We were worried!"

"I am late because I am at the mercy of cretins!" he squalled. "Cretins and thieves!"

After the library had closed he had gone as usual to fetch his bicycle and found nothing.

"Nothing! And what do you think the concierge had to say about it? 'I cannot watch your bicycle every minute, *monsieur*. The thieves of Paris are very clever!' She who had been *paid* to prevent thievery!"

A revolutionary, yes, but Vladimir Ilyich expected—demanded— impeccable service for his coin.

"Perhaps the concierge and the thief are one and the same," Nadya suggested.

The very possibility infuriated Ilyich anew. He could not eat for cursing.

The purchase of Ilyich's second bicycle coincided with our move to Rue Marie-Rose, a more secluded street with wider sidewalks that permitted Ilyich to strip and oil his new transportation on a weekly basis.

"Nadya!" he would call up through the window. "Come down at once! You must see this!"

Dutifully, Nadya would leave her papers and I as often a boiling pot to stand on the sidewalk and listen to Ilyich, sleeves rolled past his elbows, enthusiastically recount an alteration he had made to a spoke or a gear that would "improve performance immensely."

Improved performance did not prevent Ilyich's second bicycle from ending up a twisted mass of metal. A speeding car ran it and Ilyich off the road. Had he not leapt off the bicycle, he too might have been hit and injured.

Not a propitious combination, Ilyich and bicycles.

When Ilyich discovered the driver of the "high-powered car" was a *vicomte*, he put his lawyer training to use, sued the negligent, won the case and in compensation received a new bicycle—his third.

And then one afternoon he brought home a bicycle for Nadya.

"Vladimir Ilyich! It is not enough that you risk your own neck, you must now risk my Nadya's?"

"Hush, Mama," my daughter said, eyes gleaming. Already she had hiked up her skirts and swung a leg over the seat. "I shall make a test run!"

Albuquerque/Bernalillo County Libraries

Customer ID: **********3281

Title: An unfinished season / Ward Just.
ID: 39075030189275
Due: 05-17-13

Title: For you, Madam Lenin / Kat Meads.
ID: 39075041010601
Due: 05-17-13

Title: Orders from Berlin / Simon Tolkien.
ID: 39075040983303
Due: 05-17-13

Total items: 3
4/26/2013 1:15 PM
Checked out: 6

Thank you for using the Main Library
http://library.cabq.gov

"To the end of the street and back, as fast as you can," Ilyich dared and off Nadya sped, losing hairpins, showing her knees.

Ilyich clapped his hands. "You see, Yelizaveta Vasilevna? Nadya loves it."

I did see. And hear. My daughter pedaling, whooping with delight. And so I reconsidered.

Why not the recreation of cycling for Ilyich and Nadya? Why not speed through Paris on bicycles? The Revolution in Russia had stalled.

A Visit to Draveil

"Nadya, you are like a schoolgirl with a crush!" her mother observed.

It was true. She was excited, ridiculously so. Moreover, she could not talk herself into being or behaving otherwise.

"Imagine, Mama! To meet the daughter of Karl Marx!"

"I do not have to imagine, Nadya. You will come back and tell me all about it. Now turn your head."

Her mother had suggested extra hairpins to combat the effects of the 25-kilometer bicycle ride from the Rue Marie-Rose to Draveil and she had submitted to the reinforcements. At the moment she felt no inclination to refuse anything—even Yelizaveta Vasilevna's primping on her behalf.

"And you will bring back an autograph for your mama?"

"I will do no such thing!"

Her mother brushed at her collar, smiling.

"Do not pretend you would not like one."

The visit was enough, more than enough. She and Laura Marx Lafargue! To talk of revolution together!

"Ilyich," her mother commanded. "You must watch the roadway for two. And if another *vicomte* in a high-powered car swerves in your direction, I rely on you to knock my daughter to safety. She is too giddy to do so herself."

"Who is giddy?" Ilyich asked.

"Not another word, Mama!"

Ilyich would not approve of giddiness. She did not approve of it herself. They were all revolutionaries. They were all Marxists. But the Marxist she was to meet was *Laura Marx!*

"Nadya, make haste. We will be late."

Rushing, her shoulder knocked against the doorjamb; a hairpin fell to the floor.

"And the wind will undo the rest of my good work," her mother said with resignation.

Ilyich wore a dark suit and a shirt with a stiff white collar. Very carefully he rolled up his trousers before climbing onto his bike. Now it was Ilyich who was delaying!

"The oil splatters," he said because her foot impatiently tapped. "It is my one good suit!"

The ride? Since she did not crash into Ilyich or a *vicomte,* she must have paid sufficient attention to roads and spokes and rocks and passing traffic. But it did not seem so.

"You are pedaling too fast!" Ilyich complained. "We are not to arrive until one."

Would it be inappropriate to mention that, while in England, she and Ilyich had often taken the bus to Primrose Hill, to the cemetery, to stand at the grave of the hostess's father?

At the gate to the house, she stammered: "Ilyich! A moment! I cannot go in looking so windswept!"

But already he had stored his bicycle behind bushes and was striding up the path. Now that they had arrived, Ilyich too revealed a bit of nervous excitement. He had sent a copy of his *Materialism and Empirio-Criticism* in advance, eager to discuss reactionary philosophy with Paul Lafargue. Ilyich felt Lafargue would appreciate his arguments against the "Marxist mystics."

She was still in the doorway when Ilyich unceremoniously settled into a worn chair and launched into conversation with the figure in shadow.

"Such a pensive face!" Yelizaveta Vasilevna had remarked on seeing a photograph of Laura Marx.

The woman standing next to her in the doorway seemed less pensive than detached. Cordial, but detached.

"Perhaps you and I will stroll in the park while our husbands talk?"

"That would be lovely."

And it was lovely: the autumn day, the chestnut trees, but she could not talk to Laura Marx about trees and weather! Along with her husband, Laura Marx had devoted decades to political work, translating her father's work into French, diligently promoting Marxism in France and Spain.

Because her companion walked slowly, she walked slowly. Should she mention the latest news from Piter? Ilyich's feud with the Mensheviks? She would have been honored to discuss the Lafargues' current work but hesitated to inquire. *She* could not bring up the topic.

Tongue-tied and horribly embarrassed, she loped alongside Laura Marx.

It was obvious Ilyich had suffered no similar embarrassment. When they returned to the house, the two men were deeply engaged in conversation. Ilyich continued to talk as Paul Lafargue rose from his chair and came to stand beside his wife.

"Paul will soon prove the sincerity of his convictions," Laura Marx said.

"He has proved them already," Ilyich replied but neither of their hosts acknowledged the compliment. They looked only at each other, smiled only at each other. And then they said goodbye.

Back on the Rue Marie-Rose, she and Ilyich had barely finished wiping their shoes before Yelizaveta Vasilevna launched her interrogation.

"Come now, Volodya! You have spent the afternoon with Marxist celebrities and you have no gossip to share?"

"They are both old and feeble."

"Ilyich!" she protested.

"He had spilt butter on his sleeve."

"Ilyich, enough!"

"And does he look like a Creole and she like her father?" her mother quizzed.

"Yes to the one, no to the other. Nadya? You agree?"

"Leave me out of this rudeness."

"Very well," her mother said, directing the next barrage solely at Ilyich. "What color was the wallpaper? Did the house smell of fish or stew? Were there flowers in vases? And the father and father-in-law's books? Reverentially displayed on the mantle or fashioned into a separate altar piece?"

Her mother had gone too far. At that last snideness, Ilyich also turned peevish.

"I could learn more from a jackdaw," her mother complained, dismissing them with a wave of her arm and returning to the stove.

"All joking aside, Volodya. Did you notice? They showed no interest in the work ahead. They said nothing of the future."

"He was not as complimentary as I had hoped about my book,"

Ilyich brooded. "I cannot understand why. It refuted none of his work."

"Something in that house made me uneasy."

"You went expecting too much, Nadya. They are simply people."

INTERVIEW WITH HISTORY
The Daughters Marx

"First to you, Eleanor. That morning in March when you sent the maid to the chemist for chloroform and prussic acid, took a bath, dressed yourself in white and expired before noon, age 43. Given the chance to redo, would you?"

(Silence.)

"Do speak, Tussy. This is a chance to tell it your way."

"Tussy?"

"The family called me Tussy. Never Eleanor."

"Your sister Laura has a valid point, Eleanor/Tussy. Anything you say must be recorded."

"My taste and Edward's taste were much the same. We agreed on Socialism. We both loved the theater. We staged a private reading of Ibsen's *Nora*. I translated *Madame Bovary*."

"To be clear: you're referring to Edward Aveling? The deceitful parasite who lived off you for 15 years?"

"I do not care…"

"What's that, Laura?"

"I do not *care* for your *tone* in speaking to my sister."

"Your dead sister. Oh, wait. You're both dead. Two sisters, two suicides."

"When Edward and I met, we could not *legally* become man and wife. It was not possible."

"Because *legally* Edward already had a wife."

"But ours was the *true* marriage, a Marxist marriage that set aside all false and immoral bourgeois conventionalities. Our fellow Socialists approved. They recognized our happiness."

"They did, did they?"

"Yes, yes! They did! Didn't they, Laura?"

"Don't upset yourself, Tussy. I can explain. I can steer clear of the anorexia and hysteria and the broken engagement to Lissagaray. I can gloss over the fairytale obsession, the rambling letters to Abraham Lincoln. Let me respond on your behalf."

"…Except I wish people didn't have to live in houses and cook and bake and wash and clean…"

"Laura? Interpret, please. Is your sister reminiscing about her home with Edward or your parents' swine pit of broken chairs, cracked tea cups, and filth?"

"Tussy and Edward made a pact. A *pact*, you understand. Like mine and Paul's."

"Paul Lafargue—your husband in both the conventional and Marxist sense."

"We also decided, Paul and I, to quit before we had outlived our usefulness."

"Define 'usefulness.'"

"Usefulness to the cause."

"Could we return a moment to Edward Aveling? The louse who quit the house, not the world, that March morning and left his Marxist bride to her tub and death meds. The socialist 'husband' who shed nary a tear before, after or at the funeral."

"Again, I do not appreciate your tone. Nor does Tussy. Tussy! Defend your husband!"

"Father once wrote to Engels: 'Such a lousy life is not worth living.'"

"He wrote that after Mother's smallpox, Tussy. After the disease left Mother deaf and scarred. After she had given birth to our stillborn brother."

"Pardon, sisters. Scholarly records indicate your father expressed that epistolary sentiment while suffering a case of boils. Quote/unquote: 'A truly proletarian disease.'"

"We had a brother who lived. Freddy. The maid's son. Laura, tell about Freddy. How Mother didn't mind. He became a machinist, Freddy did."

"Again, to Laura: Did you always intend to follow your sister's example?"

"My husband and I died together, as planned."

"'Healthy of body and spirit, I give me death before implacable old age paralyzes my physical and intellectual strength.' Your husband's note reads like the farewell of one, not two."

"We were in agreement."

"A hypodermic full of cyanide."

"Yes."

"At 69 and 65."

"Yes."

"You left this world in tandem with the man your father described as a Creole medical student."

"I died with my husband, Paul Lafargue."

"Quoting once more from Paul Lafargue's final missive: 'I die with the supreme happiness of having the certainty that very soon will triumph the cause in which I have given myself since 45 years ago.' I, I, I, I, I."

"We had become too feeble to carry on the struggle."

"Had you, though? Nadezhda Krupskaya didn't think so when she and Vladimir Lenin visited. Remember? You and she strolled about while the gentlemen stayed inside to talk philosophy. She was excited, embarrassed to be excited, strolling with one of the daughters Marx."

"They always came for Father, didn't they, Laura? Never for us. I was Father's secretary, his translator. For years we thought no one would marry me."

"Tussy! No one thought any such thing."

"I'm quite sure we did. I'm quite sure we all quite rightly despaired. Until Edward."

"George Bernard Shaw thought Edward Aveling resembled a lizard. But you, Tussy? I assume you found him physically attractive?"

"We had so many troubles! I would feel so completely desperate and Edward so unconcerned."

"One last question, daughters. Was Daddy right? 'Anyone who knows anything of history knows that great social changes are impossible without feminine upheaval. Social progress can be measured exactly by the social position of the fair sex, the ugly ones included.'"

"Of course."

(Silence.)

"Tussy! Agree!"

A Café in Paris

A rare occasion.

Nadezhda Krupskaya has left behind both desk and mother to join her husband at a café on the Avenue d'Orléans.

Each orders a beer.

Yes, beer.

When funds permit, Nadezhda Krupskaya and Vladimir Lenin treat themselves to one beer each.

The year: 1910.

The season: spring.

Would the encounter on the horizon play differently in winter? In summer? Before you respond, a caution: speculation is the godchild of regret.

The woman seated next to her husband amid the squawk and hiss of squabbling Social Democrats regrets that Nicholas II remains on the throne in Russia; she regrets that The Revolution of 1905 has failed to improve the workers' lot.

But personal regrets—as a woman, a *wife*?

Those Nadezhda Krupskaya has been spared until this day, this hour, this moment fast approaching.

Émigré cafes bore Comrade Krupskaya. One Social Democrat shouts. Another counter-shouts. And then everyone shouts at once like children fighting over a stolen ball. She does not consider this progress.

It is hot inside the café and getting hotter. Too many bodies, too much temper. The windows have begun to drip with condensation. Nadezhda Krupskaya's face is flushed from beer and heat. She does not need the light coat she wears and soon she will see that garment as not only hot but shapeless, priggish, dull, because momentarily she will begin to think in comparisons. And when she does, the flush on her face will spread.

Nadezhda Krupskaya is aware of an itch beneath her knee, a scratchiness near the seam of her dress, sensitivity when the beer passes over a certain back tooth. What she does not immediately notice because of hammering fists and flailing arms is the woman in the flamboyant hat making her way between tables toward their own.

Only when the woman sets down her glass in front of Vladimir Lenin does Vladimir Lenin's wife begin to pay attention.

When Nadezhda Krupskaya thinks back on this meeting, and she will think back on it many, many times, she will assume the glass contained Grenadine and soda, Inessa Armand's favorite drink.

And she will be correct.

The woman is green-eyed, stylish. The extravagant hat does not completely overshadow the fineness of her auburn hair. Her manner, approaching Vladimir Lenin, could be taken for awe. When she extends her hand, Vladimir Lenin holds it a beat longer than he would hold the hand of a female less lovely. Quiet muffles the noisy room. Watchfulness replaces contention.

Could it be that Vladimir Lenin, ascetic, has revealed himself susceptible to the temptations of flesh?

The woman says: "I am Inessa Armand. I have wanted to meet you for a very long time."

"And now we have met," Vladimir Lenin replies.

Because no one else is doing the honors, Nadezhda Krupskaya introduces herself.

She does not add: "I am Vladimir Lenin's wife."

She bites her lip.

"A pleasure," says Inessa Armand to Nadezhda Krupskaya.

But not the greater pleasure.

And Then He Met Inessa

When he was 39, my daughter's husband for more than a decade, when Ilyich was feeling his age, his mortality, the eroding of his influence, when he was still reeling from the turmoil and frustrations of 1905, Ilyich met Inessa Armand.

Another of history's sly ironies, is it not? That Vladimir Lenin should acquire a mistress in a city famous not only for revolutions but for royal favorites the likes of Madame de Pompadour and Madame du Barry?

Not so very long after Inessa introduced herself to Ilyich at the café on the Avenue d'Orléans, I found myself alone with my son-in-law. Nadya had left the apartment to mail the day's documents back to Russia, and Ilyich was using her desk to finish another letter before departing for the Bibiliothèque Nationale.

With what some might label presumption, others impertinence, I tapped his shoulder.

"Vladimir Ilyich, you realize you have shown yourself vulnerable to more than Mensheviks."

An old woman's ribbing—but not only, not quite.

He turned narrowed eyes in my direction, the calculating brain in that oversized skull no doubt assessing what ought and ought not be admitted to a mother-in-law.

I folded my hands. I waited. He turned back to his papers. But I tell you this, history: the nape of the great Bolshevik leader's neck had turned the color of a ripe plum.

People assume I disliked Inessa. On the contrary, I liked her very much. She was wonderful company, a bright presence and lively spirit. Among a crowd of drawn and pinched faces, slumped shoulders and émigré shabbiness, there would be Inessa, vibrant, animated, fiery and flirtatious. Within such a circle of depression and defeat, she stood out brilliantly. One could hardly help gravitating in her direction. Born in Paris, she remained more Parisian than Russian. She wore the very latest fashions and she wore them beautifully.

You imagine I note this with disdain?

Absolutely not. It was more than a pleasure to see a revolutionary woman so well turned out. I have often wondered why so many male Marxists resemble dandies and so many Marxist females washerwomen, my Nadya included. Plekhanov dressed as if he were a prince and, with far less funds at his disposal, Lev Davidovich gave him a run for the clotheshorse prize. Vera Zasulich with her cigarette ash and inked fingers and skirts in a perpetual twist? She made my Nadya look kempt. Only in Paris, when Inessa joined us, did I see a revolutionary woman exhibit fashion sense.

A trained musician, Inessa was a lyrical pianist. She played with great skill and greater passion. Invariably her piano performances, while delighting the rest of us, disturbed Ilyich.

"Why the frown, Ilyich?" Inessa would tease after finishing a Beethoven sonata, a Chopin étude. "Have I hit a wrong note? Have I played in a displeasing manner?"

And Volodya would answer: "I am frowning because your music makes me have stupid, gentle feelings. It makes me want to stroke peoples' heads, including the heads of idiots."

And so you see? Ilyich could also become entranced and enchanted.

As a young girl, Inessa had moved to Moscow with her aunt, who secured a position as a French tutor at the Armand estate. Inessa finished growing up among and within a family of prodigious wealth. She also made her future there. Two of the Armand sons fell in love with her. She was to marry one, Alexander, the father of four of her children, and leave him for the second, Vladimir, nine years her junior, the father of her fifth and last child.

While Nadya and others like my daughter acknowledged a woman's right to live and love in the free manner of Chernyshevky's fictional heroine Vera Palovna, Inessa exercised that freedom in life.

"To divide myself between you is impossible," she announced to her husband and brother-in-law. "I refuse to try."

Alexander Armand's acceptance of the arrangement is far more remarkable than Vladimir Armand's. The lover of a married woman knows he has entered a triangle; such knowledge generally catches the husband by surprise. I regret that no opportunity to meet Alexander Armand came my way. History will label Inessa Armand an extraordinary woman, and she was. But she had also married an extraordinary man.

Many, many times I longed to ask Inessa: "And how did your husband react to the announcement that you would not divide yourself? In that room, on that divan, what did he do? What did he say? Was your happiness, your contentment, his only concern? Did he say: 'Whatever pleases you, my darling.' Or did he say, to you both: 'Better a brother than a stranger.'"

While living openly with her brother-in-law, Inessa remained Alexander's wife. Alexander Armand financially supported the new couple and when Inessa gave birth to her last child, a son, Alexander Armand claimed that son as his own.

A woman so impulsive, so unconventional, joining forces with the ever practical native of Simbirsk.

Did I enjoy the fireworks that clash of temperament and personality created?

I did.

In her movements, in her thinking, Inessa was very quick, very opinionated. She deferred to no man, Vladimir Ilyich included. Unlike my Nadya, she did not see fit to watch and brood in silence. When she disagreed, she did so with heat and vigor.

In the future, between Ilyich and Inessa, there would be many disagreements, personal and political. Unlike Ilyich, Inessa supported the Workers Opposition. To have done otherwise, she felt, slighted the trade unions. In 1918, she adamantly opposed negotiating a separate peace. Rather than sue for peace, she—and others—favored waging a revolutionary war against the Germans.

Their relationship, *l'affaire*, did not run smoothly. There were flare-ups, recriminations, bruised feelings. But at the onset: only enchantment.

You doubt it? Then explain to me these curious exceptions to the rule. Whereas Vladimir Ilyich missed no opportunity to mock and condemn the high style of Plekhanov's morning coats and silk ties, the similarly expensive equivalents in Inessa's wardrobe—the elaborate hats, the stylish dresses—drew not a word of criticism. Inessa employed a dressmaker, a milliner, a nanny. She did not live on a revolutionary's budget; she lived from proceeds of a textile fortune that had been earned off the backs of workers. Never once did Ilyich refer to the origins of her capital or her less than frugal lifestyle.

I do not mean to slight Inessa's revolutionary service. A spoiled, extravagant, impetuous woman can also serve The Revolution and in Inessa's case did so admirably. Her skills as a linguist, her fluency in Russian, French, German and English, contributed greatly to the cause. In Russia, she had been arrested and, like my Nadya, spent time in a tsarist prison cell.

How could my son-in-law resist such a combination of feminine charm and revolutionary dedication?

He could not and did not.

Would Inessa have taken up with the second Vladimir if the first had not died? That I cannot say. But I can tell you this: whatever joy Inessa brought into Ilyich's life, it did not come without tension.

"Ilyich credits women with intelligence—but only a bit of it. Is that not so, Nadya?"

"Nonsense!" Ilyich roared.

My Nadya would not be drawn into that kind of three-part play. When Inessa engaged in Ilyich baiting, Nadya excused herself and returned to The Revolution's paperwork.

As often as not in those situations, I did not excuse myself. It was not my mission to provide Inessa and Ilyich with privacy and in exile I took my entertainment where I could find it. In this instance, I joined the discussion.

"It is not a matter of quantity, Inessa," I said. "It is a matter of ingredient. Ilyich believes a woman's intelligence is compromised by emotion. Is that not so, Volodya?"

Inessa smiled.

"Well put, Yelizaveta Vasilevna. Defend yourself and your kind, Ilyich."

But Ilyich had also had enough of the topic and retreated elsewhere with his books.

It happens often enough: an intelligent woman ruled by her emotions.

It had happened before with Inessa; during the duration of Inessa and Ilyich's love affair, my Nadya refused to allow it to happen to her. However great her distress—and Nadya admitted no distress, not even to her mother—my daughter's personal feelings never prevailed over duty. She worked daily without pique or prejudice alongside her rival for another of their common causes, The Revolution. In Paris and elsewhere, when Ilyich spoke to the workers, when he addressed other Social Democrats, when he proposed new tactics or denounced old theories, Nadya and Inessa sat in the front row together, united in their applause and in their belief in Ilyich and his leadership.

And so you are thinking: we have heard much about Inessa; we have heard about Ilyich's infatuation, but we have heard too little about the wife. What sort of mother encourages a liaison when she knows her daughter faithfully loves the unfaithful?

I will tell you what kind: the kind who is deeply concerned about the reservoirs of her daughter's strength and resilience. The sort of mother who, of necessity, makes peace with a daughter's sacrifices on behalf of The Revolution but refuses to tolerate a daughter's *raison d'être* devolving to the care and feeding of a single man.

Early on, they reached an understanding, the three of them. If Ilyich's desire for Inessa and hers for him left undiminished Ilyich's respect and fondness for Nadya, my daughter accepted Inessa the mistress.

And my reason for accommodation? Ilyich was too much for Nadya to handle, even with my help. We needed another keeper. And Inessa became that third keeper, in Paris, in Cracow, in Poronino.

Nevertheless, I did not forget my Nadya's feelings. To Nadya, I said: "You can permit it. You can accept it. But that does not mean you have to like it, Daughter."

"Inessa is a good comrade."

"That she is, and a striking, charming woman."

"He was depressed and discouraged before he met Inessa. He is less so now."

"And yourself? You, too, might look elsewhere for gaiety."

"Mama! Do not say such things!"

Despite that rebuke, I repeated the suggestion on several occasions. And why not? If husbands can seek sympathy and passion elsewhere, why not wives? If we were to thumb our noses at the attitudes of the bourgeoisie politically, why not in other realms?

So I say this as the mother of Nadezhda Konstantinovna Krupskaya Ulyanova without qualm or the slightest disloyalty: the Krupskayas needed Inessa Armand. As Ilyich's paramour, she took some of the burden off my Nadya, and anyone who took some of the burden off my daughter received my blessing.

No, I had no quarrel with Inessa. Inessa was Inessa; Inessa was Paris.

INTERVIEW WITH HISTORY
Inessa Armand

"So as not to come off *completely* chauvinistic, an acknowledgment of your vast contributions to The Revolution: editor, translator, organizer, administrator, underground agent, chair of the First International Conference of Communist Women, Zhenotdel director. Comrade Armand, the Russian proletariat and peasantry thank you. Now for the juicy stuff. The first Volodya—your husband's brother. If he had lived, would there have been entanglement with the second?"

"There are people whom I trust more than myself because I know that, even if I become the worst of women, the nastiest and most odious of people, they would remain my friends."

"Sentiments penned to your long-suffering husband, yes. We're aware of that letter."

"My husband in the old sense of the term."

"The gent who not only forgave your absconding with his brother but funded that flight."

"Sasha wanted everything for me. Clothes, servants, trips to Paris, lovers. Any passing fancy, Sasha provided. But I was not happy."

"So you took to running away from him and his house at midnight in your nightdress. Hiding out in barns while he and the servants searched woods and wells, lanterns swinging, your husband crying out your name, begging forgiveness for he knew not what."

"It was quite romantic."

"But ultimately futile."

"He was a liberal, my Sasha, but no revolutionary."

"Merely a revolutionary's wallet."

"I have acknowledged his generosity. Did you not hear me describe him as a generous man?"

"We heard described a doting man…but never mind, never mind.

Fast forward to Paris, 1909. The first Volodya dead of septicemia, his successor, the balding redhead who slurred his r's, spouting off in a café. Your introduction to Vladimir Ilyich. Describe for us that marvelous encounter on that marvelous Parisian day."

"No description does it justice."

"An auburn-haired woman in her mid-thirties, dressed in the latest belle époque fashion, a red feather in her hat. A talented pianist, an exceptional linguist. Elegant, charming, dynamic. In the words of another admirer: 'A hot bonfire of revolution.' Poor sod didn't stand a chance, did he?"

"Ilyich was magnificent, brilliant. Meeting him for the first time, I felt suddenly, dreadfully awkward, lamentably stupid. I did not know what to do with myself. I envied those brave people who simply walked up and spoke with him."

"But the salacious details? History is confused. Was it in Paris or Longjumeau or Cracow or Berne or back in Paris where you two first hit the sheets? Was it in 1911, 1914 or both that Nadya Krupskaya offered to bow out as wife?"

"I and my children had great affection for Nadya. She, too, was much loved."

"She was also, like your husband, forgiving. She was also, like your husband, quick with the alibis. 'Inessa soon gathered our Paris crowd around her,' NK writes. *All* the Cracow crowd 'became very much attached to Inessa,' NK writes. Life seemed 'cozier and livelier when Inessa was present,' NK writes. But was it? For the woman insisting such? We vote: unlikely."

"Ilyich and I were souls united. Nadya understood."

"Accepted, maybe. We'll give you 'accepted.'"

"But soon I grew exhausted, ill."

"The universal fate of revolutionaries, sensuous or chaste."

"Toward the end, the only warm feelings I had left were for my children and Vladimir Ilyich. In all other respects, it was as if my heart had died."

"Still: you'll always have Paris, *n'est-ce pas?*"

A School for Bolsheviks

Thereafter, when and where we moved in Paris, Inessa moved also, renting the apartment next door or down the hall or across the street, but never sharing the same apartment, the same house. Certain proprieties were maintained and had either Ilyich or Inessa failed to uphold those niceties of appearance, I can assure you, they would have had to answer to me.

I would not see my Nadya publicly humiliated or compromised. That I would not countenance.

Inessa's entourage at the time included her two youngest children, Varvara, age nine, and Andre, age seven, and the children's nanny, Savushka. Although the children travelled back and forth to Russia for visits with Alexander Armand, they were often with Inessa and privy to their mother's revolutionary activities.

Ilyich, Nadya and I were fond of both children, and my Nadya especially adored Varvara, a grave-faced little girl who looked more like a worker's child than the daughter of an aristocrat. Her legs were long and spindly. Her face was perpetually dirty, despite Savushka's best efforts. She had none of her mother's grace of carriage. Repeatedly she ran into the corners of tables and dropped her pens and pencils. But she could not hear enough about Piter and The Revolution of 1905.

"Tell me again, Aunt Krupa," she would beg Nadya. "Tell me again how Vladimir Ilyich hid from the Okhrana. Tell me again what dangers the night contained."

And Nadya would stop her work to tell the tale in her fashion, a tale about the hero Ilyich, shortchanging herself.

"Vladimir Ilyich worked ceaselessly in Piter on behalf of The Revolution."

Since my daughter has never been one to exaggerate, I helped.

The child wanted a story, not the dry facts.

"Night and day! Sneaking back and forth to the Vyborg, aware that every footfall behind him, every shadow ahead, may belong to an agent of the tsar."

"He did not sleep in the same bed twice," Nadya said.

"Could not! For fear of capture! Even in his fitful dreams, Vladimir Ilyich kept running, outwitting the Okhrana and the spies in their pay. After a few hours' rest in a comrade's bed, he would wake panting, as if he had sprinted to Moscow and back."

Listening to my embellishments, Varvara would also begin to pant.

"Once, the Okhrana came very close to success," Nadya said.

"They arrived just as dawn was breaking. There was a mist on the Neva, a mist on the streets. Vladimir Ilyich lay on a cot in a worker's quarters, separated from the family by a screen. As the Okhrana interrogated the worker and his terrified wife and children, Vladimir Ilyich dared not breathe. A cough, the softest sneeze, and all would be finished!"

"Beneath the screen," Nadya said, "Vladimir Ilyich could see the Okhrana's boots."

"The arrogant boots of arrogant men! Boots that stomped this way and that, heedless of what they kicked. When they kicked the family's cat, it hissed and ran behind the screen for protection."

"No!" Varvara protested.

"Mama, you have gone too far," Nadya reprimanded. "There was no cat."

I winked at Varvara.

"And when the Okhrana stomped toward the screen that hid Vladimir Ilyich, what do you think happened?" I asked.

"The cat jumped in their faces and scratched and clawed and Vladimir Ilyich escaped!" Varvara exclaimed.

"Exactly so. Vladimir Ilyich escaped. Once again Vladimir Ilyich escaped," I concluded.

If any cat had come between the Okhrana and Ilyich, it would have met with a thud against the wall and a broken neck. But why describe to a child, even in a story, how efficiently and indifferently the Okhrana dealt with impediment and obstruction?

As exiles in Europe, we were not shed of the Okhrana entirely. After the events of 1905, surveillance of revolutionary exiles markedly increased. Such surveillance was harder to conduct outside the city, the prime reason Ilyich decided to headquarter his school for Bolsheviks in the countryside south of Paris. Inessa was put in charge of organizing the venture whose purpose was to train workers in the art of agitation.

Nadya has described Longjumeau as a "straggling French village" through which farmers' produce passed on its way "to fill the belly of Paris."

Filling the bellies at the Bolshevik school was my assignment. I had assistance, of course, but it was I who planned the meals and haggled in the local markets for fruit and vegetables and tried to save The Revolution a few francs here, a few francs there. Such frugalities were my habit but in the case of the school at Longjumeau not altogether necessary. For this particular enterprise, Ilyich and Inessa had adequate funds at their disposal, provided by Alexander Armand.

We opened in June 1911 with 18 students. Inessa and her two youngest lived in the same structure as the students, which also included the classrooms and the communal kitchen. Ilyich and Nadya and I lodged in rooms at the other end of the village. Ilyich gave the opening lecture at 8 a.m. on theoretical Marxism, his vision of the Party or political economy. Then Ilyich departed and Inessa took over, leading the discussion on Ilyich's remarks. Nadya did not teach. She spent her time corresponding with Party members and sympathizers and making not strictly necessary trips back and forth to Paris to collect papers that could have been forwarded to Longjumeau. But if those trips to Paris helped my daughter escape the intimacy that existed between her husband and another woman, undeniable to anyone with eyes that sweltering summer, who was I to encourage her to stay and keep her mama company?

It was not all work and duty at Longjumeau. On the weekends, there were nature walks and picnics. Inessa insisted on the recreation. And after meals in the wilds, while Ilyich jotted down notes and Nadya, if Nadya were present, studied Italian, and I played cards with Varvara and Andre, Inessa would spread her skirts and stretch out and turn her face to the sun, a seductive, sensual creature. As thoroughly as she believed in socialism, Inessa believed in pleasure and perceived in those dual beliefs no contradiction.

Ilyich, in time, would grow to resent such duality. My Nadya? Perhaps she had always expected that part of Inessa's personality to wear badly with Ilyich over the long term. As for myself, I did not hold such propensities against her. There were times, more than a few, when I wished Inessa's capacity to enjoy life would prove contagious and infect my Nadya. But that was not to be. No criticism of Inessa ever passed my daughter's lips but in no way did she try to refashion herself in her rival's image.

Despite Inessa's beauty, wealth, wardrobe, delightful children, and understanding husband, despite her relationship with Ilyich sanctioned by *his* understanding wife, despite her work for The Revolution, at Longjumeau Inessa was not a contented woman.

In the late afternoons, after classes had finished for the day and before I began supper preparations, Inessa and I adjourned to the porch to smoke—our shared "vice." It was our habit, while smoking, to chat idly about the heat or Varvara's lessons or Andre's lost hat, mail delays or termites or flowers that had bloomed overnight—nothing of grave importance. On the porch we had never exchanged anything like confidences until the afternoon she turned to me quite seriously and caught up my hand.

"Yelizaveta Vasilevna, you blame me?"

I understood that she was speaking to me then as Nadya's mother.

"Dear Inessa, men will be men. Even those men who live for revolution."

How intently she studied my face!

"You are suggesting, Yelizaveta Vasilevna, that a certain callousness is to be expected? That callousness is the male prerogative?"

I did not say "yes"; I did not say "no." Inessa was a grown woman, perfectly capable of drawing her own conclusions.

She became pensive—unusual for her.

I began to list in my head what I would need to shop for on the morrow. I began to think of mushrooms, Russian mushrooms, and to wish that a bowl of them, plump and washed and ready to stew, would appear in the kitchen cupboard.

"And yet men believe they are the masters of creation," Inessa continued.

Another statement I found no cause to dispute.

She stood abruptly enough to rattle the table in front of us and the glasses upon it. At the edge of the porch, she yanked at a perfectly innocuous vine encircling a post. Her next comment sounded even less like the Inessa with whom I was familiar.

"Men lie endlessly and women believe anything."

The tone as well as the sentiment startled me. I cannot pretend otherwise. As a mother, I am partial, of course, but partiality did not blind me to Inessa Armand's effect on and power over members of the "stronger" sex. Before and after Ilyich in his shabby coat and bowler hat began to pay her court, Inessa enjoyed legions of admirers—Frenchmen, Spaniards, Italians, Russian émigrés. She was a sophisticated, cultured, attractive woman at ease with love triangles, immune to gossip, unfettered by convention. That such a woman would believe "anything" out of a man's mouth was inconceivable.

And yet, to hear Inessa Armand, a woman whose allure even history verifies, speak in the same breath of mendacious men and gullible women gave me then and later much to consider.

If the Inessas of the world feel themselves at unfair advantage, what hope for the rest of womankind?

Fish

As she had learned to do in Paris, in Cracow she asked the butcher for meat without bones. As soon as the request passed her lips, she began to think of things other than meat and the market list. Her mother usually did the shopping in Cracow, but her mother had risen this morning with a severe case of melancholia. What kind of daughter sends a melancholic mother to market? Now she must hurry back. Ilyich's writings on the nationalities issue must reach Piter. She must find a way to get them there without mishap. She must remember to check whether Comrade Kupchenko had proved reliable as a go-between. She must try again to determine how many pamphlets had gone missing from her last mailing. She must restock their paper supply. She must...

The butcher's squall took her completely by surprise.

"The Lord God made cows with bones!"

Distress made the goiter swell.

In public she wore a thin scarf to disguise the protrusion, but she could not, if she were to see, cover her bulging eyes.

"With bones then," she amended.

Customers on either side had begun to stare and kept staring, as if she were a leper, when she was only swelling, swelling.

A scolded woman swelling.

She took the wrapped meat from the still grumbling butcher, paid him but did not thank him. Back on the unpaved street, short of breath, she leaned against building stones and with her hand covered her heart. She must not let abusive butchers and rude stares upset her! They were nothing, nothing.

Another exiting customer, swinging parcels, knocked against her. She must move on. A few more steps and she stopped again, pretending to gaze for pleasure toward the river Vistula.

An odd sensation: fearing to inhale, as if some thief loitered in her lungs with a satchel, waiting to pirate away the prize of breath.

Once at her desk, at work, she would feel better.

Mocking that wishful prophecy, her heart began to palpitate.

The same bed her melancholic mother climbed out of, she climbed into.

"It is nothing serious. I am sure I will be fine after a little rest."

Her mother ignored that analysis, that prediction. Trepidation had eclipsed melancholy. Yelizaveta Vasilevna gathered her coat and gloves.

"You will stay, Nadya, until I return?"

"Do not go to Ilyich, Mama!"

She could not bear the idea of her mother interrupting Volodya's work on her behalf.

"You will not defy me and go to your desk, after I have gone?"

"I will not go to the desk."

"Promise your mother."

"I am going nowhere, Mama. I assure you."

But what if she could not honor that promise? What if the decision were not hers to make? If she died today, tomorrow, who would take care of her mother, of Ilyich? Inessa had returned to Paris. There was no one dependable nearby...

For weeks and weeks, she disrupted Ilyich's work, his valuable time frittered away corresponding with doctors and specialists about her condition. He would not hear of engaging anyone less than the best in the field. He researched; he consulted; he comprehensively, painstakingly, compared rank and reputation, and then he chose Dr. Kocher, a surgeon in Berne, to perform the operation every doctor agreed was necessary.

To retain Dr. Kocher's services required additional negotiations, extensive, nerve-straining negotiations.

"Volodya is taking care of all the arrangements," her mother said. "We are lucky he is such a competent, thorough advocate. You and your mama need not worry with Ilyich in charge," Yelizaveta Vasilevna repeated again and again, worry creasing her face.

She overheard them—Volodya and her mother—whispering in the hallway. Volodya lost his temper: the editors of *Pravda* should have more quickly honored his request for funds.

"This is disrespect!" Volodya railed and her mother shushed him.

It was mortifying: her wretched health the cause of so much upset and expense. She felt so terribly, terribly embarrassed…

And then she could not remember, could not be entirely sure, what she felt in truth and what she imagined.

From another bed she must have heard the procedure explained: a three-hour operation to remove a section of her thyroid, to be performed without anesthetics. A cry of protest and her mother collapsed against Ilyich—or not? She could not be sure.

She believed herself awake, waiting for the doctor and his instruments, but still somehow dreamed of the Nevaskaya Zastava, unable, even in dream, to reach the heart of Piter, her longing and ambitions confined to the suburbs.

After which they must have come.

They must have begun.

"Brave," Ilyich said and Yelizaveta Vasilevna shouted: "She does not have to be brave! My daughter does not always have to be brave!"

But she struggled to be brave regardless, for Ilyich.

Sweat slid past her elbows; the soles of her feet burned as if some fiend held a match to her arches. On damp, slippery sheets, she floated—or sank. She was moaning. She was screaming. She was weeping. Or she did nothing, was nothing.

Volodya's bald head. Her mother's chilly hand. She and Inessa, hurrying to finish an issue of *Rabotnitsa*, print it, get it to Piter. Four kopeks. They must not charge the women workers more than four kopeks. In Longjumeau, they had taken off their shoes and walked barefoot down the road. Like sisters. Like truants. Inessa had helped her learn French… no, no. That was not correct. She had struggled to learn French before France, before Inessa and Ilyich.

Walking barefoot, they had kicked up dust and pebbles.

"Nadya, Nadya, you must believe me," Inessa had said. "I would never ask him to leave you."

And she had said: "Because you ask it, you imagine it will be done? That Ilyich will turn his back on a partnership of 15 years? That he will agree to be supported by the purse of Alexander Armand?"

Or had she, instead, begged: "Do not make Ilyich choose between us. Do not make him choose!"

Because if he chose Inessa, if he chose Inessa…

The struggle must be fierce, irreconcilable. The proletariat must destroy everything that stands in its way. The working class will not be led; it must lead.

Yelizaveta Vasilevna had taken such trouble preparing the tea! A visit from a woman with funds and contacts on the continent.

"I cannot say I am pleased with the Social Democrats. With Ilyich and his stridency."

Did they not understand? Did they not realize Ilyich fought for the very existence of the Party? In what manner should one fight for the Party if not "sharply," if not "brusquely"?

The devil take so-called sympathizers who imagine their cash entitles them to influence in the affairs of a proletarian party!

Papers, so many papers. On either side of the bed, walls of papers or simply walls, she could not determine which.

"Are you in pain, daughter? Nadya? Can you hear your mother?"

In the glorious Vyborg, Nadezhda Konstantinovna Krupskaya Ulyanova disappeared and in her place Praskovaya Eugenevna Onegina taught revolution, not arithmetic, to the workers.

All had been possible in Piter. With Ilyich. Beside Ilyich.

Before the dead, dead sea of emigration.

"Ilyich, she is asking where she is. What should I tell her?"

"Switzerland, Nadya. Berne. A hospital in Berne."

Not Poland? Not Cracow?

Cracow smelled of Russia.

Had it smelled the same, 40 years previous?

In Poland in braids she had never been ill. She had romped and played with Poles and Jews and birds and dogs and waited for her father to come home.

Konstantin Krupsky adored in Poland; Inessa adored in Poland, in France, in Switzerland.

She must not behave like a bourgeois wife, a scorned woman looking to punish.

She must not wait to be told; she must offer.

"Nadya, do not disturb the dressing! You must keep your hands from the incision. The flesh is very tender."

"Volodya."

"Ilyich, lean closer. She is asking for you."

"I am right here, Nadya. You will soon feel much better. The operation was a success."

"No," she said.

"Yelizaveta Vasilevna, help me to reassure her."

"It is true, Nadya. The doctors are quite pleased."

"Volodya."

"She is trying to tell you something, Ilyich. Do not make her strain."

"I will not keep you apart, Volodya. I will step aside for you and Inessa."

"Nonsense, nonsense," she thought he said.

She had been delirious. Feverish. For several hours after the operation, she had been talking out of her head.

"But now you are our Nadya again," her mother explained.

And so, as Nadya again, once more she offered.

"Daughter! Think what you are saying!"

"Nonsense," Ilyich said. "Nonsense."

She would not offer a third time; never again would she be so brave.

INTERVIEW WITH HISTORY
Maria Ilyinichna Ulyanova, Part I

"Ah, the little sister."

"Sister *and* confidante. No one was closer to Volodya than I. "

"Oh? Not elder sister Anna?"

"No."

"Not comrade/wife Nadya?"

"Certainly not."

"What about his buddy, Lev Davidovich?"

"The impossible Trotsky? Volodya tolerated Trotsky—nothing more."

"Which leaves only Inessa Armand as your rival in closeness."

"Inessa was a superlative comrade. She was of great assistance to The Revolution and to my brother."

"And you of assistance to them, carrying private letters back and forth and back and forth."

"If Comrade Armand needed to communicate with my brother, I was happy to forward her communication."

"Because you preferred Inessa to Nadya Krupskaya."

"Who did not?"

"And you have no kind word, not one, for your sister-in-law of record?"

"Nadya revered Volodya's genius. But her mother, Yelizaveta Vasilevna, treated him with a highhandedness that bordered on contempt. And she a former governess, the widow of a civil servant."

"In the photo archives, there you constantly are: at your brother's side on the street, on the platform, in conference. Crowding his ribs. Letting no one come between you and Volodya, including—or should we say *especially*?—his wife."

"Those who can be elbowed aside will be. Ulyanovs know that."

"Even Ulyanovs of 'average abilities'?"

"You are quoting the scoundrel Trotsky?"

"And now we segue: scoundrel to fish. Are you truly the originator of that slur? Were you the first to go aquatic in mocking Nadya Krupskaya's looks?"

"I cannot recall."

"Cannot recall? You, the expert recollector? The sister who told the world what one brother famously said on the occasion of the other brother's death? And we quote: 'No, we will not follow that road. That is not the road to take.'"

"Are you contradicting that sacred memory?"

"The scoundrel has done it for us. According to Lev Davidovich, your version 'tramples on all laws of human psychology.' You were a child; Vladimir Ilyich, a high school student 'unacquainted with Marx, devoid of political interest.'"

"Volodya was never devoid of political interest."

"You are contending that Volodya never once wondered: *Why did Sasha doom himself? Why did Sasha not stick to his science and his worms?*"

"So now you slander the revolutionary convictions of both my brothers?"

"Ah. Slander. Hold that thought, will you? We shall return."

Treacheries

Father Gapon?

The priest who organized the march to the Winter Palace? Whose stated purpose was to petition the tsar for fairer wages, for bread, for education for the workers he walked among? Father Gapon who held high his religious icon and added his tenor to "God Save the Tsar" but marched behind a buffer of women and children, women and children who continued at his insistence to walk toward Cossack guns and bayonets?

Let me tell you about the perfidious Father Gapon, pawn of the Okhrana, agent provocateur. He was no friend of the Russian worker. He did not serve the cause. He served himself.

After escaping Russia, Father Gapon arrived in Geneva, asking to meet with Ilyich.

"And what would you learn from the chaplain of Kresty Prison?" my daughter asked archly.

As Nadya well knew, it was not chaplain Gapon who had requested a meeting with Ilyich; it was Gapon, founder of Piter's Assembly of Russian Factory and Mill Workers who sought an audience. My daughter's barb was meant to remind Ilyich no priest turned revolutionary could be trusted.

"Gapon understands the peasants," Ilyich said.

"Rich, Ukrainian peasants," my daughter revised, referring to the priest's lineage.

"You are suggesting I avoid Gapon?"

"Do not meet him in secret, Volodya. You, not he, must decide where and when to meet. You must make that a condition of your conversation."

"Very well. But I must hear what he says."

"What you will hear is little of the people and much of Father Gapon," Nadya predicted.

When Ilyich returned from the appointment, he did not disagree.

"He has much to learn."

"But for the moment?" Nadya badgered. "What has he read? Who has he studied?"

"Some Marx, no Plekhanov," Ilyich admitted.

My daughter sniffed.

"Worse," Ilyich said, "he is susceptible to flattery."

Again my daughter sniffed.

We were not to learn the full extent of Father Gapon's duplicity until much later, but those revelations, when they came, more than validated my daughter's early suspicions. Prior to 1905, the priest had founded his society of workers in accordance with the Okhrana's wishes; with the founder's consent and collusion, tsarist spies attended each and every meeting. After his brief stay in Geneva, Gapon settled in London and hobnobbed with society, basking in his "hero of The Revolution" status. He penned his autobiography. To generate additional publicity for his book, he returned to Piter. But there the celebrity Gapon erred. The Okhrana were not inclined to deal with the same spy twice. The very police agent who had facilitated Gapon's rescue on Bloody Sunday murdered the priest and left his corpse to dangle from a meat hook.

"And there may he rot," as my Nadya would say.

Comrade Malinovsky? Ilyich's favorite?

Roman Malinovsky was born a peasant in Russian Poland. He had spent three years in prison during his youth for crimes unrelated to revolutionary activities. By 1905, he lived in Piter, on his way to becoming a valued Social Democrat. In Piter, he organized the Metal Workers Union. His comrades referred to him as "the great Roman"; he was taken for a man who would help defeat the autocracy. Ilyich pushed for his appointment to the Party's Central Committee at the Prague conference in 1912. Malinovsky was to serve as the Bolsheviks' lead voice in the resurrected Duma. His working class origins reassured Ilyich, but my Nadya had lived among the peasants. The craftiness of character that delighted Ilyich gave her pause. She had seen a peasant's craftiness serve several masters at once.

As was later revealed, Roman Malinovsky had been recruited by the Okhrana in 1910.

In the summer of 1911, at Longjumeau, he surprised us with a visit. Ilyich was overjoyed to see him; he could not hear enough about Comrade Malinovsky's adventures in Piter, making fools of the tsarist police.

Or so Comrade Malinovsky claimed.

A ruddy man with massive shoulders, he was missing several teeth. The scar running from his elbow to his wrist in certain lights seemed bluish and not entirely healed. He had brought to Longjumeau his own supply of vodka, which he drank steadily throughout the day and night.

"He does not set a good example for the students," Nadya fussed to me, not Ilyich.

Around Ilyich and Malinovsky, my Nadya chewed her lip.

This particular evening, Nadya was helping me clean the kitchen. We could hear the two men talking through the open window.

Malinovsky had long been slurring his words, but Ilyich, usually so critical of drunkenness, had not rebuked the visitor. He had twice joined him in song.

"Vladimir Ilyich!" we heard. "You must return to Piter and seize control of The Revolution! The Revolution needs a leader in Piter, not France!"

And then Malinovsky began to clap in time with his yodel: "To Piter! To Piter!"

"A boisterous comrade," I said.

"Yes," Nadya agreed, frowning. "With tales that get away from him."

"You disagree that Ilyich would better serve The Revolution in Piter?"

"I disagree with Comrade Malinovsky's recollections. He could not have eluded the Okhrana by dashing into an alleyway beside the Narva Gate. There is no alleyway beside the Narva Gate."

A native of Simbirsk, Ilyich would pay less attention to the architectural details of Comrade Malinovsky's escape.

"Perhaps it is the inventions of vodka," I suggested.

"Perhaps," Nadya said, plainly unconvinced.

In retrospect, I realize Comrade Malinovsky was not a man entirely at ease with his conscience. At the time, I attributed the disquiet to family difficulties. His only child, a son, shunned him. When his wife discovered she had married an atheist, she threatened to end her life. He did not say whether or not she had followed through on the threat, and I did not ask.

I heard about Comrade Malinovsky's son and wife on my way to buy the day's bread. As I went about my errands, he often tagged along, sharing what I presumed were confidences.

"In the village of my birth, I cannot show my face!"

Quite apart from whether Comrade Malinovsky's stories were true or false, they were not very entertaining. Most often they were maudlin, tediously so. Very quickly I lost interest in and curiosity about my errand companion. He repeated himself incessantly and lacked even a modicum of humor.

In 1914, abruptly, Malinovsky resigned from the Duma amid rumors that he answered to the Okhrana and not to the workers. The news shook Ilyich—profoundly. Again and again he asked of Nadya: "What if it is true? What if the vicious rumors are true?"

Confirmation of Malinovsky's treachery also upset my daughter, but surprise she pretended for Ilyich's sake. Later, Ilyich would say of Malinovsky: "The swine! He really put one over on us! Shooting is too good for him! The traitor!" But initially the betrayal devastated Ilyich. He did not sleep for days.

As I have said, I wish my Nadya had detected immediately the deceitful nature of Comrade Stalin. But to be suspicious, one must credit the suspected with the intelligence and determination to do harm. And such credit in 1910, in 1915, in 1920, few extended to Comrade Stalin.

To my recollection, during our years of exile, Nadya and Ilyich had words about the Georgian on only one occasion. Nadya was displeased that Josif Vissarionovich Dzhugashvili had been named editor of *Pravda*.

"He is without literary distinction!"

"He is *there*, Nadya," Ilyich said.

"He and the rest of the editorial staff have been chosen at random, like pines in a forest!" she fumed.

"Pines in a forest in *Russia*," Ilyich said.

By the time we took lodgings with the shoemaker Kammerer in Zurich, my head, if not my heart, had accepted that I would never again see Russia. And yet I cannot claim that such a fate, however objectionable, counted as the worst of émigré fates. Weekly, it seemed, we heard of another Russian who had perished from extreme poverty or sickness or died mad in a charity ward's hospital bed. In Paris, one of the starving found his way to our door, his collarbones so pronounced they seemed a coat hanger from which hung his flesh. We gave him soup; we gave him tea, as he babbled incoherently about chariots piled high with corn sheaves and the beautiful girl who handed out that bounty to passersby. Ilyich sat with him while Nadya went in search of a doctor. The physician pronounced our visitor insane. We found a room where he could sleep, engaged another comrade to look after him, but the mad one ran away, tied stones to his neck and feet and leapt into the Seine. His floating body was noticed one midnight by lovers on the stroll.

Such tragedies grew less and less rare, more and more commonplace. Rootless Russians, Russians uprooted, losing their reason. It seemed by then wiser to resign oneself to the likelihood of permanent exile than to hope continually for a return to my country.

The suicides of Paul Lafargue and Laura Marx constituted a different kind of tragedy, of course. Believing their usefulness to the Revolution had come to an end, the couple killed themselves the autumn following our Longjumeau summer.

When we heard the news, Ilyich stammered senselessly for several seconds. Then he threw the apple he had been eating across the room.

"No, I cannot approve of it! They could still write. Even if they could no longer work efficiently, they could still observe and give good advice!"

While I cleaned up apple pulp, my Nadya sat very still in her chair, the very uniformity of that stillness an indication of how fiercely she struggled to remain composed.

Ilyich was asked to speak at the funeral service. His remarks, which Inessa translated into French, focused on the Russian Social-Democratic Labor Party and its future. The Lafargues were now part of the past.

"You remember the day Ilyich and I cycled to Draveil?" Nadya asked.

"I remember," I said.

"Laura Marx's remark—about her husband proving his convictions—puzzled me."

"Yes," I said.

"While we walked together in the park, they had already decided."

"Very likely," I agreed.

"I should have spoken, despite my embarrassment. I should have conveyed how much I admired her, them. How much I and so many others revered and valued their work."

"It would not have made a difference, Daughter."

"No," Nadya said. "For who was I? A stranger, an afternoon guest. A woman who gawked and stuttered in her presence."

The shoemaker with whom we lodged in Zurich was the craftsman responsible for Ilyich's famous hobnailed boots, footwear beloved by Ilyich and a proven menace to every floorboard with which they came in contact. Initially, Frau Kammerer, the shoemaker's wife, opposed renting to us, put off by my Nadya's drab dress with its "unfashionable hemline." She relented after meeting Ilyich, who impressed her as a man of great physical strength. She admired his "bull neck."

"At last," I said to Ilyich as we took the stairs to our rooms, "your thick neck has done us a service."

"Mama!" my Nadya rebuked.

We were all tired and peevish. I was to grow more peevish in the household of Herr and Frau Kammerer. The kitchen where I worked alongside the proprietress was scarcely large enough for one woman's hips. To prepare the simplest of meals meant squeezing past each other time and again. Frau Kammerer did not share anything graciously, including passageways. When she questioned my daughter about the desire to return to Russia—"such an insecure country!"—my Nadya, with laudable restraint, explained that she and Ilyich needed to work in Russia.

"Why not work here?" jousted the insufferable Frau Kammerer.

My Nadya must have noticed her mother's rising temper.

"Shoo, Mama," she said. "It is my turn to cook today."

We did not take turns cooking—if we had, the three of us would have eaten many more burnt and overly salted meals. But I was only too glad for an excuse to rid myself of Frau Kammerer's kitchen and the irritant of her company. Upstairs, I stretched out on the bed and tried to recover some measure of calm. I would have liked to open a window but the stench from the sausage factory across the way was far too intense during the day. To air out our rooms, we had to wait for night.

That evening in darkness I sat smoking. Nadya found me with my elbow propped on the window ledge.

"What are you doing, Mama?"

"Gazing toward Russia."

Nadya laughed. "You are sure of the direction?"

"As sure as you and Ilyich of defeating Romanovs."

At once my daughter stiffened.

"Do not mock me, Mama."

"A mother cannot have a conversation with her daughter?"

"Not to criticize the cause."

"All right, Nadya, all right. Sit with me. Look at the lights. In Piter the lights are dancing on the Neva."

"And a mad monk with the tsarina."

Mad monks, spies and counterspies. A city of strife and suffering. Our Piter, all the same. My daughter's caustic remark did not fool me; she longed for that city as much as her old mama. Ilyich and Nadya and I—all of us desperate to return home.

TO THE
FINLAND
STATION

Preparations

And now Piter no longer Piter but Petrograd.

As if a name change ensured victory in another ridiculous war fought by under-fed, under-armed peasants and workers in the name of the never hungry, seldom muddy tsar.

"The tsar is not threatened by mortar shells or mustard gas," her mother observed, "but that is not to say he has escaped the German threat."

Her mother was referring to the German-born tsarina. When the tsarina frowned, so went the scuttlebutt, the tsar quaked in his boots.

"But Nicky quakes on royal carpets, not in trenches," she said.

"Even so," her mother quibbled, "I would not want to share the royal apartments with Alexandra Feodorovna. Of the two locations, a trench would seem easier to bear."

To her astonishment, and Inessa's, Plekhanov declared himself an *oboronets*, a supporter of the war in "defense of the fatherland," at the Lausanne conference.

"Ilyich will be beside himself!" she predicted.

"Indeed," said Inessa dryly.

"Better Plekhanov declared it outright. Now there can be no mistaking his position."

"Still I do not look forward to telling Ilyich," Inessa admitted. "The messenger will not get off easy."

"I will tell him," she volunteered.

"Please, Nadya. I have not yet become a total coward."

They had returned from the Lausanne conference to find Volodya at the kitchen table, already upset, already infuriated.

"He has been reading a report from Piter," her mother summarized. "And after stopping to stomp and curse, he reads again."

"It is simply shit!" he shouted.

"Vladimir Ilyich! Again! Your language!" her mother objected.

"I repeat: *govno!*"

"Volodya, you must not become overly excited," she cautioned.

"Shit, I said!"

"If you do not calm down," Inessa intervened, "how will you be able to become suitably enraged by Plekhanov's latest declaration?"

Inessa's ploy partially succeeded. Volodya gave them his attention; he did not calm down.

And then in the wake of Plekhanov's villainy: renewed hope.

Glorious hope.

In Russia, the workers in the munitions factories had struck. The reserve troops of the Pavlovsky Regiment had mutinied. The feckless tsar had abdicated. At such turn of fortune, the tsarina, reportedly, had collapsed and wept—misery that called for celebration.

"May Alexandra Feodorovna's tears never end!" she toasted with black tea.

"The mother of a sick child, Nadya," her own mother countered.

"And four healthy," she said.

"The wife of a dull and timid man."

"Who lives off the backs of his people."

"A woman deprived of her confessor, her seer, her prophet."

At last she registered Yelizaveta Vasilevna's slyness.

"You are having fun with your own child, Mama. Is that not so?"

"I am thinking about the frozen Neva and a *starets* swirling in the currents beneath. I am thinking that if the tsarina's husband had proved as resilient as the monk Rasputin, you and Ilyich would face a much tougher fight."

Night and day Ilyich paced, scheming to get them back to Piter/ Petrograd.

"It would be quickest by air."

"An airplane, Volodya? And do you imagine we, with our false passports, would be permitted to land in Russia?"

"We could arrange to travel with Swedish passports."

"Swedish, Volodya?"

"I would be a deaf Swede. A mute Swede."

"And when you burst out with a Russian curse against the Mensheviks in your dreams, you would give us all away," she said.

"You are not helping, Daughter," her mother chided, the two of them alone.

"I am doing precisely that! Ilyich can only think of Piter and what is happening there. He is too emotional. He is not being rational. He cannot lead The Revolution if he does not get there *safely*."

Finally: a feasible plan. The Swiss Socialist Platten would negotiate with the German General Staff on behalf of a group of Russian émigrés—not solely for Ilyich.

"An excellent solution!" her mother enthused. "What German would not want Vladimir Lenin back in Russia?"

There were conditions attached to the assistance, of course. They must assume "full political responsibility" for the seven-day journey. All must sign a document stating that they accepted the risks incurred by returning to Russia and were fully aware that the Provisional Government intended to try the lot of them for treason. And so they signed, packed and congregated at Zurich Central Station.

On the train platform, a well-wisher called out to Ilyich: "I hope to see you back again among us, comrade."

"If we come back, it will not be a good sign for The Revolution," Ilyich sensibly responded.

For her part, she hoped never to step foot in Europe again. She would far rather die among a mob of striking workers on the Nevsky than to read about another uprising in Russia from the safety of a chair in Zurich.

Her mother would not have put the sentiment in quite those terms perhaps, but Yelizaveta Vasilevna had also grown impatient. She had been promised a return to Russia and did not look kindly on further delay.

Using an elbow, Yelizaveta Vasilevna insistently nudged Ilyich forward. Had he not responded, her mother would very likely have begun kicking his calves.

After the three of them had settled in their second-class compartment, Ilyich took out his note pad and began immediately to work.

But then his gaze wandered.

"What is it, Volodya? You do not trust the Germans to keep their agreement?"

He flung his arm in irritation.

"What, then? Arrest?"

"If we are arrested, we will surely be hanged. This time."

"But just now you are feeling apprehensive about something other than death," she said.

He did not agree; he did not disagree.

"I know Piter. I know Simbirsk. I know Kazan. But that is all I know of Russia. I know better 17 years of exile."

"You know what the workers want. You know what The Revolution needs," she said.

All the while Yelizaveta Vasilevna had been keeping up the pretense of reading. Now her mother reached over and gently patted Volodya's knee—a vote of confidence from Yelizaveta Vasilevna.

Trains, Ferryboats and Sleighs

An uneventful journey, in my Nadya's opinion, a trip filled with trivialities.

I beg to differ.

At very nearly three p.m., March 27, 1917, Ilyich, Nadya, Inessa, myself and assorted others met Fritz Platten at Zurich Central Station to board the Swiss train that would take us to the frontier point of Schaffhausen, where we were to transfer onto the famous "sealed" train that would take us through Germany. Our group numbered 30 or 31 or 32 émigrés; I did not perform a headcount, so I cannot, on such matters, enlighten or correct history. Although we were not all Bolsheviks, I can confirm that, with the exception of our Swiss guide Platten, all of us were Russian socialists.

A few Bolshevik supporters did show up at the train station in Zurich to wish us well but those well-wishers were far outnumbered and out-shouted by the hecklers.

"Spies! German spies!"

Even among our supporters, sanguinity did not rule. A wild-eyed gentleman grabbed Ilyich and swung him round, begging: "Vladimir Lenin! Please! Stop this mad journey through Germany!"

Ilyich extracted his arm and consulted his watch; Nadya stepped between Ilyich and the wild-eyed. Her body effectively blocked the man's access to Ilyich, but she was also preparing, as necessary, to beat him back further with her string bag of books. And I? I tried not to betray a Russian's innate superstition of being accosted by someone who resembled a flapping, squawking bird of ill omen so close to departure.

In that effort I did not succeed.

"We will be seated soon," my daughter said.

It was not to be soon enough.

Ilyich wore his one suit, the derby hat he ritually cleaned every spring, the hideous boots made by Kammerer and a serviceable topcoat. Despite clear skies, he carried an umbrella. A fortunate addition, the umbrella. During a ceremonial chorus of "Internationale," a near riot broke out along and below the platform. Ilyich used the umbrella to get himself, Nadya and me through the melee and finally onboard. Fritz Platten did not fare quite so well. A slight and slender man, he had to fight past an opponent twice his size. When he came to check on us in our compartment, his nose was swollen, his tie askew. His knuckles looked as if they had been dragged across ice.

"Even now he is wondering what he has taken on," I murmured. "If beaten as an accomplice in neutral Switzerland, what awaits the Russians' escort elsewhere?"

My Nadya shrugged.

Bruised fists, obstructionist hecklers—not worth the mention.

The train still had not left the station when Ilyich learned that a certain Dr. Blum, a spy in the *Bolsheviks'* estimation, had boarded the train. Very nearly choking with fury, Ilyich charged forth to deal with the culprit personally.

During the ensuing scuffle, which Nadya could hear as plainly as I, she rearranged Ilyich's pencils and dusted off his seat.

Ilyich returned victorious; he had tossed the "swine" off the train and stood guard at the entry until the wheels had begun to turn.

We were, at last, underway.

I had brought along a basket of Swiss chocolates. Since we had no idea how much or how often we would be fed, I had packed what I knew would sustain us. A Swiss customs official took my basket for "inspection" and returned neither container nor contents. And why was that? I quizzed Comrade Platten, who could not answer the question. His own food supplies had also been commandeered.

The transfer onto the German train came and went without incident, I will admit. But the process occurred in a hushed atmosphere of secrecy and in the company of multiple police and soldier escorts, as if we were criminals being led to slaughter.

On the German train almost instantly Ilyich began to rail against the tobacco smoke.

"I am suffocating! Suffocating!" he groused and stomped off to berate the smokers next door, Inessa among them.

"No more smoking except in the lavatories!" he decreed.

The partitions between compartments were thin. Laughter that originated on either side of us sounded like our own.

I believe the noise of it, rather than the gaiety, played on Ilyich's nerves. In any case, he demanded the laughing stop "at once."

"Vladimir Ilyich! Now you are forbidding laughter? Do you expect Russians to be solemn, heading home?"

Although I argued in favor of celebration, my own mood remained exceedingly solemn. Inessa's children had already returned to Russia. I wished Varvara had been travelling with us. Her constant chatter would have been a welcome distraction.

"But you will see her soon—in Piter," Inessa consoled as we smoked in the cramped lavatory.

"I do not think any of us can predict who or what we will see once in Piter," I replied.

"Yelizaveta Vasilevna!" Inessa scolded. "Where is your faith in the people?"

In individuals I have faith. In the aggregate, less. If history is to be believed, "the people," when thwarted, too easily turn into a vengeful mob. We were not returning simply to Piter; we were returning to Piter in the midst of another revolution. What my daughter relished, her mama feared.

In Berlin, there was real reason for fear. In that city, without warning or explanation, we were ordered off the train, our entire number led into a shed where we remained sequestered for more than an hour.

Do you imagine I was the only Russian who assumed herself moments from being lined up against a German wall and shot?

I can assure you that I was not.

In Sassnitz, we changed our mode of transport as well as the surface on which we travelled. Although I was ready—more than ready—to leave Germany, I did not look forward to substituting water for land. On the boat to Trelleborg, the sea winds united against us. During that rough, rough crossing to Sweden, the Bolshevik standing next to me held his belly and cried out with each roiling swell. Weak from vomiting, many of us despaired of setting foot on the solid ground of any nation ever again.

"You will feel better once we reach Finland," Nadya said.

From such prophecies, I derived no comfort.

In Sassnitz, in Trelleborg, in Malmo, my daughter incessantly urged: "Close your eyes, Volodya. You must try to get some rest."

But he would not or could not. None of us slept, my daughter included, until we reached Stockholm and the Hotel Regina. Even there our peace was fleeting. Once the reporters discovered our arrival, they filled the lobby and staked out the surrounding streets. Regardless, Ilyich and Nadya went about their business, shopping for the books on Ilyich's list, trailed by an uninvited entourage.

It was in Stockholm that Inessa confronted Ilyich about his wardrobe and demanded an upgrade.

"You cannot return to Piter looking so shabby," she declared.

"I do not look shabby," Ilyich argued. "I look perfectly respectable."

"You look threadbare. What you are wearing will not do."

"Nadya!" Ilyich whined. "Help me crush this ludicrous proposal! Inessa wants to turn me into a dandy!"

"Dandy" was the generality Ilyich used but both Nadya and I knew precisely, if Inessa did not, who personified such vanity for Ilyich: the Menshevik Plekhanov, followed closely by the Menshevik Lev Davidovich. Under no circumstances did Ilyich want to be linked, sartorially, with his two adversaries of the moment.

"This is not only about you, Volodya," Inessa pestered. "Nadya, explain to him. When he steps off the train at Finland Station, he steps off as more than Vladimir Ilyich. He steps off as the leader for whom The Revolution has been waiting."

She could not have chosen words more likely to bring Nadya round to her viewpoint.

"If Inessa believes you must have new clothes, then you must," my daughter said, and Ilyich threw up his hands.

Inessa, outfitted in a new blue and flattering cape, first separated Ilyich from his atrocious boots. Gradually she persuaded him into a better pair of trousers, coat, shirt and tie. He also left Stockholm wearing a felt hat, quite smart as well as distinguished. But not even Inessa could separate him from his topcoat or his fighting stick, the umbrella.

During Ilyich's clothing acquisitions, I did my best to get a smart hat on my daughter's head. The wheel-shaped horror she wore exaggerated, and not becomingly, her round face. But my Nadya refused and, unlike Ilyich, kept refusing.

For You, Madam Lenin

"Do not speak to me again of *hats*!" she warned.

Obstinate, intransigent. The Bolsheviks were fortunate to call her their own.

The train trip from Stockholm around the Gulf of Bothnia?

Interminable.

But it was shortsighted of me to complain about tedium, the alternative being so much less pleasing, so much more fraught.

No one had expected difficulty at the Finnish border. No one. And yet, trouble we encountered. The British soldiers on duty proved unwilling to let us pass without further investigation.

We had to hand over our bags, each of which was meticulously examined—linings slashed, handles broken. One by one we were taken off and interrogated.

"Decide on a statement and never vary it," my Nadya whispered in my ear before I was called in to account for myself.

My daughter had weathered multiple interrogations by the Okhrana. I would have been a fool to disregard her advice.

"I am an old woman with one daughter. If she goes to Russia, I go with her."

By no means a lie.

Each of us was required to fill out an extensive questionnaire.

Why did you leave Russia?

What are your reasons for returning?

Where will you be staying once in Petrograd?

What is your profession?

What was your last address on the continent?

Ilyich signed his true name, listed the Hotel Regina in Stockholm as his last residence and his profession as "journalist."

I listed my profession as "mother."

The hours passed. The sleighs waited, as did we.

Easter Morn

Is snow a comfort to Russians? Consolation, curative, religion?

At the border, Bolsheviks and luggage pile into sleighs to ride snow and the incline into Finland proper.

In the lead sleigh, Vladimir Lenin, an old exile headed toward a new revolution. At his side: Nadezhda Krupskaya.

And farther back?

Where?

Nowhere near?

The former mistress in the blue cape.

Unlike in stuffy, smoky trains, Vladimir Lenin can breathe in a sleigh. As their caravan picks up speed, he throws back his head, delighted by the prick and sting of frosty air.

There are ice crystals on his nose, his ears, his eyebrows, his chin. But the gut of Vladimir Lenin is hot and thrumming.

After Finland, Russian Finland. After Russian Finland, Piter.

Nadezhda Krupskaya's gut? Its state?

Thus far, she has avoided elation. She has occupied herself with reading and study, with arranging in so far as possible her mother's comfort, a quiet atmosphere for Vladimir Lenin. If, in an unguarded moment, she has felt her pulse race at the prospect of Piter, she has countered that excitement by counting dust motes or threads in her mother's sleeve. But soon, not even Nadezhda Krupskaya will be able to hold her emotions in check for she is fast heading toward white birch and scattered pines. The wooden depots of Raivola, Jalkala, Terijoki, Kuokkala. Station platforms crowded with peasants and Russian soldiers. A third-class Russian coach with rickety benches. Everything, everything so familiar and so very, very dear.

Vladimir Lenin turns toward Nadezhda Krupskaya who is always,

always, turned toward him.

The snow, the air, is working its magic.

When Vladimir Ilyich grins, she grins. When he laughs, she laughs. And when he raises his fist and pumps it in defiance, in determination, in joy, Nadezhda Krupskaya, Bolshevik and atheist, does something even she cannot believe: she blesses snow.

Twenty Miles

We were to arrive at the Finland Station on Monday evening, but first we arrived in Beloostrov, greeted by Comrade Kollontai on behalf of the Bolshevik Party Bureau.

Who else met us in Beloostrov?

Ilyich's sister, Maria Ilyinichna.

Alexandra Kollontai had barely finished her speech of welcome before Maria Ilyinichna inserted herself beside Ilyich in a position she would thereafter claw to maintain.

"Shove any harder," I said to Maria Ilyinichna at the time, "and you will topple your brother."

"What are you muttering, Yelizaveta Vasilevna? If you want me to hear you, you must do better than mumble like an old woman."

I had neither muttered nor mumbled. Alexandra Kollontai heard me plainly enough. As a courtesy to Vladimir Ilyich, Comrade Kollontai had permitted herself to be shunted aside, but thereafter her eyes did not look warmly on Maria Ilyinichna. My Nadya, in contrast, took an additional step backward to provide her sister-in-law ample space and did so betraying no sign of resentment. As for Comrade Kollontai, I wish I could say that being shunted aside at Beloostrov counted as an isolated incident during her career as a Bolshevik, but it did not. Very regrettably, it did not.

Among those *not* part of the welcoming party at Beloostrov: the Georgian.

Despite accounts rewritten at his order, to suit his whim, to corrupt and alter history, Comrade Stalin was not part of the welcoming party and most certainly not the first Party member to embrace Ilyich upon his return to Russian soil. That story is pure fantasy.

Another fantasy: that Ilyich's vociferous reception in Beloostrov pleased him. Ilyich did not like being jostled and flung about—even by jubilant proletarians. When the workers from the Sestroretsk Armaments Factory swarmed round and hoisted him onto their shoulders, he protested the elevation.

"Careful, comrades. Careful! Go gently there!"

"The workers will not have him walk," my daughter proudly declared while Ilyich bobbed and grimaced.

In a brief speech, Ilyich castigated the Provisional Government and repeated the necessity of its demise.

"And now let us hear from Comrade Krupskaya!" someone shouted.

My daughter demurred; never would she compete with Ilyich.

The entire train, including the snub-nosed engine, had been strung with red bunting. We were twenty miles from Piter, a mere twenty.

In our compartment, the fifth car back, Ilyich paced; my Nadya and I sat side by side, holding hands. For those last miles, we kept on our coats; Ilyich kept on his hat.

"You are certain?" Ilyich asked his sister repeatedly. "We will not be arrested?"

And each time Maria Ilyinichna smugly smiled.

"We shall see, Volodya. We shall see."

A minx enjoying her secrets, reveling in our suspense.

As our train pulled into Finland Station, even above the engine's noise, we became aware of a tremendous roar.

"What the devil!" Ilyich sputtered.

Maria Ilyinichna at last ceased speaking in riddles.

"The sound of Petrograd cheering, Volodya!"

And so it seemed.

As soon as Ilyich stepped off the train, a brass band struck up the Russian "Marseillaise." An honor guard of Kronstadt sailors, their blue uniforms sporting red pompoms, formed a barrier around us. When their captain saluted, Ilyich, completely befuddled, raised his hand in turn.

"What is this about?" Ilyich shouted above the cymbals.

"The greeting of the revolutionary troops and workers," the captain shouted back.

A student from the Longjumeau school, a red sash around his shoulder, rushed toward us, waving a bouquet of red roses. He embraced Nadya, then me, then Nadya again and during the extended reunion we somehow became separated from Ilyich, ushered steadily forward.

Beyond the platform, out into the square, stretching into the streets, banner after red banner, torches lit and waving. In the sky, the light streams of searchlights mounted on armored cars crisscrossed with the searchlights of the Peter and Paul Fortress. Hundreds upon hundreds of faces, hundreds upon hundreds of voices, chanting Ilyich's name.

"Mama! Mama!" my Nadya said, incapable of saying more and needing to say no more to her mother. My daughter saw in that whirling madness confirmation that the soldiers and workers of Piter had been waiting for Ilyich. And now he had come. Now he had come.

But had they turned out for Ilyich?

History will forgive an old woman's skepticism. It was Easter Monday, a holiday. Was it not equally probable that the workers had turned out for the free beer?

"Len-in! Len-in! Len-in!"

Hoisted high again, Ilyich lost his new hat. It was a bald and bobbing head we followed toward the tsar's former waiting room. Admittedly, I am not the most reliable witness to report on the official welcoming ceremonies, arranged and attended by the delegates of the Executive Committee of the Petrograd Soviet of Workers' and Soviets' Deputies. My own fatigue made me see signs of that malady everywhere: in the circled eyes of the Social Democrats, Bolshevik and Menshevik, who had remained in Piter; in the drooping shoulders of statuesque Comrade Kollontai; in the thinness of Inessa's wrists; in Ilyich's sallow cheeks; in my daughter's nervous fidgets.

We were tired, terribly tired, all of us.

Revolutions are not for the tired.

The Menshevik Chkheidze opened the proceedings.

He looked a bit like a turtle, Chkheidze, constantly pulling his head into his shoulders, compressing his neck. Rather timidly he expressed the hope that Vladimir Ilyich had not returned to "split the ranks of the revolutionary democracy."

I leaned my head on Nadya's shoulder. I could no longer hold it upright. As a child, she had leaned her head on my shoulder and now her mama leaned on hers.

While Chkheidze spoke, Ilyich gazed at the ceiling. In retrospect, one might have described him as ominously composed. The instant Chkheidze finished, like a steppe hound sprung from his leash, Ilyich bolted for the dais.

"What is it? What?" I stuttered, already half in dream.

"Shush, Mama. Listen to Ilyich."

I listened without hearing anything I had not heard a hundred times before:

No compromises.

A fight to the finish.

A fight against the Provisional Government.

A fight to the full victory of the proletariat, nothing less.

On that evening, Ilyich was 46 years old, a week shy of 47. If those in Piter/Petrograd imagined 17 years of exile finished off with seven sleepless nights in transit had turned Ilyich into a more cordial, cooperative, conciliatory opponent, tolerant of dissent and magnanimous with power, they were not students of character.

He had never run from a fight and would not in April 1917.

We rode past bonfires; we rode past rubble. Shop fronts had been stripped of the double-headed eagle, the imperial symbol. The statues of Nicholas II that had not been destroyed had been wrapped in shrouds of red. Illuminated by searchlights, those remaining statues looked like shrouded corpses. I cannot say that such sights, glimpsed from the back seat of an armored car, encouraged optimism about the future. Bloodlust is bloodlust.

"Where are we heading now?" I asked between yawns.

"To the cemetery, Mama."

During our second exile, Maria Alexandrovna Ulyanova had died and been buried in Piter.

A good Bolshevik, Ilyich; a better son.

The Struggle Transferred to Piter

Did the stars immediately realign and favor the Bolsheviks, simply because Ilyich returned to Piter in 1917?

They did not.

The workers only sporadically listened to Ilyich and the specifics of his platform. Also striving to be heard in Piter at the time: Constitutional Democrats, Socialist Revolutionaries, Mensheviks, and the apparatus that replaced the Romanov autocracy, the Provisional Government. The Bolsheviks had no shortage of competitors. In April, in July, in September, the fight for control and power was far, far from over.

Between April and July, Ilyich wrote more than 170 articles, pamphlets and resolutions. During that same time period, he also prepared for and addressed the First All-Russian Congress of Soviets, directed Central Committee activities, spoke at countless rallies, visited the factories to speak with the workers within them and refined his All Power to the Soviets program. The Bolsheviks conducted their business in the appropriated mansion of Mathilde Kshesinskaya, Piter's former prima ballerina and Nicholas II's former mistress. A grand palace, to be sure, but hardly designed for the business of revolution. Space was at such a premium even the gilded bathrooms held desks and secretaries. Meetings ran all day and into the night. Telephones rang ceaselessly.

Certainly Ilyich had his hands full after we returned to Piter. The situation on the streets and inside the Provisional Assembly seemed to change hourly. There were many demands on his time and person. Even so, he should have spoken up in my Nadya's defense.

"A moment, Ilyich."

"I do not have a moment, Yelizaveta Vasilevna."

"Not even for Nadya?"

"What is it? Is she ill?"

Ilyich feared illness above all else. To be ill was to be sidelined.

"No, not ill, but hurt. Deeply hurt."

"What are you talking about?"

"Did my Nadya not prove herself in 1905 as well as in the years before and since? Has she not always been at your side, working as hard as yourself on behalf of The Revolution?"

"Have you ever heard me deny it?"

"And yet you appoint Elena Stasova as head of the secretariat. A Party member whose experience does not begin to match Nadya's."

"Nadya wanted to return to the Vyborg."

"Only when it became clear she would find no place at your side here."

He shuffled his stack of papers; he frowned.

"Nadya has told you this?"

"Of course not! She would never complain."

"And do you worry about Nadya in the Vyborg?"

"No more than I worry about her walking the Nevsky. But that is not my point, Ilyich."

"I cannot worry about everything and everyone, Yelizaveta Vasilevna! Nadya, at least, can take care of herself."

A compliment, yes. But not one that countermanded the injury of appointing to the secretariat my daughter's inferior.

I will tell you what my daughter will never admit: she returned to Piter expecting that she and Ilyich would continue to work in tandem, an extension of the partnership they had developed in exile. It did not happen. Perhaps it could not have happened. Their revolution no longer counted as the intimate affair it had been. There were new faces, new players, appearing daily. The stakes were high and growing higher. And so, for the sake of The Revolution, my daughter swallowed her resentment and adjusted her expectations accordingly.

"I will be of better use in the Vyborg," she declared.

"Of better use," I repeated. "And yet you scowl, daughter. Why not train that scowl at Ilyich?"

"I do not need Volodya to speak for me. I can speak for myself."

"And in this speech to Comrade Stasova you will say…?"

"That I would rather be in the Vyborg with the workers than with Bolshevik secretaries in a ballerina's palace. There is much to be done in the Vyborg."

And those many tasks my daughter endeavored to do.

Ilyich went his way; she, hers.

In June of 1917, Piter looked more like a cesspit than Russia's illustrious capital. The streets stank of urine and feces. The wind rearranged and redistributed pile after pile of fetid rubbish. While walking, one never knew what filth might land and stick on the shoe or cheek. After three years of war, the cost of food in the city had quadrupled. Foolishly, and cruelly, the government had banned vodka—not the wines favored by aristocrats but vodka, the workers' drink and solace. In consequence, vast numbers of Piter workers poisoned themselves guzzling eau de cologne and varnishes. Along the Russian front conditions were no less deplorable. What bullets missed, typhus killed.

When Alexander Kerensky succeeded Prince Lvov as the Provisional Government's prime minister, an actor replaced a prince.

Why do I call Kerensky an actor? When he addressed an audience, his fainting fits were scripted. He painted his face. He polished his nails. Very theatrical, the Socialist Revolutionary Kerensky, even before he moved into the Winter Palace and began to sleep in a tsar's bed.

The power-mad do sleep, you know. Typically, quite soundly.

Ilyich's usual arsenal of pejoratives—imbeciles, cretins—proved unequal to the task of expressing his wrath at the mention of Kerensky. In consequence, many tea glasses sacrificed their form.

Although there was very little to jest about during those unsettled months, I did tease Ilyich about sharing a hometown with the latest prime minister.

"A Simbirsk native like yourself, Volodya! A small town with so many statues to erect!"

Sweeping up glass shards, Ilyich swore even more vehemently. He was not swearing at me. To his credit, my son-in-law had no interest in statues—his rivals' or his own.

Can you blame a mother-in-law, a mother, for losing track?

As July approached, intrigues began to branch from intrigues. I could not keep straight who sided with Ilyich and the Bolsheviks and who plotted against. Very soon I gave up trying to chart the shifting alliances and intrigue of what history calls the July Days.

One happy consequence of the tumult: Lev Davidovich returned to the Bolshevik fold. I caught sight of him in the hallway of the palace, looking peaked but dapper as ever, dressed in a black silk coat and flowing tie. To properly greet me he had to break stride. Everyone ran from one destination to the next, everyone.

"Yelizaveta Vasilevna!" he exclaimed and kissed my hand. "What a pleasure to see you here!"

"And you, Lev Davidovich," I replied.

"And how is it that you look not a day older than you looked in London?" he asked, inveterate flatterer that he was, no matter the woman's appearance or age.

"And you, Lev Davidovich," I parried. "Older, wiser, but with hair no less thick."

It is the only exchange of light banter I can recall from the entire summer.

"They're getting ready to shoot us all," Ilyich predicted.

Such an outcome did not seem unlikely.

We did not live together then—Nadya and Ilyich and I. To do so would have been sheer folly. After Lev Davidovich was caught and arrested, the net drew ever tighter around Ilyich. A warrant had also been issued for his arrest.

"You must leave Piter, Volodya," Nadya insisted.

If he left, he would, at least, be able to write. If he stayed in Piter, his time would be devoted to avoiding detection.

In the apartment of a Vyborg worker, where Nadya had arranged for Ilyich to spend the night, we met him in secret to say goodbye.

Before I kissed him, quite ridiculously I said: "Remember to sleep."

He was already disguised as a worker, the telltale Ilyich beard shaved off.

He and Nadya embraced, a long and emotional embrace. They both understood they might never see the other again, but only Ilyich was willing to admit it.

"If this is the last…," he began before my daughter cut him off.

"You will return to Piter," she vowed. "And then again we will fight together."

In Ilyich's presence, as long as we remained in his presence, my Nadya's faith in that claim appeared unshakable, but when the door closed between them, she bowed at the waist and covered her face.

Her sobs shook us both. Her grief was immeasurable.

Ilyich's flight from Piter—to the hut near Razliv and on to Helsingfors—has been called an act of physical cowardice. If so, cowardice saved his life. In this instance I wholly agree with Nadya's conclusions. If Ilyich had given himself up in July, his enemies in Piter would have torn him to pieces.

For You, Madam Lenin

The Recurring Nightmare
of Comrade Nadezhda Krupskaya

Again and again and again: August 1917.

Nadezhda Krupskaya hurries, pants, darts between shadows, between trees, a thick shawl covering her head. To fool the border guards, to get to Vladimir Ilyich waiting for news of the mood on Vyborg streets, she hurries in the disguise of a Sestroretsk peasant.

Border guards care nothing about squatty peasant women crossing from Russia to Finland and back again.

Border guards are only interested in finding the Bolshevik leader who once hid in a haystack, once in a Razliv hut, and now hides…where?

Nadezhda Krupskaya knows where.

On a Helsingfors side street, in a stale apartment that stinks of burnt soup, tea breath and arm pit.

Haystack, hut, Helsingfors. Haystack, hut, Helsingfors.

In Nadezhda Krupskaya's dream, the chant is meant as encouragement, a chant to keep the revolutionary disguised as peasant pushing forward, regardless of setbacks, obstacles, confusion, darkness, chilly air, spongy earth, the tsarist trees and their whisper leaves.

A left, a right, a circling.

Where did she start?

In which direction should she hurry?

The too-pale moon refuses to serve as comrade guide.

She left Piter too late, started for Olilla too late, entered the forest too late, even the dream knows she is late, late, and now Vladimir Ilyich is waiting, worrying.

She should have gone first to the Emelyanovs, crossed again in their company.

She should have memorized the directions.

She should have remembered the way.

Five *versts* to Olilla, the soldiers' train from Olilla to Helsingfors, a final steep hike up Vladimir Ilyich's street.

"And the soldiers on the train?" Vladimir Lenin had quizzed Nadezhda Krupskaya when last they met in Helsingfors. "What did the soldiers say? What did you overhear?"

"That they had thrown their officers into the river."

Even in that wretched, wretched room, such news had made Vladimir Ilyich prance and clap his hands.

She had promised to come again, in two weeks, with fresher news of soldiers and strikes and comrades.

For in the dream she possesses such tidings: The Revolution is escalating; The Revolution is succeeding. After years of exile, prison, treachery, Mensheviks and the disappointments of February, she and Ilyich will live to see the people triumph!

If she gets through the dark forest.

If she can again reach Ilyich, who is expecting her, *counting* on her, peering through shabby window curtains, searching the street for a peasant woman with a shawl over her head, the woman who wanders left, right, wrong, in a forest of rot and darkness, trying so desperately to succeed and failing because she is lost.

Lost, the comrade/wife.

The Krupskayas, Alone

When I looked out onto the street from whatever window in whatever apartment my Nadya and I had passed the night, I saw corpses. In summer no cloak of snow draped and disguised those bodies. The dead lay, abandoned and exposed, for all who still breathed to contemplate. Will you believe me when I say there were mornings when I envied those corpses? Quite true. I envied their indifference. The dead no longer fear.

We will die, all of us. And while we live, we must endure the deaths of those we love. Never a day passed that I did not miss and mourn my Konstantin. But to say I wished him alive and with us in the summer of 1917? No. Even I could not be so selfish. Konstantin would have been appalled, then heartbroken, by the condition of his city, by what the citizens of Piter witnessed and suffered during the summer of 1917.

Daily we stepped over the dead to queue in bread lines, the rot of flesh mixing with the scent of yeast.

Rarely did the bread supplies last beyond noon and often the shelves emptied by midmorning. One left early to buy bread and left prepared to wait. There were customers who spent the night in front of bread shops to guarantee their purchase. Once the shop doors opened, patrolling officers refused to permit lying or sitting in line, but to hold a place overnight, a sleeping body sufficed. Desperate mothers alongside starving children alongside deserter soldiers in ragged uniforms, their boots missing toes and heels, their bodies missing arms, legs, fingers, ears.

To watch a fly attack a man's severed flesh?

It is an insult to the living. An insult to Piter.

Few in Piter knew my face and fewer connected it with Nadezhda Krupskaya, wife of Lenin; regardless, I took precautions. I went out with my gray hair unpinned and swinging; I wore a patched and tattered dress.

It was imperative that I escaped the notice of any military officer or cadet, that I gave none of Kerensky's minions reason to single me out among a crowd of unfortunates.

Most in line behaved with stoic dignity. Their stomachs growled, their mouths watered, but they did not push and shove. Others showed less restraint, civility lost to the torments of hunger. A frantic man knocked over a woman holding a baby. Two other men went at once to the woman's aid. The line surged forward. For their kindness, those Samaritans forfeited their place.

When history mentions bread lines, it concentrates on the scarcity of rations. The lack of food is but one of the hardships. Guilt is an equal torment.

"Please, please. My wife is ill. We have not eaten for three days. I cannot go home without bread. I must bring her bread."

Moment to moment the citizens of Piter had to re-harden their hearts. Their own family's survival depended on such callousness.

One morning I could not seem to summon the energy to leave as soon as I should have left for the nearest bread shop. When I arrived, the line already coiled past the corner. Nevertheless, I took my place. Almost immediately, a young girl filled the space behind me. She must have run a long way. It was some time before she did not gasp for breath. When I crossed the shop's threshold, only five loaves remained. Mine was the final purchase of the day. I cannot adequately describe the extent of her anguish as she confronted the empty rack. Those words do not exist in my vocabulary.

In 1917 in Piter, I had walked past much suffering without stopping. This girl I could not walk past. I divided the bread I had and refused the payment she tried to push into my hand. After I had succeeded in finding out where she lived, I suggested a different bread line, a different bread shop. In distance, it was closer to her starting point. She would not get thinner—or thinner any faster—running there.

Please do not think my altruism came at my daughter's expense. Nadya's share I would never have given away or sold at any price. But an old woman grown marginally weaker for lack of sustenance? Of what consequence?

Kerensky's men did not find Ilyich in Finland, but twice in Piter they found the Krupskayas.

The first group comported themselves in gentlemanly fashion. They asked, politely, that I step aside and when I did they fanned out across the room. They neatly sifted through our clothes and papers and very quietly confiscated the documents on Nadya's desk.

My daughter was not so foolish as to leave incriminating papers on her desk. What they confiscated were documents pertaining to the construction of playgrounds in the Vyborg.

Next we were invaded by a gang of cadets—younger, more savage men. What they did not steal, they made sure to damage. And when my Nadya appeared and protested the ransacking, they tied her hands behind her back and took her.

I fell to the floor weeping. I vomited into my skirts. I believed I had lost my daughter forever.

When she returned many hours later, I was still on the floor.

"Mama, get up. Get up."

My legs would not support me. My Nadya had to lift and hold me upright.

"They have no real interest in us, Mama. They want information about Ilyich. The bastards care only about capturing Ilyich."

"I cannot endure this, Nadya."

"You can. You are," she said.

"No longer."

"Yes, Mama," she said. "We must show them they cannot intimidate the Krupskayas."

Thereafter I slept, when I slept, in a chair pushed beside the window.

Why, you may wonder? To view corpses?

To scout for enemies and allies. By watching the street I hoped to identify cadets and Kerensky's ghouls in advance of their reaching our building. By constantly canvassing the dissolute, bereaved and indigent of Piter I hoped to intuit who among them might assist a mother and daughter in sudden flight.

And where would Nadezhda Konstantinovna Krupskaya and mother have gone?

It is not an idle question.

The countryside was no safer than Piter. Long before, the peasants had ceased waiting for their promised reward. In village after village, they took back the land by force, murdering any who stood in their way. The simple, peaceful, obliging peasants Count Tolstoy had once idolized had become barbarians, merciless in their destructions. On the Count's Tula estate, his widow and daughter armed themselves with hammers, prepared to fight for their lives.

By the merest happenstance, they survived.

When the marauding peasants saw the unlit house, they assumed it had already been pillaged.

A Lutheran Minister

In early October, Ilyich slipped back into Piter, disguised as a near-sighted, beardless Lutheran minister. Almost, she failed to recognize him.

Not because of the disguise. The disguise was laughable: Ilyich a minister! Ministers did not look hunted; they did not look world-obsessed.

"It is you? It is really you!"

"Of course it is Ilyich!" her mother said. "With bags under his eyes and a belt too loose. Embrace your mother-in-law, Volodya. We are now of equal size."

She had not wanted her mother to accompany her to the comrade's borrowed apartment.

"Mama! Be sensible!" she had argued. "It is too dangerous. Ilyich is a fugitive."

"Ilyich is Ilyich," her mother disputed in turn. "And if he is in Piter, both Krupskayas should welcome him back."

And now while she stood, aloof and awkward, alarmed by his thinness, the gash in his coat, afraid of showing too much emotion, too much relief, her indomitable mother had jumped in with her usual gruff affection and succeeded in making the gray-haired, bespectacled faux minister laugh.

"That wig!" her mother clucked. "Surely you could have found better!"

"Mama! Please! We have more than wigs to discuss."

Nonetheless, she agreed with her mother's assessment: even judged as fake hair, Ilyich's headpiece looked unconvincing. Like straw sewn together.

"You received the news about Lev Davidovich?" she asked Ilyich.

"That he bought his way out of Kresty Prison?"

"Last month," she verified.

"With whose three thousand rubles?" Ilyich quizzed.

"Do not worry about that. He is out."

"And once again chair of the Petrograd Soviet," Ilyich said. "As in nineteen 'five."

The reference, the comparison, did not bode well.

"We will not repeat the mistakes of nineteen 'five, Volodya."

"We cannot make *any* more mistakes! Old or new!"

Her mother pushed a plate in front of Ilyich. They had brought food with them.

"More than likely he will be hungry," her mother had predicted. "And if he is to continue hiding, he will need to eat where and when he can."

"Eat while you talk, Volodya," Yelizaveta Vasilevna ordered in the borrowed apartment. "You are capable of both feats at once."

"Kerensky has not rearrested Lev Davidovich?"

"No," she said.

"Cretin!"

"His own press has gone to his head. He believes those who call him the 'ideal citizen.'"

"Then we must use that vanity against him," Ilyich plotted.

"I can stand the suspense no longer," her mother interrupted. "Which comrade provided that hideous wig?"

"Careful whom you disparage, Yelizaveta Vasilevna! This was fashioned by a very reputable wigmaker employed by the Mariinsky Theatre. A famous craftsman in Helsingfors."

"Then he must never stray from Helsingfors."

"Mama! Enough about the wig."

But Yelizaveta Vasilevna would not be diverted.

"This is how it looked? The first time you stuck it on your head?"

Ever so slightly Volodya began to squirm.

"It looked better before falling in mud."

"Did it fall or did you fling it, Volodya?"

This, Ilyich would not answer.

"Just as I thought. Give it to me!" her mother demanded.

"I cannot give it to you! I need it!"

"While you continue your discussions, I will wash and fluff it."

"If you ruin it…"

"I cannot ruin matted rat fur!"
Her mama and a minister, tussling over a wig!
And who won that contest? Not the minister.

The Smolny

Once the Bolsheviks occupied the Smolny, I felt less anxious. It was not an entirely rational response; there remained much to fear. But at least, at the Smolny, the Krupskayas did not face Kerensky's men alone. If government forces attempted to invade the Smolny, they would be met with machine guns and cannon and Bolshevik soldiers. In such men and armaments, I took comfort.

Once a school for the daughters of aristocrats, by late October 1917 the Smolny more resembled a fort. Guns on the rooftop and portico, firewood barricades across the lawn. Inside, chapped-faced soldiers tramped up and down the hallways, chewing on sunflower seeds and spitting out the husks. No mere broom could hold in check the widening gyres of rubbish. In the basement, where I assisted in the kitchen, the aromas of the overly excited and under-washed combined with the aroma of continuously boiling cabbage. Round the clock we served comrades soup and black bread. It was not nearly enough, the portions we served, but it was something. When I left the basement, it was usually to carry food to Nadya or Ilyich or Lev Davidovich or Alexandra Kollontai or the rest of the Bolshevik Executive Committee. None of them would take the time to come to the basement to eat.

Ilyich's sister, Maria Ilyinichna, did not like the food served at the Smolny. And, as always with Maria Ilyinichna, whatever she felt or thought she said without considering how her comments might be received or interpreted.

"And you call yourself a cook, Yelizaveta Vasilevna!"

You remember Maria Ilyinichna's face? In certain lights, remarkably porcine.

"I call myself a woman in a kitchen making the best of poor rations, Maria Ilyinichna. What are you now calling yourself?"

If stung, I sting back. That is my weakness, but a character failure I was never to regret in the company of Maria Ilyinichna. Too many others deferred to Ilyich's sister. She had been riding her brother's coattails, trading on that kinship, since he had returned from Finland. At the Smolny, she made no personal effort to earn the respect of the other workers in the kitchen or even to treat them with minimal civility. Already, you see, she had become used to the deference, to expect it automatically. And when such obeisance was not forthcoming, she lashed out tartly.

In the kitchen of the Smolny, she behaved as if we, the toilers in that space, had conspired against her. As if we had deliberately concocted a less than savory dish so that Maria Ilyinichna's taste buds would suffer.

"Even I could cook a better soup!"

"Then by all means," I invited, "cook it."

She swept behind the serving table into the kitchen proper. She picked up a spoon. She sniffed it. She peered into one pot, then another.

"Here is your problem," she majestically announced. "You have overfilled this pot and shortchanged the others."

The comrades in aprons snickered.

"Ah," I said. "Perhaps you are right. I am sure you would be more successful in finding the correct amount and quality of ingredients. May I inform Ilyich you will be taking on that responsibility, Maria Ilyinichna? No doubt he will be enormously relieved to hear that his sister has put her talents to just such a service on behalf of The Revolution."

To a resurgence of titters, she flounced out, glaring.

Let her flounce. Let her glare. If Maria Ilyinichna ever dreamed I would treat her other than the spoiled younger sister, she dreamed in vain.

If you expect from the mother-in-law an inspiring, heart-thumping version of the triumph of the Great October Socialist Revolution, you too will be disappointed. From my small and blinkered perspective, it seemed as unlikely as likely that Ilyich and the Bolsheviks would command greater power on October 26 than they commanded on any other day. In any case, history does not need my account. The victory has been recorded by countless others, including Comrade Kollontai, who described quite prettily the gathering in the White Hall of the Smolny, October 25.

On that "dark night," a "blustery wind" blew "fitfully" in from the river, according to Comrade Kollontai. Ilyich and cohorts sat beneath an electric bulb's "dim light" at a "small square table," drinking a "few glasses of hot tea," awaiting the Aurora's first volley.

I am very fond of Comrade Kollontai, but affection does not prevent my saying she is an unregenerate romantic who has been known to err on the side of melodrama. The short novel she would pen in a few years' time about a revolutionary love triangle did not alter my affection for her, but it did confirm my opinion that she was not shy about exaggerating when and where she felt exaggeration heightened the effect of her story.

Although wonderfully important as a *symbol* of rebellion, the Aurora, in fact, contributed little to the success of the October Revolution. The Kronstadt sailors who would in 1921 turn against Ilyich, in October 1917 solidly supported the Bolshevik cause and did, by means of the Aurora, steam up the Bolshaya Neva and linger in the waters opposite the Winter Palace, prepared for battle. However, the few shots fired from the vessel fell harmlessly into the water. The Aurora did little damage to the Bolsheviks' enemies.

While the Aurora idled, inside the Winter Palace governmental ministers supped in the Malachite Chamber, served by green-coated servants who had previously served the deposed tsar. Already Kerensky had fled for Gatchina, but neither the Bolsheviks nor the dining ministers were aware of the desertion. All assumed the prime minister remained somewhere inside the Winter Palace.

Units of Lev Davidovich's Military Revolutionary Committee had been mobilized and stationed throughout the city. At Comrade Trotsky's order, they were to seize the utilities and railroads. Red Army troops encircled the palace. The telephones were cut off first, the electricity next. The ministers now sat digesting in candlelight. Some of them, it was later reported, crawled beneath the last tsar's dining table and cowered beneath that canopy.

A few moments past midnight, in search of Nadya, I came upon Ilyich and Lev Davidovich. As usual, Ilyich paced. Lev Davidovich perched on a chair, his heels clacking against the rungs.

"When have you last eaten? When have you last slept?" I harangued.

Ilyich never slowed his pacing; Lev Davidovich's heels continued to clack. And so I began to issue directives of my own. I called for a blanket and two pillows and when they arrived I spread those provisions on the floor and pointed.

"Gentlemen, you can still give orders in a state of recline. If you will not rest your minds, at least rest your backs."

I did not expect to be obeyed—not without further wrangling. But what did I have to do on the night of October 25 if not wrangle? No revolution was being decided on the basis of my activities inside the Smolny.

"Ilyich. Lev Davidovich."

Again I pointed to the floor and improvised bed.

Lev Davidovich began to jabber about wrinkling his coat, a garment already thoroughly wrinkled, although he did not seem to realize its state.

"Take off your coat. I will hang it for you."

Like a child he held out his arms for me to take his coat. And like an obedient child he tried to stand still, but exhaustion made him wobble.

"She will not leave, you realize, until we are flat on our backs on floorboards," Ilyich said and I, to eliminate any doubt about that assertion, nodded that such was the case.

The two of them stretched side by side. Lev Davidovich put his arms behind his head. Ilyich held his elbows against his belly.

"You, Vladimir Ilyich," Lev Davidovich said. "There can be no other choice."

"And why not?" Ilyich disputed. "You are head of the Petrograd Soviet."

"Only because you were in hiding," Lev Davidovich replied.

As I left them, Ilyich had raised a hand above his head and there it circled and circled in air that did not resist.

"Dizzying," he said. "This sudden transition to power."

Nonsense.

Fatigue and only fatigue inflicted the dizziness. If Ilyich had not been so physically depleted, the moment the Provisional Government conceded defeat to the Petrograd Soviet he would have leapt onto that square table Comrade Kollontai so prettily described and danced for joy.

INTERVIEW WITH HISTORY
Alexandra Kollontai

"Your fancy party frocks. Unbecoming, for a Bolshevik."

"We are to start with insult, are we? Very well. But understand: I supported Ilyich's All Power to the Soviets. It was not initially a popular platform. The allegiance earned me many enemies."

"Enemies who criticized your attire?"

"Not only my attire."

"For quite some time, you wavered. Neither Bolshevik nor Menshevik, then Menshevik, then Bolshevik."

"Ultimately, I felt closer in spirit to Bolshevism and its uncompromising belief in revolution."

"And yet…?"

"The personal charm of Plekhanov restrained me from condemning the Mensheviks."

"The personal charm of men, your susceptibility to. Let's discuss."

"Is a man ever judged by his love affairs? Never."

"Be that as it may, *your* love affairs were defended by Trotsky, vulgarized by Stalin, and used by Vladimir Lenin to discredit the Workers' Opposition faction."

"So it would seem."

"When your affair with Alexander Shlyapnikov ended, you embarked on another with Pavel Dybenko, Commissar of the Navy."

"Pavel was the soul of the Baltic Fleet."

"And 17 years your junior."

"What of it?"

"That erotic, passionate attachment prompted Vladimir Lenin to question 'the reliability of women whose love affairs are intertwined with politics.'"

"And thereby reveal himself a hypocrite."

"You allude to his love affair with Inessa Armand, his political crony."

"I have done more than allude."

"By writing a 134-page roman à clef."

"What Ilyich and Inessa shared did not diminish their affection for Nadya."

"But did its novelization diminish Comrade Krupskaya's affection for you?"

"You must ask Nadya that question."

"You stated, publicly, that Inessa's death was more than Ilyich could bear."

"It precipitated his fatal illness."

"Oh? Fanny Kaplan's bullets didn't accomplish that feat?"

"You are putting words in my mouth."

"As you did in theirs."

"My generation of women grew up at a turning point in history. Love still played a tremendous role in our lives."

"*Free* love."

"I advocated the foundation of a new sexual morality that liberated women from the servitude of marriage. I did not advocate 'free love.' I have been misquoted."

"These are not your words? 'Satisfying one's sexual desire should be as simple as getting a glass of water'?"

"That is not what I wrote. In *Communist Morality in the Sphere of Martial Relations*, thesis 18, I wrote: 'Sexuality is a human instinct as natural as hunger or thirst.'"

"And failed to convince Vladimir Lenin."

"Despite his attachment to Inessa, Ilyich was a prude."

"Quite a few of your male comrades openly referred to the Zhenotdel as the 'Babotdel.' Translation: peasant hags united."

"Is this to be a recitation of male boorishness?"

"Many have argued that history, by definition, is simply that."

"I am not, nor was I ever, a bourgeois feminist. I am a Marxist. Six million proletarian woman worked 12-hour shifts, starved on 12 rubles a month and slept in vermin-infested barracks. Neither the government nor society assisted them in times of illness, pregnancy, or unemployment. The Party needed to address those appalling conditions and end the exploitation."

"The Party. Back to the Party. Quick review. Your comrade/lover Shlyapnikov: tortured and murdered, 1937. Your comrade and greatest love Dybenko: shot stepping off a train, 1938. The only 'old Bolshevik' left standing: Comrade Kollontai."

(Silence.)

"Your apologia?"

"It is not necessary to die to be rendered irrelevant."

"Irrelevant? The first woman ambassador? The Russian envoy to Norway, Mexico and Sweden? The only female People's Commissar? How could such a woman find herself relegated to the dustbin of history?"

"Do not insult my intelligence. You know as well as I."

"Because she is a she?"

"In time, the family in which a man is everything, a woman nothing, will cease to exist. No true Marxist should be frightened by the prospect."

"What or whom did Comrade Stalin fear?"

"Ilyich, while he was alive, while he was well."

"Never a woman?"

"One woman, briefly."

"Nadezhda Krupskaya."

"Wife of, widow of. Briefly."

The Conspiracy Against Sleep

Another glass of strong tea and back to work, for new tasks awaited. Monumental tasks. The "destruction of the (previous) machinery of state." The organization of a new state "apparatus" that would follow through on the revolutionary promises: bread, peace, factories in the hands of the workers, land for the working peasants. Defeat Kerensky's forces in Gatchina. Implement socialism in a country reeling from war and revolution.

Ask Lev Davidovich. He will tell you how regularly Ilyich, into the fifth hour of a meeting, burst into a fit of laughter from sheer exhaustion. And when that happened, Ilyich bent beneath the table so as not to "disorganize the meeting." Ilyich, Nadya, Lev Davidovich, Alexandra Kollontai and so many others worked 18-, 20- and 24-hour days. Up and down the halls of the Smolny, one heard the cry: "I cannot work any longer like this!" but the crier went on working nevertheless. When I read the November 12 decree that established an eight-hour working day for the masses, I myself rocked with laughter—the laughter of disbelief. None in the Smolny would have considered working so few hours.

Do not misunderstand. I do not condone idleness. I appreciated that The Revolution had promised much to the people of Russia and that to renege on those promises would have been worse than contemptible. But one cannot continue to work without rest. The body simply will not stand the strain.

Once Ilyich became chair of the Council of People's Commissars, he and Nadya and I again lived as a trio in a trio of rooms on the second floor of the Smolny. Lev Davidovich's assigned rooms were directly across the hall.

Our long delayed trunks from Switzerland at last arrived and we added those contents to the furnishings departed students had left behind:

beds, dainty chairs and decorative desks. Nadya now worked at a "lady's desk," painted white and green—far too whimsical for her style or taste, but as always my daughter made do. Ilyich had the electric lamps refitted to burn kerosene because the electricity was turned off in the building at midnight and, without fail, both he and Nadya worked past midnight.

I think of my Nadya in her scuffed shoes and unruly hair seated at that prim furnishing. She was constantly pulling in her legs and hunching her back as an adult might seated at a child's desk. But once she became thoroughly absorbed in her work, her legs would relax their holding pattern and smack against wood. And then my work-interrupted daughter would swear like a Kronstadt sailor.

Although our Smolny accommodations were perfectly adequate, by November 1917 I am unashamed to admit that I longed to live in more comfortable quarters. I would have liked to have been able to sit in a chair with adequate padding, to set plates on a serviceable table, to nestle with my book in a warm and welcoming corner not constantly beset by drafts of wind. Occasionally I still worked in the Smolny kitchen, but my legs had begun to give me trouble. I could not stand for too many hours before my knees began to stiffen, the pain to radiate. Nonetheless, I did insist on continuing to cook for the three of us. We now had, for our private use, a small kitchen. To avoid the chaos of the dining room, we often ate the evening meal in our rooms, just we three. My dining companions were distracted, always distracted by work and projects, but at least for an hour we sat together, a remnant of normalcy I cherished.

Outside our rooms, outside any room that contained Ilyich, day or evening, sentries stood guard.

"It is foolish," Ilyich objected. The guards' presence made him feel confined. It reminded him, I suspect, of his stay in a tsarist prison cell.

"It is a precaution, Volodya," Nadya countered sternly. "I will not have you sending away the guards."

As a further precaution, the three of us had access to a private elevator whose last stop was the back courtyard. Successful revolution notwithstanding, the chair of the Council of People's Commissars might still need, on a moment's notice, to sprint for his life.

During daylight hours, Ilyich worked in room 67, so identified by a handwritten number tacked to the doorframe. Alongside Ilyich worked two secretaries feverishly attempting to diminish pile upon pile of telegrams, decrees and reports. At the Smolny, let no one tell you otherwise, the paperwork seemed to replace itself by fairy dust. Every day, when my Nadya returned from the Vyborg, she went to room 67 to help Ilyich.

One of those afternoons, I passed her in the hallway. Or rather, she passed me.

"What? No kiss for your mama?"

She had not even recognized me.

"You are staggering on your feet!"

"I am fine!" she denied. "I simply need tea."

When she went in search of her tea, I followed.

"And what must be done this hour that cannot be done the next? Are Kerensky's soldiers at the city gates? Has the tsar reoccupied the Winter Palace?"

"We must make use of everybody's experience to construct a new type of state. We must create a state such as the world has never seen, one that relies on the masses, that remakes the entire social fabric in a new, socialist way, that reshapes all human relations…"

"One that reshapes human relations? Come, Nadya. That will not occur even if you never sleep again."

"We must extricate ourselves from the imperialist war in a revolutionary manner…"

My daughter sounded like a recording wearing down.

In the hallway I found Zheltishev, an Ufa peasant, who had been assigned to run errands and take care of the little necessities for Ilyich. That afternoon I appropriated his services on behalf of my daughter. Between the two of us we got her in bed, where she continued to recite.

"Tremendous difficulties have to be overcome…a desperate fight must be waged…if necessary, against one's colleagues. We must continue to work without a moment's respite. We must…we must…."

Zheltishev pulled a trinket from his pocket. He and some of the other machine gunners had pried open the students' trunks in the attic and confiscated their contents.

"For you, Madam Lenin, for you."

So saying he curled my Nadya's fingers around a tiny, round mirror, the word "Niagara" carved in English letters on the back. I believe he meant it as a charm, a talisman for my daughter's health and protection.

"Thank you, Comrade Zheltishev, for your help and kindness," I said. "She is resting now. I will stay beside her. Ilyich may need you elsewhere."

He nodded and took his leave but several times during the next hour returned to make sure that Nadya continued to rest and I needed no further assistance. Nadya slept with Zheltishev's gift in her hands. I did not remove it from her grasp nor did I consider doing so. If a peasant's superstition helped my daughter endure the rigors of creating from scratch a Soviet state, so much the better. A mother's efforts alone were insufficient.

The work went on, at that accelerated pace, into the new year. Ilyich took to saying: "Commune plus one, Commune plus two," savoring every day that his regime outlasted his model, determined that the Soviet experiment would avoid the Commune's fate of collapse.

"Are you forgetting what you said last week to the Swedish reporter, Volodya?"

"Why bother to remember, Yelizaveta Vasilevna," he replied, bloodshot eyes twinkling, "when I have you to remind me?"

"The Swedish reporter asked about your enormous workload. And you agreed, yes, the workload was enormous. But despite it, you said, you felt fine. And then the reporter asked: 'And there is time for sleep?' And you admitted there was very little time for sleep. 'But when I do sleep,'—do you remember saying this, Volodya?—'when I do sleep I have but one dream and that is to get a little rest, if only for half an hour.'"

Ilyich laughed, folded the notes in his lap and, smiling, closed his eyes.

"I will try again for that dream," he said.

For perhaps ten minutes he snored, sitting upright in his chair, and then with a startle and snort he woke and hurried off to room 67.

In January of 1918, Ilyich dissolved the Constituent Assembly.

"Volodya," I chided. "Surely this is not necessary!"

"To declare itself the supreme parliamentary body is counterrevolutionary," he seethed.

"And the suppression of newspapers?"

"The newspapers are in the hands of the bourgeoisie," my Nadya yipped.

"*Every* newspaper?" I unwisely doubted. "If so, it is a first in the history of Piter."

Any in Russia who did go to sleep, and slept past midnight on January 31, 1918, woke on the fourteenth of February. Replacing the Julian with the Gregorian calendar reduced the complications of dealing with the Western world. That particular Ilyich edict I understood and support-ed. Nevertheless, starting my day, February 14, New Style, I prepared for intervention and argument. If my Nadya felt she had lost 13 days' labor overnight, she would not rest until she had made up the deficit.

Lev Davidovich, you will remember, negotiated the "shameful peace" with Germany in accordance with Ilyich's wishes and over the objections of Inessa and others. Inessa came to tea to argue the matter personally with Ilyich. His office was too public a theatre. Along with the rest of the Bolsheviks, Inessa had been pushing herself beyond the limits of her natural strength. Just as The Revolution had accelerated the aging of my Nadya and Ilyich, long hours and faulty nutrition had told on Inessa. She was still Inessa, but a faded version of her former self—more somber, less lively.

She hugged me; she hugged Nadya. Ilyich she did not hug. Nor did she stand on ceremony.

"Reconsider. This is not the way to go about it. Many in the Party feel as I do."

"Then, like you, they are wrong," Ilyich replied.

"Because only you can be right?" Inessa challenged.

My Nadya stepped back, out of the fray. Whether she secretly agreed with Inessa, I would never know—nor would Inessa. What Ilyich de-cided, Nadya supported and in that support never wavered until Ilyich abandoned one plan to test another. Comrade Stalin and his revisionist hacks would have you believe that in the wake of the Great October Socialist Revolution socialism in Russia moved steadily forward. It did no such thing. Ilyich and Lev Davidovich were often grasping at straws, inventing "solutions" to countcract the latest developing crisis.

"I repeat, Volodya: you are acting against *much* opposition."

"And I repeat: it must be done. And Trotsky will do it."

As did most of those who debated Ilyich, Inessa gave up first. She did not, however, give in. She had not changed Ilyich's mind; none of his explanations had persuaded her over to his viewpoint. They had fought to a stalemate and as a stalemate they left it.

On her way out, again, she hugged Nadya and myself.

"And how are your legs, Yelizaveta Vasilevna?" she inquired. "Nadya tells me you battle Smolny stairs."

"And with as much success as you enjoyed just now," I answered.

"Varvara sends her love to you both."

"She is in Moscow?" Nadya asked.

"With her father, yes," Inessa said, "but far from content. She complains she has too little to do there."

Ilyich, who had resumed his work, turned at the mention of Varvara.

"Do you or the children need anything, Inessa? Here or in Moscow? You must let me know."

"I will, Volodya," Inessa promised.

They were no longer lovers nor were they comrades in full agreement, as their standoff indicated. Neither alteration diminished Ilyich's concern for Inessa and her children. Although The Revolution had not entirely obliterated the Armand fortune, a memo from the chair of the Council of People's Commissars produced faster results than a payoff of rubles. If Inessa or her children needed a doctor, medicine, firewood, tickets on a train already overbooked, it was Ilyich, or Nadya operating in Ilyich's name, who saw to those needs. If you imagine my daughter resented helping Inessa and her children, you are mistaken. Long before, she had begun to think of Inessa as less a rival than a sister. She was Aunt Krupa to Inessa's children. As much as Ilyich, she wanted Inessa strong and well. Inessa was one of the trusted.

In 1918, when Ilyich decided the name "Social Democrat" equaled "dirty linen," only the thinnest crust of hoarfrost covered the linden trees each morning. Spring had come early to Piter, uncovering banks of brown, shriveled leaves.

We were henceforth to call ourselves Communists, Ilyich decreed.

"You cannot erase history, Volodya," I said. "The Revolution triumphed because of Social Democrats."

"And because of Communists, The Revolution will proceed."

"That is how you now talk at the supper table? Reserve your speeches for assemblies."

"Mama!" Nadya warned. "Ilyich has explained himself. That you do not like the explanation does not justify criticism."

"Then what does justify criticism, Nadya? I await your answer from the edge of my seat."

The Neva was once again a running river when Ilyich announced his decision to relocate the government to Moscow.

After hearing that pronouncement, before I spoke, I looked toward my daughter. When I saw that her bottom lip had completely disappeared inside her mouth, I knew such news made her equally unhappy.

"To remain in Piter will jeopardize The Revolution," Ilyich said. "If we are in Moscow, the Germans will be less tempted to seize Piter."

"But the Smolny…," I began and got no further.

"Why does everyone prattle on about the symbolic importance of the Smolny?! The Smolny is what it is because we are in it."

That practicality again—Ilyich's trademark.

At this remove I cannot remember how I meant to finish my protest. Certainly I would not have argued the structure's amenities. I did not feel sentimentally attached to the landmark as did, apparently, other Bolsheviks. Yes, we had been physically in the Smolny when the Provisional Government fell, but we had been in countless apartments and hallways and meeting rooms agitating for that collapse. Were any of those locations less noteworthy, less integral to revolutionary lore? I could not think so. Nor could I plead on behalf of my heart and my daughter's: "No, Ilyich, no! Do not take us from Piter! Do not make us say goodbye to our city again. We are just home. Do not make us leave our Nevsky, our Neva. Do not insist the Krupskayas move to Moscow, even for the sake of The Revolution!"

As history knows, we left Piter—Ilyich, the Krupskayas, the Communists, the committees, the government and its burgeoning bureaucracies. In the spring of 1918, we moved to Moscow. There would be no further Piter homecomings. We would not see our city again.

MOSCOW

Behind Kremlin Walls

Nadya forgets, or dismisses, that it took no small amount of time and no little amount of proletarian labor to make our Kremlin apartment livable. Our assigned rooms, in fact the whole of the Kremlin in 1918, showed appalling neglect. One could hardly find an inch that did not cry out for repair: stoves broken, ceilings fissured with cracks, walls coated with grease and grime. The hallways smelled of carbolic acid and rodents. Doors did not properly close; doorknobs went missing. Winter's icicles seemed to have found conditions inside the Kremlin quite as hospitable as the outside turrets and eaves. Water had pooled beneath the windows, leaving floors discolored and furry with mold. The tsar's former palace had become a shanty of gigantic proportions.

Genuinely dismayed by the scale of the improvement project and dubious about my ability to mount it, I reminded Nadya: "I am a humble Communist, not a magician."

At the time, my daughter and I had just stepped across the threshold of the caretaker's apartment, the filthiest of the lot, and our newest address.

"So the head of the Soviet state is to live in the caretaker's apartment. Very appropriate," I sniped. "But why did the caretaker not take better care?"

"Mama!" Nadya said. "Enough! The place needs doing up."

Until that doing up had been completed, the three of us lodged in the National Hotel, accommodations only a little less squalid than the derelict Kremlin.

Moscow did not charm me. A gray city, a rough city. A city of coarse men and conniving women. The inhabitants of Moscow seemed equally unimpressed by the *arrivistes* from Piter. We were viewed as outsiders, usurpers, treated with the kind of blatant suspicion one associates with a peasant village. In no manner did the populace of Moscow open its arms to us. We remained unwelcome.

Nadya and Ilyich claimed to have found the market stalls surrounding the National Hotel "quaint"; I found that pocket of commerce foul and dangerous. We were told, with pride, that one of the shop owners had not hesitated to knife a student he suspected—but had not proved—guilty of stealing. Had I been able to see into our future in Moscow, I would have taken that example of lawless vengeance as portent.

I am not being entirely facetious when I say that making the Kremlin livable was very nearly as difficult a task as the running of the new Soviet state. I could not count on the carpenters to show up as promised; I could not, even with Ilyich's signature, find anyone to repair the sink drain. I haggled over wall paint; I despaired over door locks. The health and girth of Kremlin rats made killing them a bloody business, but in bloodshed, the amount and extent of bloodshed, my comparison falters. Russians were now killing Russians. We had exchanged an imperialist war for a civil war.

"We are against civil war, but what are we to do? We must defend The Revolution," Nadya said. "The people wanted a bloodless revolution, but their enemy forced them to take up arms."

The people's latest "enemy," in my Nadya's view?

The White Army.

"You think because Kerensky is done for, the opposition has no leader?"

"The opposition": another term with which we would all become overly familiar.

I picked up a basket of darning. When my daughter shouted doctrine, I tired quickly of her company.

In Moscow, the incompetence and laziness of "bureaucrats," the city's "bloat of officials," exhausted Ilyich's always minimal patience. He railed nonstop at such hindrances. Was he partially responsible for the proliferation of officials? Certainly. Yet in terms of work ethics, Ilyich remained endearingly naïve. Given the enormous amount to be done, he simply could not comprehend any comrade taking off his boots, putting up his feet and having a smoke.

The workers of Moscow were equally disgusted.

"Where are the chickens? Where are the sausages?" they asked. "Have the bureaucrats eaten them all and left us nothing?"

Throughout the city, throughout Russia, people went to bed hungry and rose hungrier. For worker, soldier or bureaucrat in Russia, there simply was not enough food.

A "difficult time," my Nadya said of the summer of 1918.

In Piter, the Moika and Fontanka floated refuse and bodies. An influenza epidemic had killed thousands, cholera and typhus thousands more. Shops and factories had shut down. Now the daughters of aristocrats competed with the daughters of workers for street favors, selling themselves for a crust of bread, a sliver of soap. Hoping to find provisions in the countryside, thousands left Piter on foot, only to meet death, not relief, along the way.

In Piter, in Moscow, there were few kind words for Vladimir Lenin. From Lev Davidovich, Ilyich heard the blunt truth.

"They are saying on the streets: 'Take your comrade and go to hell.' They are saying: 'Down with Lenin and horsemeat! Give us the tsar and pork!'"

"We are failing them," said Ilyich miserably. "The Revolution is failing them."

In penance, in recompense, he ate less than his rations. When the Council of People's Commissars voted to raise his salary, he flew into a rage and severely reprimanded those responsible for proposing such an "obvious illegality." Night and day he scribbled angry notes which he attached to angry, insistent memos, every word thrice underlined as if lines of ink would speed the fulfillment of his wishes: _Read, grasp, follow through very quickly and let me know the result_. Increasingly frustrated at his desk, he went into the factories to speak directly to the workers.

"If he could," Nadya said to me, "he would speak individually with each worker in each factory in all of Russia to reassure them."

Her tone was not altogether approving. Ilyich did not look well. He had all but given up sleeping. He sometimes appeared light-headed, shaky on his feet.

To Ilyich, Nadya said: "You cannot do it all yourself. It is not possible."

He waved off such fretting.

"This is my life. One fighting campaign after another."

To outwit the Whites, the Red Army needed an able leader. Very soon after we settled in Moscow, Ilyich appointed Lev Davidovich to the post. It was not a reflexive decision. Ilyich deliberated long and hard.

"Do you think Trotsky could handle it?" he asked Nadya.

"Lev Davidovich?" She frowned. "He is dedicated," she praised cautiously. "A good organizer." Another pause. "In the field, he would give fine, stirring speeches…."

But she stopped short of an endorsement and I knew why. Wars are not refined; they are not genteel. My daughter, quite reasonably, doubted Lev Davidovich's capacity to put aside his scholarly ways for the blood and gore of combat, the mud and mess of battlefields. I shared my daughter's reservations. Neither of us appreciated at the time the relish with which Lev Davidovich would undertake the strategic challenges of battle. As it happened, he made an excellent Red Army Chieftain and of course looked quite dashing in his Red Army uniform.

The majority of Red Army recruits did not wear their uniforms with Lev Davidovich's style or flair. Even to march in parades across Red Square, they did not suit up tidy.

Watching from a Kremlin balcony, Ilyich cursed and flung his fist as unit after unit passed below.

"Look at them. Their uniforms are half buttoned. They march like bags of sand!"

But march and fight and die they did, defending Ilyich's and Nadya's revolution.

When we came to Moscow, Ilyich's face was not well known. Often, within the Kremlin, he went unrecognized. If Nadya insisted, and kept insisting, he would sometimes agree to a brief stroll along Kremlin walls, midday. From the upper paths, one had a sweeping view of the city and Grand Palace; the lower paths offered more greenery and greater privacy. You will recall that in Shusha, as well as in Europe, both Nadya and Ilyich allowed themselves the occasional recreation: a hike, a bicycle ride, a tramp about the neighborhood. How I wish they had kept up that practice on a regular basis! Recreation is not a bourgeois indulgence. It was not in 1905 or 1910 and it would not have been in 1918.

One rare afternoon they returned to the apartment having ventured beyond the Kremlin, out into the streets. Giggling, the two of them. Such a joy to hear, those giggles!

Near the marketplace, they had stopped to converse with a peasant. He named his village; Nadya failed to recognize the name. Insulted, the peasant asked where she could have come from to be so ignorant.

"Oh, a Petrograder!" the peasant dismissed with contempt. "I will

For You, Madam Lenin

tell you what I think of another Petrograder. That Lenin is a nuisance. Muddle-headed, if you ask me. His wife wanted a sewing machine, so he gave orders for all sewing machines to be taken from all the villages, my niece's among them.'"

Ilyich clapped his hands throughout Nadya's recital.

"Just think, Yelizaveta Vasilevna! *All* the sewing machines in Russia collected for your daughter."

"And these sewing machines are now where?" I played along.

"In the Kremlin hallways!"

"*Cluttering* the Kremlin hallways!" Ilyich corrected.

"And throughout the discussion, there stands Volodya," Nadya reported, "nodding his head, commiserating with the peasant, affronted by the husbandly indulgences of Vladimir Lenin!"

You see how willfully I reminisce about the lighter moments? There were to be so few as the Whites—and Reds—resorted to terror.

"Red or white, terror remains terror," I reminded my daughter, snow falling on Red Square, on Moscow, on Red Army and White Army soldiers, all of them Russian and so many of them dead. "Remember your history. If not Russian, French. Terror can be mandated; it cannot be controlled."

My daughter sat at her desk, squinting over the latest bulletin from Red Army headquarters.

I spoke to her back. I spoke and received no response. I spoke to no effect.

Tea with Louise

As if there were not enough to do, Ilyich had to sit for insufferable interviews with foreign journalists curious to take tea with the Soviet leader but ignorant of the most rudimentary of socialist principles. Stupidly imagining they complimented, they addressed her as "First Lady." As if she, an experienced Party member, had given up working for a socialist system of education, an end to illiteracy and the promotion of proletarian culture to stand in reception lines, shake hands, and exchange vacuous pleasantries!

"Think of it as educating the fourth estate," Ilyich advised.

"They have no interest in *learning*," she argued. "They come merely to snoop on where and how we live."

"And we shall encourage them to do so," Ilyich placidly replied. "In courteously numbing detail, we shall describe our four-room living quarters and the steps we must climb to get there: an ostensible three-story climb the Kremlin's high ceilings turn into six. We will freely admit that our dining room is a converted hallway. We will joke that we had more floor space as the tsar's convicts in Siberia. And when they inquire about 'First Lady' fashions, you will force them to take copious notes on your one belted overcoat, two skirts and simple hat."

Her jaw clipped air.

"I would not count on that discussion taking place, Volodya," she warned. "A First Lady ought not choke on her words, addressing visitors in the Kremlin."

Her mother, who had joined them in time to hear Ilyich's scheme to advertise her wardrobe, sighed as Yelizaveta Vasilevna always sighed regarding the matter of clothes.

"Hear me, Volodya! I will not talk long and hard on skirts! Even for The Revolution!"

"Then talk of cats," her mother suggested. "And when they ask about the cat in Ilyich's lap, say it is a newborn Communist kitten, not the runt of a Romanov stray."

"Perhaps you would like to take my place, Mama?"

"Nadya! Do not saddle me with Western journalists and Yelizaveta Vasilevna at one and the same time!" Ilyich protested.

"You doubt my ability to carry off a performance comparable to your own, Volodya?" her mother inquired.

"On the contrary, Yelizaveta Vasilevna. I am quite certain the next headline would read: 'Soviet Leader Inferior to Delightful Mother-in-Law.'"

"I do not pretend that it would not be a *gamble*," her mother allowed. "Very often a mother-in-law outshines the competition."

"Join the circus! Both of you!" she exploded.

Whereas they saw the sport in performing for the Western press, she saw only interruption, interference, a trial to be endured.

Whatever the conveyance, propaganda was propaganda, Ilyich reminded. "The process may be tedious, but we cannot forego the opportunity."

"Even if the reporter is an idiot," she sulked. "Even if the idiot reporter insists on idiotically addressing me as Russia's First Lady."

"Yelizaveta Vasilevna, some assistance! She is your own stubborn daughter."

"And your own stubborn wife," her mother countered.

"All right, all right!"

She would ruin her afternoon. She would smile and sit and chat while minute after minute ticked away, never to be reclaimed. She would stifle all grumbling and grousing in the presence of unwanted company. She would do it, but she *would not like it*.

Ilyich, she and the cat assembled on schedule to greet a certain Louise Bryant, wife of the American John Reed. The couple had been in Piter when the Soviets assumed power. Based on a smattering of articles published in radical journals in America, Bryant called herself a Communist. Emma Goldman thought otherwise: "Louise is not a Communist— she merely sleeps with one."

Prior to being interviewed by a pretender, solely to be contrary, she changed from her clean jumper into the striped jumper with the torn pocket. When the pin fell out of her hair in transit, she did not replace it. Their visitor came dressed in a tapestry cap, dangling earrings, a black vest edged with white rickrack, her dark eyes outlined in kohl. An American who looked like a gypsy.

Once seated around the table, Ilyich continuously teased and tormented the cat, but his frank and cordial smile never wavered. In contrast, she must have seemed cool to the point of sullenness. She could not help it. She had no patience for this kind of masquerade. None. To distract himself for the duration, Ilyich had a wriggling cat. She had only a tea glass.

"Madam Lenin, what a pleasure to be introduced at last! I cannot fathom how we missed seeing each other in the halls of the Smolny."

"My wife," Ilyich said, "concentrated her efforts in the Vyborg."

"Tea?" she asked, pouring.

"As you may know, John and I bunked at the Astoria Hotel…"

Why would she or Ilyich know where American reporters slept—or care?

"…though we rarely saw our beds. We preferred to be out on the streets with the workers and soldiers."

Did their visitor expect to be congratulated for that unsingular feat?

"Your husband accompanied Comrade Kollontai to the Obukhovo Arms Factory," Ilyich flattered.

"And addressed the workers, along with Comrade Kollontai."

Ilyich nodded as if he had all the time in the world for such tripe. A journalist! Telling *Ilyich* what transpired in Piter! An American waxing nostalgic about The Russian Revolution!

"Your services to The Revolution will not be forgotten," Ilyich said.

"And we will never forget your exciting revolution."

Exciting.

To hide a curled lip she gulped tea.

"I remember as if it were yesterday. On the morning of October 24, we left the Astoria for the Winter Palace. We showed our Smolny passes—nothing. Luckily we had our American passports with us. Those did the trick. We got as far as the door of the Malachite chambers, determined to speak with the ministers. We knocked and shouted, but they refused to let us in."

It almost made one respect Kerensky's devils—that turn away.

"And so we wandered the halls and came upon a young officer swigging a bottle of wine. Château d'Yquem 1847. The tsar's favorite vintage."

Ilyich did not bother to clarify that he had ordered the tsar's wines poured into the gutters once the Winter Palace had been secured. A wise omission. Although the order had been obeyed, it had not achieved the desired results. Soldiers, workers and children had dropped to their bellies and licked the streets.

"We were there when the ministers filed out of the palace under Red Army guard. They left behind sheets and sheets of doodles. John and I both took a page to commemorate the great event."

She could scarcely contain herself. Such papers did not belong to interloping Americans! They belonged to the people of Russia!

"A souvenir of the Revolution, a keepsake," Ilyich murmured, mouth still smiling.

The cat yowled and leapt to the floor.

"At three a.m., we returned to the Smolny to hear Comrade Trotsky consign the revolution's enemies to the 'dustbin of history.'"

—Which meant Lev Davidovich had calculated correctly: the phrase did and would stick.

"And then we celebrated with the workers, eating cabbage soup and boiled beef in the basement."

As if it were a lark, a camping expedition. A trip to the zoo.

It was over. It was done. She could not be more delighted to be shed of the American Louise Bryant.

Several weeks later, as she and Volodya were rising from the supper table to return to work, her mother impishly ordered them to stay put.

"Not yet, children. Your work will wait. Tonight we have entertainment."

"What are you hiding, Mama? What is that folded in your hand?"

"You will see, you will hear," her mother said and with great merriment lifted and twirled a piece of newsprint.

"Have you been stealing mail, Yelizaveta Vasilevna?" Ilyich asked, already entertained by her mother's antics.

"I have indeed. And what do you suppose I have stolen this day?"

"Must I chase you around the table to find out?" she asked irritably.

"No. To find out you must *sit*," her mother repeated.

"Sit, Nadya, sit," Ilyich chimed in.

"So now there are two of you engaged in mischief?"

"Quiet, daughter. What I have here"—another twirl of newsprint—

"is the Russian translation of the French translation of the English account of journalist Bryant's visit to the Lenins."

Ilyich roared. "Then we can blame the French for all inaccuracies?"

"'Mirror of Moscow: Leon Trotsky and Nikolai Lenin.'"

"Nikolai," she grumbled. "A bad start."

"And worse to come," her mother said gleefully. "We begin, first, with the 'Soviet warlord' Lev Davidovich."

Warlord.

Ridiculous.

"'Trotsky cannot bear Russian slothfulness. He is constantly irritated by Russian indifference to sanitation. He insists on the utmost fastidiousness and neatness from all who work with him.'"

Ilyich slapped his thigh. She continued to scowl.

"And now for 'the Lenins,'" her mother trilled as if introducing the next sideshow. "Nadya, are you listening? You will want to pay close attention to this passage."

"I have not left the room, Mama," she answered. "Be satisfied with that concession."

"'Nikolai Lenin is very proud of his wife. How different the state of the Soviet Premier's temper might be if Madam Lenin were the sort of woman who wept because her apartment in the Kremlin was small, who quarreled with the other commissars' wives, who felt jealous of the Premier's secretaries.'"

"Wept, quarreled, jealous??! Does she take me for a member of the bourgeoisie?"

"Vindicated!" Ilyich crowed. "For our next interview we must again expound on our poor, cramped quarters."

"'Everything in their small apartment is spotlessly clean, although, as Madam Lenin explained, she has no servant.'" Here her mother broke away from the text to interject: "No servant, but a mother, a mother! 'There were quantities of books, a few chairs, a table, beds, no pictures on the walls. When you have an appointment with Lenin, he jumps up to greet you, shakes hands warmly and pushes forward a comfortable chair. Once you are seated, he draws up another, closer chair, leans forward and begins to talk as if there was nothing else to do in the world but enjoy your visit.'"

Volodya had anticipated and choreographed every reaction.

"'Madam Lenin has the same charm which Lenin has, the same way of focusing all her attention on what the visitor is saying.'"

Now she did laugh. How could she not? Ilyich grabbed and hoisted the cat in triumph.

Her mother waved her hand. "One more sentence, one more. 'It does not matter how determined one is to ply them with questions, one goes away astonished because one has talked so much, answering questions instead of asking them.'"

Finished, her mother shook from head to toe, wiped her eyes, fell momentarily silent and began again to shake.

Almost worth it, that idle hour spent with the American Louise.

They had not laughed like this since Shusha.

The Woman with the Umbrella

Beneath a tree, she waits.

Ask anyone to describe the woman beneath the tree, 30 August.

The *woman*, they will sneer. None will call her *comrade*.

Ask anyone about the woman standing beneath the tree, prior to *the event*. As if coached, the descriptions will cohere: a birdlike woman with a hooked nose, stringy dark hair. An ugly, commonplace woman—shoes cheap, dress dirty. A woman who appears haunted and hunted before she actually is.

Of Fanya Kaplan, as if to seal the case against her, all will say in perfectly modulated disgust: she smelled like a bleeding woman.

Blood for blood, comrades.

Blood for blood.

It is not raining. It has not been raining. Dismiss any report or after-the-fact gossip that includes drizzle. All day the skies have been stunningly clear, free of tumult. Fanya Kaplan's umbrella is a prop. She brings it as a prop but during her wait grows attached to incidentals. She begins to think in terms of symmetry. In her mind's eye, she begins to picture herself as standing beneath the dual canopy of umbrella and tree.

In one hand: umbrella.

In the other: scuffed briefcase.

In the briefcase: a Browning pistol.

In the Michelson Factory: the traitor Vladimir Lenin.

Beneath the double shadow of umbrella and tree, Fanya Kaplan first attracts the attention of a fly. The fly circles Fanya Kaplan's nose, brushes her eyelid, lands on her chapped lip.

If Fanya Kaplan were obliged to call out "Vladimir Lenin!" at this moment, she would likely swallow fly. If the fly remains, it may interfere with Fanya Kaplan's concentration, skew her aim. If, on the other hand,

214   *For You, Madam Lenin*

the fly departs before Vladimir Lenin exits the Michelson Factory, its service to The True Revolution must be recognized and rewarded. Before they hang or shoot or burn her, she will insist that the Moscow fly's collusion, its contribution to the death of the traitor, be duly and suitably noted.

It is a lot to manage: umbrella, pistol-packed briefcase, fly.

How does Fanya Kaplan manage?

Where the briefcase touches skin, she sweats. Where she sweats, she chafes. The fly rides her lip.

The traitor will be surrounded: at the door of the factory, on the steps, on the sidewalk. To kill Vladimir Lenin, she may have to kill others.

Perhaps she should start with the drunk soldier at her elbow.

Dirty whore. Scrawny, ugly, dirty whore, he slurs, pinching at the fabric of her dress.

A nearby man is easier to shoot than a distant man.

If she shot the pestering soldier at her elbow, very likely the pestering fly would leave her lip to investigate his gaping belly.

But Fanya Kaplan does not shoot; she waits.

Her feet are tired. Her arms are tired. Her eyes are tired from squinting. What a long time Vladimir Lenin has been inside the Michelson Factory, telling lies! She would like to look elsewhere, but she must watch for the bald head to bob in the crowd like a turd on the river.

"Vladimir Lenin!" she calls at last.

How foolish he is to turn toward the summons!

How quickly she must open the briefcase, extract the gun, dump the incidentals!

Raising her arm to shoot, she steps forward.

The fly flies off; the drunk soldier runs.

For one accustomed to bombs, a gun's discharge is utterly unspectacular.

Beneath a tree, Fanya Kaplan waits for what will happen next.

Shot

A car had come to fetch her.

Ilyich had been attacked, shot by a woman, she was told. Shot and slightly wounded. At seven-thirty this evening. It was now a few minutes past eight.

She looked deeply into the informant's face.

This was not the truth.

"On my word of honor!" her informant swore. "Vladimir Ilyich is only slightly wounded!"

She did not believe him.

The door to their apartment stood open, strangers were spilling into the hallway. There were unfamiliar coats on the rack, on tabletops.

"Comrade Krupskaya," a stranger greeted. "Please be assured arrangements have been made."

Then he was gone. Arrangements could only mean undertakers, coffins. Her heart still raced from rushing up the stairs but all feeling fled her limbs. She willed herself to remain standing. She must retain her composure. She must do nothing to embarrass herself or Ilyich or the Party.

The memory of Ilyich.

"Nadya!"

Her mother's voice.

Almost then, she wept. To hear Yelizaveta Vasilevna struggling to overcome her own pain and sorrow, attempting to convey quickly, without histrionics, what had occurred.

"The driver got him into the back seat and drove him here. They thought the Kremlin safer than the hospital. Ilyich did not lose consciousness. He climbed to the apartment without help. Maria Ilyinichna was here when he arrived. Maria Ilyinichna had come for papers on Ilyich's desk. It was Maria Ilyinichna who opened the door to him."

Maria Ilyinichna, not she, also had been with Ilyich the first time they tried to kill him. In Piter, in winter, at the Mikhailovsky Riding School. After he had spoken to a detachment of the newly formed Red Army, he and his sister and Fritz Platten had walked through a dark courtyard to the car. Once in the car they had travelled fewer than fifty yards when shots rang out. The driver accelerated; Platten pushed Ilyich's head to the floor. Three bullets broke through the windshield. Ilyich escaped unharmed, Maria Ilyinichna escaped unharmed. But the hand covering Ilyich's head was bloodied. Ilyich had dismissed the incident with a joke. "It gives Platten something to brag about," he said. And when she had protested the joking, the lax security, he had said: "Nadya, if they want to kill me they will find a way to kill me—and what if they do? None of us lasts forever."

Her mother was still holding her arm, still talking. "There were three shots. The third bullet only tore his coat."

Three bullets. Why must there always be three?

"We helped the doctors pull the bed from the wall. The surgeons are with him now. They fear internal bleeding, but he remains conscious. Go to him."

"But the doctors are working???"

"Let Volodya see you. He needs to know you are here."

A dressing table had been set up beside his bed. It overflowed with inhalators, gauze, bandages white and stained red. Those standing between her and the bed parted like curtains.

"You have come," Ilyich said.

"I have come."

"Do not look so frightened. It is a minor wound."

His face was pale, sweating. He breathed with great difficulty. His voice was weak.

"Volodya," she said too plaintively.

"You seem tired. You must lie down."

"I do not need to lie down."

"Lie down and rest. What is there to look at here?" he asked.

One of the surgeons motioned. She followed him outside the room. If the path of the second bullet had deviated "one millimeter in either direction," the surgeon told her, "Vladimir Lenin would be dead." They dared not operate. They would wait and watch, monitor pulse and temperature, change the dressings. The rest depended on Ilyich.

"We must issue a bulletin," someone said while another someone whispered: "one millimeter in either direction."

"Say *that* in the bulletin to the people!"

"Nadya!" her mother objected.

"Say it! Let the people know how close we came to losing Vladimir Ilyich!"

But her wishes were not implemented. In Ilyich's office, others wrote and published the decree.

> *Soviets of Workers, Peasants*
> *and Red Army Deputies*
>
> *A few hours ago a villain-*
> *ous attempt was made on the life*
> *of Comrade Lenin. The working*
> *class will respond to attempts on*
> *the lives of its leaders by still fur-*
> *ther consolidating its forces against*
> *all enemies of The Revolution.*

Everywhere she turned she saw another member of the Cheka. But where were the Chekists when Ilyich had been shot? Why had a state security organization of their own making proved so inept? If Ilyich had not been the victim, if he were not now lying in the other room, if Lev Davidovich or any of countless others had been shot, she and Ilyich would at this very moment be working to correct such appalling incompetence.

But she could not now work with Ilyich.

Ilyich had been shot.

To the Chekist crowding her shoulder she raged: "You are here but not there? When Vladimir Ilyich needed you, you were not there? You are sworn to protect his life at the cost of your own! You are *sworn!*"

"Nadya," her mother said, pulling in the opposite direction. "This helps no one. No one."

"Who did this to Vladimir Ilyich? Answer me!"

"We have arrested a suspect. A Socialist Revolutionary. A woman."

"You are certain? You have not made another mistake?"

"She has confessed."

"Where is she?"

"Here, in the Kremlin, transferred from the Lubyanka Prison."

"Where in the Kremlin?"

"A basement strong room."

"Take me there."

"Nadya, no!" her mother begged.

"I must *see* the Russian accused of shooting Ilyich!"

Maria Ilyinichna sneered. "And what do you, Nadezhda Konstanti-novna, think you will discover that the Cheka has not?"

To her mother, not to Ilyich's sister, she said: "If Volodya asks for me, tell him where I am. Tell him I went to talk to the assailant."

"He will be told nothing of the kind!" Maria Ilyinichna ordered.

"*Tell him*, Mama," she said.

Her mother followed her out into the hallway.

"And send a Chekist immediately to tell Inessa. If she has not heard already, she must not learn this from the streets."

Comrade Krupskaya Speaks with the Prisoner/Assassin

In a corner sits the would-be assassin, staring into space. Filthy, she is. No larger than a child.

The sound of a locked door unlocking. The prelude to another someone disrupting her reverie.

She turns, squints, recognizes.

"Ah. The comrade wife. But does she come as comrade—or as wife?"

"I come as Nadezhda Konstantinovna Krupskaya."

"*Nadezhda.* Hope. To remain hopeful in Russia is not easy. It is not easy."

A guard joins them.

At once she stands.

"My name is Fanya Kaplan. I shot at Lenin. I did it on my own."

"Leave us," commands her visitor.

The guards obey Nadezhda Konstantinovna Krupskaya.

This is impressive. This is power.

"I am here to ask why."

"Vladimir Lenin betrayed The Revolution."

"Vladimir Lenin saved The Revolution!"

Such a claim deserves no reply.

A trickle of blood runs past her knee. With a bloody finger she draws circles on her calf.

Another Chekist enters without knocking.

Again she stands.

"My name is Fanya Kaplan. I shot at Lenin. I did it on my own."

"Do not interrupt us again!" her visitor brays. "I am in no danger!"

When a guard leaves, she sits. When a guard enters, she stands.

It is a simple formula.

"Perhaps you would like to hear what happened after I shot the traitor? I will tell you. You will have no trouble remembering the sequence. I threw down the revolver. I stayed beneath the tree. Others ran about, shouting: 'Catch the killer of Comrade Lenin! Catch the fiend!' A man of authority, holding his own gun, glanced in my direction, then again. 'What are doing? Why are you standing here?' he asked. 'Why do you want to know?' I replied. He came toward me. He kicked the umbrella at my feet. He searched my pockets and briefcase. And then he saw the Browning. 'Why did you shoot Comrade Lenin?' he demanded. 'Why do you want to know?' I replied because I thought I had succeeded. I thought I had killed Vladimir Lenin."

"If Vladimir Ilyich is murdered, he will be replaced by men madder for power than your Kerensky."

"He is not my Kerensky. Kerensky fled Piter. A true revolutionary does not flee. Sophia Perovskaya did not flee. She went content to the gallows."

"Sophia Perovskaya died a martyr to the immorality of the old regime."

"And I will die a martyr to the immorality of the new."

"You are deluded."

"And your big eyes are blinder than mine. They will tell you I am alive. Held in a prison camp on Solovki Island or Kolyma. That is what they will say. Do not believe Vladimir Lenin's men, Nadezhda Konstantinovna Krupskaya. Do not believe your husband."

INTERVIEW WITH HISTORY
Fanya Kaplan

"My name is Fanya Kaplan. I shot at Lenin. I did it on my own. I will give no details."

"Please wait for a question to be asked."

"My name is Fanya Kaplan. I shot at Lenin. I had resolved to kill him long ago."

"All right. We'll do our best to catch up. Fanya/Fanny/Dora Kaplan, a Jew from the province of Volhynia, the daughter of a schoolteacher, the sister of six others, trained first as a milliner, later as a Socialist Revolutionary. As an Eser, in Kiev, you tossed a bomb at a tsarist lackey and missed. Eleven years of hard labor ruined your eyesight but stoked your revolutionary fervor. How are we doing so far?"

"My name is Fanya Kaplan. I shot at Lenin. I will not speak about the revolver."

"We were speaking about the bomb, not the Browning. But since you jump ahead.... In Moscow, as in Kiev, you failed to kill the enemy."

"My name is Fanya Kaplan. I shot at Lenin. I consider him a traitor to The Revolution."

"August 30, 1918. Vladimir Ilyich arrives at the Michelson Armaments Factory to deliver his second speech of the day. It's no secret he's there. His appearance has been advertised. *Every* Friday he exhorts the workers in one or another Moscow factory. As usual, he begins with a rallying cry. Feel free to elaborate at any time."

"My name is Fanya Kaplan. I shot at Lenin. I favored the Constituent Assembly and still do."

"Since you're not inside the factory, naturally, you hear none of his speech. You're merely waiting for the orator to finish his yammering and return to his chauffeured car."

"My name is Fanya Kaplan. I viewed the October Revolution negatively."

"With you were an umbrella, a briefcase, a Browning pistol. Quite a lot of paraphernalia to manage—and juggle."

"My name is Fanya Kaplan. I shot at Lenin. I fired several times. I don't remember how many."

"Three bullets hit the mark. One damaged Vladimir Lenin's coat. A second pierced his neck. A third lodged in his left shoulder."

"My name is Fanya Kaplan. I have not always lived in Moscow."

"The chauffeur ran toward you, thought better, returned to his downed boss and hefted him into the back seat. With the bleeder, the chauffeur sped toward the Kremlin. In the meantime, you made no attempt to hide or escape. You were captured standing beneath a tree: a tiny, sallow, old-before-her-time woman, dressed in faded black, spine bent, stare fixed."

"My name is Fanya Kaplan. The idea of shooting Lenin had matured in my consciousness a long time ago. His very existence erodes faith in socialism. What this erosion of faith in socialism consists of I do not want to say."

"Nor are we especially keen to hear. We're striving to separate speculation from fact, fact from myth."

"My name is Fanya Kaplan."

"Agreed, but about your four-day interrogation—first at Cheka headquarters, next in a Kremlin basement. Is it true? Had you been taught by comrades in Siberia to outstare your interrogators? Did the tortures cooked up by Moscow Chekists in their leather jackets exceed the tortures of their sadistic brethren in Siberia?"

"My name is Fanya Kaplan. I shot at Lenin. I did it on my own."

"So you've indicated. Still, you must be aware of persistent rumors."

"My name is Fanya Kaplan."

"That Fanya Kaplan couldn't hit a tank with a cannon at a distance of five feet. That the Browning in your possession had never been fired. That the bullet eventually recovered from Vladimir Ilyich's right sternoclavicular joint did not match the bullets from a Browning."

"My name is Fanya Kaplan. I shot at Lenin."

"Shot *at*, you say? Forgive us, dear. History can be dense. We missed entirely that transitive clue."

Revolutionaries Shooting Revolutionaries

Scrawled on the walls of the Cheka's interrogation chambers: *Death to the Bourgeoisie.*

The woman in custody does not disagree with the wall art. Vladimir Lenin is a bourgeoisie.

Strapped in a chair, the prisoner/assassin has been kicked, punched, spat at, shat on.

"Comrades, notice! Skin so yellow she shows no bruise," one Chekist declares as metal scrapes her cheek.

The detained admits she shot at Vladimir Lenin.

The detained refuses to say where she obtained the Browning.

The detained denies she had accomplices—even after a Chekist sticks his hand up her skirt, diddles her privates, smears her own blood across her nose.

"There will be no trial. No opportunity for grand statements. No clemency."

The detained does not blink.

"We could shoot you now, you realize. No one would care or protest. Certainly not Vladimir Lenin."

Three full nights, four full days of this.

If the woman in the chair is still thinking, she is considering sleeplessness a comrade. Already her mind has begun to pull away from her body, her body to cease.

Among themselves, the Chekists argue. Some want to continue the interrogation, intensify it. Neither knives nor blunt instruments have yet been applied. They have not yet harmed Fanya Kaplan's person in all the ways a woman's body can be harmed.

Then, from the floors above, the order: *End it. Shoot her now.*

Summoned: Kremlin Commandant Pavel Malkov, former sailor with the Baltic Fleet.

The execution of a human being, especially a woman, is not easy, he tells himself. *But her sentence is just. And I have been ordered to carry it out.*

"When?" he asks the others.

"Immediately."

Gathered with the prisoner in a Moscow garage, 4 a.m.: Chekists, Commandant Malkov, proletarian poet Demian Bedny—who attends for "revolutionary inspiration."

To mask the noise of a single shot: idling car engines.

To finish off Fanya Kaplan: a bullet to the brain.

To increase the drama/melodrama: a swooning proletarian poet.

If there is no corpse, there is no woman, and if there is no woman, there is no blood, brain or menstrual. And if there is no blood, there is no life and if there is no life there is no death and if there is no death there is only disappearance and where there is disappearance, hope.

INTERVIEW WITH HISTORY
Angelica Balabanoff

"In a twenty-two-room mansion on the family's estate near Kiev you lived with your tyrannical mother."

"In my childhood, yes."

"And within that hothouse of luxury, Angelica the child, rebel-in-training, audaciously demanded: 'Why, Mother, do some command and others obey?' Truly? It sniffs of the apocryphal."

"That is my recollection."

"Your recollections have been challenged before. By your one-time protégé Il Duce, for example."

"Who are you going to believe: Mussolini or a woman who gave everything to The Revolution and took nothing? Who lived all her life like a poor student in barely furnished rooms. A few books, a teapot, a jar of jam, no servant for miles."

"Even so, you did instruct Benito in Marxism."

"Marxism, not fascism. Fascism he learned on his own."

"Braggarts you have known? The short list?"

"Trotsky was supremely arrogant, always 'more royal than the king.' In time he became a great orator, but in the beginning he talked entirely too fast. Ilyich was single-minded—ruthless but never vain. To mock his vain comrades, he coined a special word: *komchvanstvo*. The boastful communist."

"You're forgetting...?"

"The megalomaniac parvenu? No one forgets Stalin. He made certain of that."

"And you? Your legacy? How would you like to be remembered? Italian Socialist, Bolshevik convert, anti-Bolshevik?"

"I would like to be remembered for what I am: a revolutionary who refused to believe that everything done in the interest of the proletarian cause automatically transformed into a just and honorable act."

"Meaning: you disagreed with Vladimir Ilyich."

"I disagreed with Vladimir Ilyich."

"You returned to Italy."

"I returned to Italy."

"You stated that anyone who believed Vladimir Ilyich developed his political sensibilities as a result of his brother's execution was 'to put it mildly, naïve.'"

"Yes."

"An opinion shared by the arrogant Lev Davidovich."

"Yes."

"And yet you, Comrade Balabanoff, insisted Fanny Kaplan was alive and well and boarding in Siberia."

"I did."

"So who's being naïve now?"

"Nadya Krupskaya assured me. In the Kremlin, she threw her arms around my neck, sobbing. She said about the fate of Fanya Kaplan: 'A revolutionary executed in a revolutionary country! Never!'"

"But Nadya Krupskaya did not rule the Kremlin."

"I would rather be a victim of power than a holder of it."

"So you've written. But—last question—would any man write, much less believe, the same?"

"Tell Inessa"

"Nadya," Inessa said, sweeping toward her with outstretched arms.

Even in distress, Inessa moved with grace.

Unwittingly she remembered her own awkward rush up the stairs. Twice she had tripped. The first time she had caught herself; the second time the driver had helped her to her feet.

"Have you hurt yourself?" the driver asked.

Beneath her skirts her knees burned—trivial pain. Ilyich had been shot. Scraped knees were nothing, nothing!

Her clumsiness, Inessa's grace.

She did not want to cry on Inessa's shoulder but could not seem to stop. Her tears wet the collar of Inessa's dress.

"I am ruining your dress," she said, raising her head.

"A dress is only a dress."

Those words would have sounded absurd spoken by Inessa in any other circumstance, in any other context.

But not now, not now.

"Ilyich is tougher than any bullet. You know that. *We* know that."

"Three bullets," her mother whispered in correction. "There were three."

Then it was Inessa who pulled away—in alarm.

"But now he is…improving," Inessa said carefully, watchfully.

Neither she nor her mother could confirm that claim.

"Nothing is certain," her mother said.

Inessa's face had grown so thin, so hollowed. The tumults of Paris had never seemed longer ago, farther away, of so little consequence than at this moment, Volodya struggling for breath, surrounded by surgeons. To be in love was to be alive. What did it matter whether Ilyich and Inessa had fallen in love, as long as they were alive?

She bit hard into her lip. She must not again start weeping.

"Varvara is on her way," Inessa said. "She was delayed. I did not want to wait.…"

"Go, sit with him," she urged Inessa. "Talk to him. Soothe him."

"Yes, Inessa. Do as Nadya says," her mother echoed. "We will be here. We will greet Varvara."

Inessa went to Ilyich; she and her mother settled in chairs beside the bedroom door. Amid a constant flow of doctors and messengers and strangers, they sat in silence, gripping hands. Without the anchor of her mother's hand she might fall to the floor and keep falling, for the universe had lost all dimension.

Maria Ilyinichna returned—from where, she could not conceive.

"Why are you out here? Who is with Volodya?"

"Inessa," she said. "And Varvara is on her way."

"Then I will join Inessa."

"Leave them in peace," her mother said.

Through the closed door, she heard Inessa coughing. She heard in bits and spurts Ilyich's own hoarse voice. Looking up, she saw a young woman she did not at once recognize. Varvara! She could not believe the young woman was truly Varvara. Simply at the sight of Inessa's daughter, no longer a child—almost 17!—she began to cry.

"I would have been here much sooner, but the trains…," Varvara apologized.

The trains did not run on schedule. The food did not reach the people. The committees did not agree on solutions. And now Ilyich had been shot.

Who would lead The Revolution, who would run the state, if not Ilyich?

Rejoining them, Inessa herself looked wounded.

"I had not expected so many…bandages."

"Volodya was gravely injured, Inessa!" Maria Ilyinichna flared. "Of course there are bandages!"

Inessa held out a trembling hand to her and she took it, squeezing bones.

"I did not hide my shock well, Nadya. Ilyich noticed. He saw my fear."

"And mine as well," she said. "We are not made of stone."

And yet she worried the same as Inessa. If Ilyich read hopelessness in their faces, he might lose courage. He might not fight.

But of course he would fight!

What was she thinking?

Ilyich always fought, harder than anyone.

"Volodya is also frightened," her mother said. "He has been shot; he has not grown stupid."

"He is *not* frightened!" Maria Ilyinichna insisted. "And I thank you, Yelizaveta Vasilevna, to refrain from putting forth that rumor!"

Inessa had begun distractedly wandering the outer room. "What was it you used to say, Yelizaveta Vasilevna? How did you phrase it? 'If Ilyich is the brain of The Revolution, Nadya is its spine.'"

Her mother nodded.

"But I am not," she said miserably.

"Yes, Nadya, you are. You have more strength than all of us. You have always had more strength."

"May I see him, Aunt Krupa? Would it disturb him if I went in for a moment?"

"Another time, Varvara," Maria Ilyinichna ruled.

"Nadya?" said Inessa. "Would Ilyich want to see Varvara?"

"It is not a good idea, Inessa! Please abide by a sister's judgment!"

"But Inessa did not ask permission of Volodya's sister. She asked it of his wife," her mother said.

Inessa had begun to shiver, to blow on her fingers as if to warm them.

"Come with me into the hallway, Nadya," Inessa said. "I will be brief. I will not keep you."

But in the hallway, Inessa could not speak for coughing—a dreadful cough that went on and on.

"You must take care of *yourself*, Inessa!" she pleaded. "We need you. Volodya needs you!"

"Yelizaveta Vasilevna! Join us!" Inessa called in pieces. She had coughed up blood. Red flecks dotted her lips.

At the sight of Inessa's blood, her mother sent Varvara back into the room to retrieve a handkerchief from the dresser. To Inessa, her mother said: "Do not be a stranger, 'Nessa. Come again soon."

Inessa's answering smile was too faint, too fleeting. "But should that prove impossible..."

No, she wanted to shout. *Do not speak this way! Do not dare talk of endings!*

"…I leave you, Yelizaveta Vasilevna, with a mission."

"You are only to name it."

"Protect wife from sister."

"That you can depend on," her mother said.

"I can defend myself against Maria Ilyinichna!"

"But hesitate to do so," Inessa said, wiping her mouth with the handkerchief.

"Mama is right, Aunt Krupa. You are too forbearing of Maria Ilyinichna."

"You see, Nadya? Even Varvara has noticed," Inessa said.

"Stop this talk! Stop it! Ilyich has been shot! Nothing else matters!"

"But it does, Nadya," Inessa said slowly and simply, as if speaking to a dim-witted child. "Maria Ilyinichna is taking this opportunity to push you farther aside. Do not let that happen. For your own sake and for Ilyich."

Comrade Stalin

You are perhaps thinking that I have been slighting the Georgian in this account? I wish I could slight him further and forever. Unfortunately permanent avoidance of Josif Vissarionovich Dzhugashvili was not possible for the Krupskayas or the world.

I am aware that many consider Lenin and Stalin two of a kind. As someone who knew them both, I give this opinion: they were not. Compared to the Georgian, my son-in-law was a gentleman scholar of conviction and principle. Comrade Stalin was not a man of refinement; he had no delicate parts. He had no honor. He had no scruples. But his will bested even the willful Ilyich.

By 1918 Comrade Stalin had successfully insinuated himself into the highest ranks of the Party. Stealthily and, though I shudder to praise him, ingeniously, he had succeeded in building up influence within the Kremlin and beyond. Prior to Ilyich's shooting, his vaulting ambitions had little effect on the Krupskayas. Nonetheless, in any palace coup, successful or otherwise, those closest to the reigning king also find themselves at risk. Ilyich's sudden debilitation left the Krupskayas exposed and vulnerable in ways we had not been previously. The same might be said of Russia. Since, to the near exclusion of all else, my daughter and I focused on Ilyich's comfort and recovery, we did not pay sufficient attention to the machinations of Comrade Stalin. We did not recognize the gravity of his threat. Ilyich's shooting provided an excellent pretext for Comrade Stalin to consolidate and solidify his base of power. I offer such conclusions in retrospect. At the time I did not know or care about Comrade Stalin's activities as long as I was spared the man's presence.

My memories of Friday, August 30?

Before Ilyich left the Kremlin to speak at the Michelson Factory on the Serpukhovaya, I insisted he change into the fresher shirt that I had that morning laundered. A fresh shirt for the bloodying, as it happened. As usual, my fiddling with his clothes both irritated and relieved my son-in-law. He did not appreciate the delay but someone else seeing to his presentability meant he need not bother. Even a man as fastidious as Ilyich ignored his wardrobe in 1918.

"Now I am at my loveliest?" Ilyich asked as I stood back to inspect the broader view. "I am officially approved?"

"You are an improvement," I said. "Beyond that, I will not vouch."

My regret?

That I did not embrace him during that bout of foolishness, that I did not remind him of my affection with at least a kiss on the cheek. You can understand such sorrow, surely? Those teasing moments would be my last with an Ilyich who was completely Vladimir Ilyich. In a few hours' time, a shooter's bullets would turn a sleep-deprived but otherwise fit and capable man struggling to lead Russia into a man gasping for breath.

Whether the bullets that struck him came from Fanya Kaplan's revolver or another's, I cannot definitively say. The Chekists were convinced. The woman confessed—but confessions can be extorted, particularly when they serve expedience. After visiting the accused in custody, Nadya believed Fanya Kaplan to be mad. But the deranged are not always murderous; sometimes they are merely dupes.

Ilyich, I suppose, could be considered lucky. He survived the attack. He did not die on Serpukhovaya pavement. He returned to work. Within a week of the shooting, he was sitting up in bed, arm in a sling, reading through telegrams. "Eager," as my Nadya praised, "to get back into harness."

But now in the Kremlin there were others issuing orders and being obeyed.

At Ilyich's bedside, Comrade Stalin behaved like a dog with its master. Elsewhere his obsequiousness disappeared. You recall him in his Red Army uniform? It was as if a tailor had tried to dress a beast of burden. His face was craterous. He had a withered arm and, according to rumor, several fused toes. That gossip had supposedly been put about by Comrade Stalin's wife following one of their more violent marital altercations. In time if I had been told his boots covered a demon's hooves, I would not have been surprised.

Nadya entered and left the bedroom with Comrade Stalin when he visited. At no moment did she leave him alone with Ilyich. On his way out, invariably, he commented on Ilyich's progress.

"Vladimir Ilyich is looking almost himself today," he would say. Or: "A strong one, Vladimir Ilyich. Stronger by the hour." And once: "We must make sure his recovery continues, Comrade Krupskaya. He must not take on too much too soon."

"Ilyich and his doctors will be the judge of that, Comrade Stalin," my daughter answered coolly.

Out of "concern for Vladimir Ilyich," Comrade Stalin had personally taken charge of Ilyich's security, we were informed. Thereafter, Comrade Stalin would vet Ilyich's bodyguards, drivers and office staff.

"Five security men will accompany Vladimir Ilyich whenever he leaves the Kremlin. An armed bodyguard will remain at Vladimir Ilyich's side at all times. If his personal bodyguard is assaulted, Vladimir Ilyich will be able to press an alarm at his desk. Vladimir Ilyich must have a new chauffeur, a dedicated Party member. We are also replacing Vladimir Ilyich's office staff. They, too, must be dedicated Party members, without blemish."

There was no "we." There was Comrade Stalin.

"You have not discussed these changes with Ilyich," Nadya objected.

"I have discussed them with Maria Ilyinichna."

"Who is sister, not wife," I said.

It was not the first time I had argued the point but to insist that Comrade Stalin recognize and honor the distinction was reckless of me. Reckless and extremely unwise.

"Vladimir Ilyich was shot by a Socialist Revolutionary. He was gunned down by an enemy of The Revolution. There was a security failure. This must not happen again."

My Nadya disagreed with nothing in that litany and yet she was breathing like a horse.

"You plan to institute such changes without consulting Vladimir Ilyich?"

"Why trouble Vladimir Ilyich with such details? He must concentrate on his health."

You see how the Georgian maneuvered? How was Nadya to oppose increased security for Ilyich or arrangements that allowed Ilyich to focus on getting well?

To me and only to me, she seethed: "He is trying to isolate Volodya. He is positioning himself as gatekeeper."

And Maria Ilyinichna is helping, I thought. But what I said, I believed: "He cannot outmaneuver Ilyich, Nadya. Even a recuperating Ilyich."

A Stalin primer: the general amnesty that followed the February Revolution freed him from prison. Back in Piter and in control of *Pravda,* he supported Kerensky and refused to publish Ilyich's call to overthrow the Provisional Government. He did not, at the onset, support Ilyich's All Power to the Soviets program. Then he realized the wagon to which he ought to hitch his star.

We underestimated him, all of us.

The refined and sophisticated Lev Davidovich underestimated him because he was a "crude mediocrity" whose theoretical writings were strewn with "sophomoric errors."

Vladimir Ilyich underestimated him when he appointed him General Secretary of the Central Committee, calling him "Comrade Card Index" to the Georgian's pockmarked face.

My Nadya underestimated him. As General Secretary, Comrade Stalin created a network of Party bosses throughout Russia who viewed him as a "man of the people," someone who spoke their idiom, unlike the "silver-tongued Jews."

A Red Army political commissar.

The People's Commissar of Nationalities.

A member of the Revolutionary Military Council.

The member of the Central Executive Committee of the Congress of Soviets in receipt of monthly reports from the Cheka on both the lowly and the grand.

Such was Comrade Stalin's revolutionary trajectory. He was here, he was there, he was everywhere. And in 1918 where he could not be, he installed his wife. Now serving as the second of Ilyich's private secretaries, the other Nadezhda, Nadezhda Alliluyeva, Comrade Stalin's battered bride.

INTERVIEW WITH HISTORY
Nadezhda Alliluyeva Stalina

"Another Nadya. Another revolutionary. Another female under her husband's thumb. Why pay attention? Why listen to you? Why bother?"

"Because in this story I am cast as Lenin's betrayer. The personal secretary who shared his secret files with Josif."

"And such is not the case?"

"History is too concerned with Vladimir Ilyich. There were other good Bolsheviks."

"Your husband, for instance?"

(Silence.)

"Rumor or fact: You were 16 when you married 39-year-old Josif Vissarionovich Dzhugashvili. Prior to the legalities, he raped you on a train. Previous to bedding you, he slept with your promiscuous mother."

"I was 16. Correct."

"You, yourself, disliked being a mother and were no stranger to the abortionist's knife. Friends and enemies of the people alike described you as 'hysterical,' 'insanely jealous.' A good Bolshevik, yes, but 'professionally discontented.'"

"If you didn't work, you were just a *baba*."

"Nadya Krupskaya distrusted you."

"Nadya Krupskaya distrusted many."

"Josif Stalin disliked Nadya Krupskaya."

"He had no fondness for homely women."

"Your husband called you 'excess baggage.' You called him a 'tormentor'—of you, his children, of Russians in general. It was then he grabbed you by the throat."

(Silence.)

"Prior to putting a Mauser to your head, you were a woman who: regularly threatened suicide; no longer shared her husband's bed; tried to enrage the man with whom you no longer slept by dancing with a Bolshevik comrade partial to ballerinas under twenty."

(Silence.)

"Alas, your husband was too drunk to notice the provocation."

(Silence.)

"Or: your husband noticed and didn't remotely care."

(Silence.)

"Tell us, Nadya Alliluyeva, was yours a suicide of despair or spite?"

(Silence.)

"Thank you for the clarification. We suspected as much."

"They Needed To Be Shot and We Shot Them"

Ilyich's shooting at the Michelson Factory did not count as the only famous or infamous shooting during the summer of 1918, of course. In July, the last tsar and tsarina, their daughters and son, were lined up and shot in an Ekaterinburg basement. Nicholas II's royal English cousins had refused his family sanctuary. His royal German cousins had no further use for him after the signing of the Treaty of Brest-Litovsk. Who, then, would save them?

The monarchists, the Whites, Nadya believed.

"Nicholas and his family had become a rallying point," my Nadya justified. "They needed to be shot and we shot them."

It has been reported that when Nicholas II learned that he and his family were headed for the merchant Ipatiev's house in the Urals, thereafter known as "The House of Special Purpose," even affectless Nicky emitted a groan of despair.

"I would have gone anywhere but to the Urals," he supposedly said. "The people there are bitterly hostile to me."

Had she been in the room to hear that comment, Nadya would unquestionably have taken exception—not to its conclusion of hostility, to its presumption of choice. The deposed tsar no longer controlled where he and his family went or did not go. That, the Bolsheviks decided. They also decided when the family should perish.

Originally, Lev Davidovich was slated to oversee the executions. For reasons I was not privy to, the Ural Soviet in consort with the Cheka actually fulfilled that revolutionary duty.

An angry mob met the train that delivered the captives to Ekaterinburg. The tsarina and the duchesses were pelted with dirt and spittle. Nicholas II carried his own luggage. He wore an officer's greatcoat with the epaulets removed. At the back door of the Ipatiev house, a member of the Ural Soviet greeted the prisoner thus: "Citizen Romanov, you may enter." Nicholas II protested the "impertinence." His protest was cut short. "Continue to argue and we will separate you from your family," he was told.

In their new quarters, Alexandra etched a symbol of faith into the windowpane. Faith, symbols, the intercession of monks and prayers. When did the former tsarina realize she had used up all her saviors? When did she admit, if only to herself, that doom, forestalled, had finally arrived?

Not even with her expiring breath, judging by the tsarina's behavior.

Red Army soldiers surrounded the perimeter. Former workers from the Zlokazovsky and Syseretsky factories in Ekaterinburg stood guard outside the rooms where Nicholas read and the tsarina and her daughters sewed diamonds and rubies inside their bodices.

Is the hiding of jewels the act of a woman who believes the end has come?

When the soldiers sang revolutionary songs, the former empress and her daughters sang hymns.

A few moments after midnight, July 17, the Romanovs were ordered to the basement. Nicholas II wore his military cap. He and his military cap fell first.

"They needed to be shot and we shot them," my daughter said, believed, and you could not have found a Bolshevik who disagreed. Vladimir Lenin? You imagine he suddenly felt pity for the emperor he considered responsible for his brother's murder? An eye for an eye or, increasingly, a head for an eye, a body entire for an eye.

Like Ilyich, my daughter had grown callous. The sufferings of her enemies she considered deserved. It gives me no pleasure to say it but, like their revolution, Nadya and Ilyich had become indifferent to brutality in all forms. Prior to 1918, although imprisoned, exiled and embroiled in factional Party strife, Nadya retained a bit of softness. No remnant of softness survived the events of 1918.

In Moscow of that year I had again taken to sitting at windows, gazing at blue skies, gray skies, snow falling or snow melting—atmospheric and surface conditions that did not discriminate among Russians, Red or White.

"What is it, Mama?" Nadya asked, coming upon me in such a pose, an edge to her voice. "What are you thinking that makes you wag that sharp chin?"

"You do not want to hear what your old mama is thinking, Nadya."

"A criticism of Ilyich?"

"A criticism of mankind."

"You have been reading history again," she said with exasperation. "You must know by now that it is more difficult to make history than to read it."

"There are lessons to be found in those chronicles, regardless."

"I cannot talk to you in these moods!"

"But you inquired, Nadya, *you* inquired, and now you will hear. I was thinking of descriptions of the Place de la Révolution, of guillotines, of humidity. I was thinking of springtime in Paris, 1794, of the terrible vapors said to arise from blood-soaked wood and stone, menacing the health and peace of mind of even those spared the slice of the blade. I was thinking that I should feel grateful to live where the snowfalls of autumn and winter and early spring turn red blood white and freeze its stench."

"Mama! You dare compare…"

"And I was thinking of the blood-demented women who brought their knitting to the foot of the guillotine to revel in death and its splatter. Real women Dickens immortalized in fiction. And I was thinking, Nadya, that in Russia now there is little need for fiction because it is almost as if we live in a fiction, driven by plots and counterplots."

"Fiction is a frivolity."

"Not every fiction," I said and returned to my window gazing.

Nadya had given up talking to her mother but not to the villagers and peasants. To explain Soviet policy, she set off for Kazan. I offered to accompany her—without enthusiasm but I offered. She preferred I stay with Ilyich and I ceded to those wishes. Ilyich did not share my pastime of staring out windows, but more and more I came upon him staring at the wall across from his desk. He was now prey to terrible headaches. As much as the head pain, the "rotten bureaucratic swamp" of commissariats tormented him. A practical man seeks practical solutions to the problems of a government and its people. By definition, bureaucracies do not advance practicalities. Deep furrows now scored that broad expanse of forehead. He had developed a habit, in his anxiety, of clicking his teeth.

In Nadya's absence, each time I passed, he asked: "How is Nadya? Have you heard from her? Is she well?"

"I have not heard from her in the twenty minutes since last you inquired," I replied.

"Even when she is ill, she pretends she is well," he fretted.

"As do you, Volodya."

He flinched but did not argue.

"You may be right, Yelizaveta Vasilevna, but what is the alternative? What is the alternative?"

Ilyich's concern about Nadya's health was not unfounded. She had nursed Ilyich while continuing The Revolution's work and one morning in December a Red Army soldier came upon her lying in a Kremlin hallway. She had fainted on her way to a meeting. Her face and ankles were terribly swollen from a resurgence of Basedow's disease. She suffered persistent pain from a heart ailment, first diagnosed by Ilyich's doctors. All of this physical misery she dismissed as inconsequential. She was not carrying two bullets, you see. How could her pain compare to Ilyich's pain?

I knew that she would be angry with me for interfering, but as her mother interference was not only my prerogative, it was my obligation.

"She must go away to recuperate," I told Ilyich. "While she is here, she will only look after you, not herself."

Ilyich immediately agreed; it was Nadya we had to convince.

Ideally, Nadya would have boarded at a rest home but nothing suitable could be found nearby. She refused to be parted from Ilyich and the Kremlin by any appreciable distance. Finally it was decided that she and I would stay at a secluded children's school outside of Moscow. The setting was lovely. We were surrounded by forests, not bureaucrats. I could not and cannot complain about the accommodations, but they did not restore my daughter's health.

Had I been less consumed with worry about Nadya, I might have predicted that Ilyich would be the one of the two unable to bear the separation. For months Nadya had barely left his side. Night and day she tended to him. Before he had relied on her as comrade and confidante; now he relied on her at all times for all things. My daughter would not have had it otherwise, but as her mother I tell you those expectations exerted a tremendous strain. Tremendous.

We had not been at the school a full day when Ilyich showed up for a visit. Every evening thereafter he came, driven by his chauffeur. He put in a full working day at the Kremlin and then he spent the evening with us. On each visit he brought a jug of milk for Nadya and pestered her until she drank every drop.

"Do you insist I lick the rim?" she asked.

Nevertheless, she was touched. Milk was not easy to come by, even for someone in Ilyich's position.

On January 19, Ilyich, his driver and bodyguard got a later than usual start because Maria Ilyinichna had decided to join them for the drive and did not show up at the agreed upon hour.

The bodyguard, Maria Ilyinichna, Ilyich and the jug of milk rode in the backseat. Near Kalanchevskaya Square a man in military attire shouted for their car to halt. Quite rightly, the driver began to accelerate. It was Ilyich's decision to speak to the man.

A moment later, they had all been yanked from the car and revolvers aimed at their heads.

Showing even less sense than usual, Maria Ilyinichna protested. "How dare you! This is Lenin!"

Unimpressed, the bandits took Ilyich's gun and overcoat. They wanted the milk, but that he refused to give over.

When they arrived at the school, all four looked quite queer.

"What is it?" Nadya blurted. "What has happened?"

I cannot speak for my Nadya in this instance, but I looked for blood, dripping from one or more of them. In my own panic, I did not notice that Ilyich in January wore no coat.

Maria Ilyinichna opened her mouth, but Ilyich spoke across her.

"The snow delayed us. The heavy snow."

In the hallway, he handed me the milk.

"What is this nonsense about snow, Volodya? Russians fly through snow."

"I did not want to upset Nadya," he said.

To me, he told what had happened.

"Do not tell Nadya. Even later, do not tell her," I said.

And of course it was not Ilyich or I who told. It was Maria Ilyinichna who could not resist spreading the tale.

The Death of Inessa

"Hard and merciless is the task of communism," Ilyich once wrote.

Harder and infinitely more merciless it was to become. To call it a task was euphemism. Communism had become thousands upon thousands of ever proliferating tasks. And now, helping Nadya and Ilyich carry out The Revolution's objectives were fewer and fewer trusted comrades.

Inessa Armand died in the Caucasus.

The news should not have shocked us. At Ilyich's bedside she had looked as fragile as he. And yet, we were shocked. Shocked, stunned, overcome.

To lose Inessa!

"I urged her to go to the Caucasus. It is my fault."

"No, no, Volodya. It is not your fault," Nadya said, tears streaming.

Inessa's letters of the past year had been increasingly despondent. More than once she had openly questioned the past and the choices made within it.

I fear the war will last a long time, Inessa wrote.

We are still very far from the time when the personal interest and that of society will coincide, Inessa wrote.

Maybe other people can find a bit of time and a little corner of happiness. I do not know how to do it for myself, Inessa wrote.

The letters were addressed to the three of us jointly. But there were certain letters Nadya and I kept from Ilyich. Physically, politically, he was struggling. Inessa's misgivings would have further upset him. We shielded him from Inessa's crisis of revolutionary faith. I would do the same again.

After reading one of those letters, I said to Nadya: "Ilyich chose correctly."

Never would my Nadya disappoint Ilyich with a crisis of faith.

"Inessa has given up much, Mama," she defended.

Yes. Inessa had given up Ilyich. Perhaps in my daughter's true heart that sacrifice seemed more difficult than any The Revolution required.

We were to hear of Inessa's last days from her son, Andre, who had accompanied her to the Caucasus. Ilyich had sent instructions that Inessa and Andre were to be given "the best accommodation" available in Kislovodsk, a spa town whose curative mineral waters had once been popular with tsarist officers on leave. Although the civil war had purportedly ended in April of 1920, in late August, when Inessa and Andre arrived in Kislovodsk, White Army bandits had made a command post of the surrounding hills. At night, they exchanged gunfire with the populace. His mother, Andre said, played her last sonata at the sanitarium in Kislovodsk at the request of the other guests. But she had not played with pleasure, he said. She had simply played.

Eventually, inevitably, we were to hear other reports of Inessa in Kislovodsk—blunter summaries uncolored by a son's love, descriptions of an agitated, withdrawn, emaciated woman "drunk on loneliness and despair."

Mother and son left Kislovodsk for supposedly safer Vladikavkaz, 130 miles south. But they did not stay in Vladikavkaz, continuing to Nalchik on a filthy train that lacked even rudimentary sanitation. Inessa fell ill with cholera. On September 24, after much suffering, she died, a mere 46, the same age at which Ilyich had returned from exile.

Her funeral was held in Moscow.

Much has been written about Ilyich's naked grief on that occasion. I do not deny his grief, only multiply it. All three of us grieved for Inessa. In our very different ways, we had all loved her and loved her dearly.

Comrade Armand

On the platform of Kazan Station, huddling in dark and blustery air: four motherless children, Vladimir Lenin and two Krupskayas.

Funds had been wired to the Caucasus, a guard sent to assist the fifth motherless child, stranded with the dead.

There had been difficulties finding a zinc-lined coffin.

There had been difficulties finding a suitable rail car to return Inessa Armand to Moscow.

But there had been no difficulties deciding who would write the obituary. Nadezhda Krupskaya volunteered.

On the train platform, between the two Krupskayas, Varvara Armand vows to be as strong as her once-strong mother. "I will not weep." But as the red-draped coffin appears, there are no dry eyes on the train platform.

Everyone weeps.

Everyone.

The doctors have told Vladimir Lenin he must not follow the coffin on foot, and Vladimir Lenin has told his doctors to go to hell. Only the elder Krupskaya rides to the House of Trade Unions. The rest trail the catafalque, drawn by two white horses.

The walk to the House of Trade Unions is long, ugly, a route filled with soldiers' debris, dilapidated buildings, the hissing of feral cats.

Workers en route to morning shifts start and turn on their heels.

"Is that Vladimir Lenin?"

"Is that Nadezhda Krupskaya?"

It is and it is.

Under a bier of white hyacinths, under the banner "Leaders may die, but the cause lives on," Inessa Armand will lie in state overnight.

The burial morning dawns clear and cold. At noon, the ceremonies begin. Comrade after comrade praises the fallen. The Bolshoi Theatre Orchestra plays Beethoven. The workers sing revolutionary ballads.

Inessa Armand's body, Inessa Armand's bones, are destined for the Kremlin wall. In its final procession across Red Square, the coffin is followed by Inessa Armand's children, who are followed by Vladimir Lenin and Nadezhda Krupskaya, who are followed by Communist Party officials, who are followed by the masses.

Vladimir Lenin is hatless, shrunken with grief. Nadezhda Krupskaya's hat is atrocious, huge, but still does not conceal her blotchy face.

The speeches are done. The tributes are done. Words are done. Wind rush replaces music. Red Square is empty; the crowd has dispersed. Comrade Inessa Armand once lived; she lives no longer.

One by one by one Nadezhda Krupskaya embraces the children of the dead, a second kiss for each on behalf of Yelizaveta Vasilevna, watching from the window.

"You must visit us in Gorky. Promise you will come."

Do they promise? Do they come?

Yes and yes.

For Vladimir Ilyich is also dying. Even the young recognize death at work.

Slipping

One of Ilyich's doctors, a German surgeon, suggested an operation to remove the neck bullet. The specialist believed Ilyich's violent headaches derived from lead poisoning. Our family doctor, Rozanov, strongly disagreed.

"Never have I read of lead poisoning from bullets causing headaches, Yelizaveta Vasilevna!" he said. "I am against the surgery."

We gathered together—Rozanov, the German, Nadya, Ilyich and I—to discuss the matter further.

The doctors' conflicting opinions made my Nadya very nervous. How were we to judge the better option? In whose advice were we to trust?

Ilyich was acting oddly, smiling inappropriately. It was almost as if he considered the conversation a game of wits and strategy, unconnected to his own wellbeing.

I turned toward the German, a haughty man with a cleft chin. "Our Rozanov remains skeptical. On what evidence do you base your argument?"

"I am a world-renowned surgeon, Madam. My experience speaks for itself."

I did not consider that reply an explanation; I considered it conceit.

Throughout Rozanov's description of the medical risks, the German glowered.

Contempt won the debate.

Suddenly Ilyich clapped his hands.

"We shall operate!"

"A minor procedure," the German declared, "easily performed in a Moscow hospital under local anesthetic. You will be back in the Kremlin within the day, if not the hour."

I looked at my Nadya. She did not believe the German. I did not believe the German. Rozanov's disbelief was frankly apparent. Which meant only two in the room believed the prognostication: the arrogant surgeon and the fearless patient.

On the appointed day, escorted by guards, we reassembled in the Moscow hospital. I had asked Rozanov to wait with us during the performance of this supposedly minor procedure. An array of medical instruments had already been laid out beside Ilyich. A surgeon's tools are not a comforting sight.

Ilyich remained unfazed. He jocularly advised the medical staff how *he* would go about the surgery.

"First, I would pinch the flesh"—he demonstrated on his arm— "then cut. The bullet will jump out. All the rest? Decoration."

The German surgeon laughed with Ilyich. Nadya contributed a weak smile.

The bullet was removed but its excision did not cure the headaches. Rozanov forbore from stating the obvious: the surgery had not accomplished its purpose.

Historians will attest that Russia's precarious position in 1921 was more than conducive to headaches. The Kronstadt rebellion badly rattled Ilyich. In 1905 and 1917, Kronstadt sailors had fought with him, not against. Although the Red Army successfully suppressed the Kronstadt uprising of 1921, that victory by force served to accelerate, rather than quell, discontent. The economy was in shambles. Alternatives had to be tried, even if those alternatives stank of capitalism. To rally peasant support for Ilyich's New Economic Policy and state-assisted modernization, Nadya again went to the countryside. Ilyich argued the case in Moscow: the NEP was *not* a betrayal of Communist principles, merely a temporary adjustment.

Of course the NEP constituted a "betrayal," as Ilyich well knew. To offset the ravages of war and revolution, to prevent the economy from collapsing, it was also a dire necessity.

By the Eleventh Congress, Ilyich could no longer ignore or deny the limitations imposed by illness. He simply did not have the strength to continue to run every facet of the Party himself. Such an admission injured more than his pride and manhood. For Ilyich, incapacitation represented defeat, a failure of will and character, a job half done. In retrospect, it is tempting to say that it would have been better for Russia if Ilyich had, for a little while longer, stayed in charge, regardless of diminished capacity. But perhaps by then the extension would have made no difference. Perhaps by then the Georgian's ascendancy had been secured.

Rightly or wrongly, to this hour, I blame Lev Davidovich. He was Ilyich's natural successor, the man Ilyich wanted to lead Russia if he himself could not. Ilyich had tried earlier to appoint Lev Davidovich deputy chairman of the Council of People's Commissars, but Lev Davidovich would not accept the title. Showing rare and uncharacteristic modesty, he declared himself unworthy.

"Then no one is worthy," Ilyich scoffed.

"I am a Jew," Lev Davidovich said.

"I am part Jew," Ilyich rebutted.

"You are also a political genius," Lev Davidovich said.

He was not fawning. His and Ilyich's talents were complementary but not identical. Lev Davidovich knew his strengths but feared his weaknesses. And fear kept him from accepting what he should have accepted for the sake of Russia.

Ilyich continued to exhort and argue but failed to change Lev Davidovich's mind. The latter felt too strongly that a Jew should not lead the country.

Better a Jew than a Georgian, someone should have said to Lev Davidovich, but no one did.

Gorky

In Gorky in 1922, I had cause to remember 1907, the year Ilyich first cheated death.

Fleeing Piter, en route to our second European exile, for Ilyich's safety and our own, we travelled separately from Finland to Stockholm. As an extra precaution, at the Abo docks, Ilyich engaged two Finnish workers to guide him across the ice to a nearby island where he could board the boat with less risk of arrest. In December there was also the risk of unstable ice. To reach the island, the trio had to traverse three *versts* of it in darkness.

When the ice began to slide beneath his feet, Ilyich later confided, his first thought was: *what a silly way to die*!

In Europe, hearing that sentiment, instantly, instinctively, Nadya grimaced and turned her head. She did not want to contemplate Ilyich's death then or later. In Gorky, such contemplation could not forever be avoided, but my daughter avoided it longer than anyone.

A mere month after the surgery to remove the bullet from his neck, Ilyich suffered the first stroke. He had just turned 52. He and my Nadya had been husband and wife for 24 years. We had been back in Russia for seven years, Ilyich in full command for fewer. To speed recuperation, or under the guise of that excuse, we left Moscow for Gorky. We had gone first to Gorky in 1918 after Ilyich was shot; by the summer of 1922 Gorky had replaced the Kremlin as home.

Since I could do little for Ilyich in 1922, I concentrated my efforts on protecting my daughter who had become, in those dangerous times, incapable of protecting herself. Exclusively she focused on Ilyich, on nursing Ilyich. He was her partner, her compass, the hero of The Revolution, the Soviet premier. In 1922, Nadya believed Ilyich would recover because she needed to believe in that outcome—for herself and for Russia.

If different circumstances had taken us there, I believe I would remember Gorky fondly. Prior to requisition by the Communists, the massive estate belonged to the former governor of Moscow, a man named Reibot, who had acquired the property by marrying the widow of a wealthy industrialist. Acres of cultivated parks, expansive orchards and flower gardens rimmed a palatial manor house and several smaller structures. Graceful palm trees and bowers of fern lined the walkway to the manor house. Inside were carpets and curtains of the gayest colors, the comforts and conveniences of electrical lighting and abundant bathrooms. On first sight, the manor house delighted me, but my Nadya balked.

"Too opulent.

"Too ostentatious.

"Velvet chairs? What are we to do with velvet chairs?"

I could easily imagine what to do: lounge on those plush seats, listening to birdsong and bees. There was even a telescope for viewing the night sky.

In 1918, we stayed in one of the smaller houses on the property. In 1922, we occupied the second floor of the manor house. The first floor had been given over to physicians and medical equipment. For the sake of Ilyich, in 1922, Nadya acceded to extravagant surroundings. I did not require a selfless excuse. Even the dying light of evening was lovely to behold in Gorky.

Comrade Stalin's accomplices in wresting power?

You know them as well as I.

Arteriosclerosis, paralysis, strokes one, two, three and four.

But Comrade Stalin had other accomplices, numerous others.

No prisoner in the Peter and Paul Fortress was more closely watched than my ailing son-in-law in the Gorky manor house. Comrade Stalin knew how many drops of soup Ilyich ingested at noon, when his linens were changed, what my daughter said to her husband in private. We were surrounded and encapsulated by informers.

Lydia Fotieva, who claimed to be Ilyich's loyal secretary?

She could not telephone Stalin fast enough to disclose the contents of Ilyich's letters.

Nadya Alliluyeva, Stalin's young and brutalized wife, long used to the lash of the tongue and the blow of a fist? A woman who spoke in the cadences of a terrified child and kept to the edges of every room she entered as if walls were her safety net? She would stand up to Stalin? She would not reveal what the doctors said, what my Nadya said? She would not share the gossip of the guards?

Even Maria Ilyinichna looked to the future and saving her own skin.

When Ilyich first turned against the Georgian, he had not yet lost his ability to speak.

"No more visits from Comrade Stalin," he told my Nadya.

To her brother's bedside Maria Ilyinichna came to plead the Georgian's case.

"Volodya, Comrade Stalin is distressed. He feels he is being treated like a traitor."

Nadya bent her head and straightened Ilyich's blankets.

The blankets did not need straightening; the sister needed reprimanding.

"Maria Ilyinichna, why do you bother Ilyich with such inanities? Be so good as to let an hour go by without the mention of Comrade Stalin's name."

"This is not your concern, Yelizaveta Vasilevna."

Of course it was my concern. What upset Ilyich upset my Nadya.

"Stalin loves you, Volodya," Maria Ilyinichna coaxed. "He sends warm greetings. Shall I deliver your warm greetings in return?"

"If greetings will keep him at bay."

"He is very intelligent, Volodya," Maria Ilyinichna praised.

"He is not in the least intelligent," Ilyich said and closed his eyes. "But he is working to bury me all the same."

She Did Not Like the Manor House

She, who had grown so fat and wide, felt small in the manor house, diminished. She could never get used to the distances between rooms, the lengths of the staircases, the corridors that echoed.

Why could she not adjust? The Kremlin had endless corridors. She had not minded those.

"In the Kremlin, you were too busy to notice echoes," her mother said.

"We are also busy here," she said.

Her mother patted her cheek.

"Tending to the sick is a different kind of labor. It permits the mind to wander."

Ilyich's wandering thoughts tortured him. They had failed the workers, he said. They had failed Russia.

"We have made colossal blunders, Nadya. We must correct them."

"And we will. You will, with the help of Lev Davidovich," she promised the invalid in the narrow wooden bed.

In the evenings, to soothe and distract him, she had begun to read fiction.

About echoes, about illness, her mother would not tease. But about fiction, Yelizaveta Vasilevna still teased.

"Read Volodya *Cricket on the Hearth*," her mother suggested, freshening the bowl of lilacs beside the bed.

Ilyich waved his hand: no.

"No, Volodya, no? When you so enjoyed the stage version?"

And then Ilyich reached to pinch her mother.

In Moscow, as a treat for Yelizaveta Vasilevna, the three of them had attended the theatrical version of the Christmas yarn penned by Charles Dickens. The curtain had scarcely risen before Ilyich began fidgeting.

During the exchange between the old toymaker and his blind daughter, he abruptly left his seat. She and her mother found him scowling in the theatre's lobby.

"Saccharine sentimentality," he spat. "I cannot watch such rubbish."

She completely agreed with Ilyich. But she had remained in her seat until intermission for her mother, who in the lobby stood between them, sulking mightily.

"You promised me a night at the theatre, Volodya. Not a partial night."

"It is insufferable! Unendurable!" Ilyich said. "Do not subject me to your Dickens again, Yelizaveta Vasilevna!"

In Gorky, striking a theatrical pose at the end of Ilyich's bed, her mischievous mother said: "You would prefer me to act the parts, Volodya? Where shall I begin? With the toymaker or his daughter?"

Ilyich grinned. A crooked grin, but a grin.

"And for tomorrow's entertainment, perhaps I will return with scarves and dance as Isadora Duncan. You will be quite impressed, Volodya! Your mother-in-law has been practicing her dancing steps!"

Her old, shrewd mother.

She could not have endured Gorky without her mother.

Fighting Back

Photos from the summer of 1922 wrench my heart not only in what they reveal but in what they portend. Nadya and Ilyich in the sun: she, sad and watchful in her ankle-length jumper; Ilyich, in his workman's cap and orthopedic shoes staring quizzically toward the camera as if he cannot comprehend what is happening to him.

And yet during Ilyich's long, terrible decline, there were stretches of lucidity and mobility. More than once he overcame the effects of paralysis and regained control of his writing arm as well as his speech.

Until the next stroke reversed the progress.

Until he had to restart the fight all over again.

Predictably, the better he felt, the more difficult he was to treat. If the doctors agreed that he could read for one hour, he read for two. If he was allowed to dictate for fifteen minutes, he continued for thirty. Such actions placed my Nadya in an untenable position. She did not wish to upset Ilyich; she did not want to disobey the doctors' orders. Despite Comrade Stalin's attempts to isolate us, my daughter was not entirely ignorant of developments in Moscow and shifting alliances within the Party's innermost circles. Nonetheless, there were Politburo decisions she did not share with Ilyich. Another burden for my Nadya, that nondisclosure. For decades, she and Ilyich had shared every detail of political strategy and struggle.

My daughter's ability to hide her feelings improved markedly during our years of exile. In the hallways of Gorky, for the most part, she maintained that talent. Facing Ilyich, she was less successful.

"You are keeping things from me! Which is dearer to you? Me or the Party?"

"Volodya!" I protested at that harshness.

"The one and the other," Nadya answered. "You are dear and the

Party is dear."

An evasion and utterly the truth.

Certain letters Ilyich dictated to Lydia Fotieva, his official secretary. It was Lydia Fotieva who copied down Ilyich's rebuke to Comrade Stalin, excoriating the general secretary's "violent high-handedness" and "chronic insubordination." Since it was a letter written to Stalin, copied personally by Lydia Fotieva, her spying duties that day were rendered lighter than usual.

Ilyich also dictated letters to Nadya. It was Nadya who conveyed Ilyich's congratulations to Lev Davidovich for successfully thwarting Stalin on the issue of foreign trade.

While Ilyich dictated that letter to Nadya, the other Nadya listened behind the door.

How do I know this?

I found her with her ear to the wood, eyes gleaming.

Occasional bouts of euphoria spun Ilyich toward a false optimism—that I cannot deny. But even as an ill man, he remained predominantly a realist. The lime trees were in bloom when he asked Nadya to bring him a copy of the remarks he had made at the dual funeral of Paul Lafargue and Laura Marx. I remember that detail because I remember apprehension mixing with the fragrance of lime blossoms.

"I do not think we have a copy of it here," Nadya said.

"It is here," Ilyich insisted. "You would not have left it behind."

When my daughter returned to the room, she held what she would rather not have held. At Ilyich's request, she began to read aloud.

"Comrades, on behalf of the Russian Social-Democratic Labor Party, I wish to convey our feelings of deep sorrow on the deaths of Paul and Laura Lafargue, gifted disseminators of the ideas of Marx."

My daughter read on.

Struggling to sit straighter, Ilyich grimaced. I repositioned his pillows but not to his satisfaction. Nadya set aside the speech to help.

"I had wanted to say over their graves that their work had not been in vain."

"Yes," Nadya said.

"There was not much to celebrate in 1911," he acknowledged. "The movement was fragmented. We could count the number of supporters on our fingers."

"Yes," said Nadya again.

"It was not a good time for revolutionaries."

Neither Nadya nor I disputed that statement. It had indeed been a dark time.

"Once they felt they could no longer contribute, the Lafargues were content to die. Perhaps I should feel the same."

"Volodya!" I rebuked because my Nadya was too stricken to speak.

Can I say beyond doubt that he did not wish to die to escape excruciating pain? Of course I cannot. But never did he ask Nadya to help him accomplish such a task. That notion, that lie, is Maria Ilyinichna's villainy at work. It is Maria Ilyinichna who put about the story that Ilyich asked my daughter for poison and Nadya lacked the courage to administer a fatal dose. Of Maria Ilyinichna, history should ask this: why did the devoted sister, so contemptuous of my Nadya's failure of nerve, not fulfill the supposed request herself?

You see?

Maria Ilyinichna cannot have it both ways. If she accuses my Nadya of cowardice, she must also admit to her own.

The people of the village of Gorky brought us fruits and vegetables and, occasionally, butchered meat, depriving their own tables to feed Vladimir Lenin's household. Nadya accepted the gifts because to do otherwise would have insulted. But when the basket of fruit or vegetables arrived in the arms of an underweight child, she invited that child into the kitchen for a chat, made up two plates, and insisted her guest finish every bite.

It was I who opened the door to the peasant with the gift dog: a mutt of indeterminate breed, but bright-eyed and frisky, tail wagging. The peasant who brought him sometimes worked in the gardens of Gorky. Whenever possible, Ilyich spent part of the afternoon on a garden bench. The open air always improved his spirits. The peasant had noticed Ilyich playing fetch with the groundskeeper's dog.

"This one is better with the stick," the peasant explained. "He will not make Vladimir Lenin wait so long between throws."

Just then my daughter came up behind me. Because Nadya is tall and I am short, she had no trouble seeing the prancing dog.

"Ah, a little performer," she cooed, dropping to her knees to pet the creature.

Objection was pointless; she had already taken him into her heart.

"And what are we to call our new friend?" I asked. "His fur is almost red. As such he qualifies as 'Comrade.'"

"Why not a name from Piter?" Nadya proposed instead, scratching the dog's belly. "Something that reminds us of home."

And so he was christened "Nevsky."

Thereafter wherever Nadya went, her companion followed. Now the hallways of the manor house echoed the clacking of a dog's toenails. A relief, you see. A comfort. How could I truly object to the presence of an animal that consoled my Nadya?

After Ilyich's second stroke but before his third, the doctors proposed a multiplication exercise to test his mental acuity. Like the star student he had been, Ilyich eagerly accepted the challenge. He was to multiply twelve times seven. That evening, when I brought his dinner soup, he smiled triumphantly.

"I have solved the mystery, Yelizaveta Vasilevna! The answer is eighty-four!"

My daughter, on her stool by the bed, breathed shallowly, as if a strap had tightened across her chest.

"Show her, Nadya!" Ilyich proudly insisted. "Show her my calculations."

He had covered more than half the pages of his notepad with numbers—sprawling, awkwardly formed numbers. For more than three hours, the great Vladimir Lenin had worked to calculate twelve times seven.

"You are too clever, Volodya," I said with tears in my eyes. "You have put us all to shame."

Less than a week afterward, while ferrying Volodya's bed sheets from his room to the laundry, I interrupted a conversation between Lydia Fotieva and the other Nadya.

"Comrade Stalin says Lenin is kaput," Lydia Fotieva confided. "A sick man surrounded by womenfolk."

When Nadezhda Alliluyeva saw me, she backed closer to the wall, on guard for reprisals. Lydia Fotieva showed neither fear nor embarrassment. She did not retract her statement; she did not soften it. She merely returned to her desk.

I had become no one of consequence, you understand: the mother-in-law of a man no longer in power. Behaving with discretion in my presence was no longer required. Nor was courtesy.

A Call from Comrade Stalin

The telephone rings in Gorky's manor house. Lydia Fotieva, Vladimir Lenin's secretary, answers and goes in search of Vladimir Lenin's wife.

"Comrade Stalin wishes to speak with you."

When Nadezhda Krupskaya rises from the bedside stool, Yelizaveta Krupskaya takes her place.

The distance between stool and telephone is substantial; nonetheless, when her daughter screams, Yelizaveta Vasilevna hears and runs as best she can. Her legs are old and faulty; she does not get there first.

The telephone is off the hook, the receiver swinging free. The dog is barking furiously.

On the floor, knees pulled to her chest, Nadezhda Krupskaya rocks and screams. Above her stands Maria Ilyinichna, the jeering sister.

With the strength of fury, Yelizaveta Vasilevna slaps the sister of Vladimir Lenin in the face.

"Leave us!"

"Your daughter is pathetic."

Which earns the sister a second, harder slap.

"Stay and I will beat you senseless. Do you doubt, Maria Ilyinichna, that I possess the will in this moment to beat you senseless?"

He may have been drunk when he called—Comrade Stalin is often drunk.

Even so, the communication is no spontaneous act.

The General Secretary is fully aware of the fragile state of Vladimir Lenin's wife, the precariousness of her physical and emotional balance. He has been apprised of the defects of her still beating heart. And should their conversation cause Nadezhda Krupskaya to collapse, Comrade Stalin can be reasonably certain of the effect of that collapse on Vladimir Lenin.

And so, when the wife of Vladimir Lenin picks up the telephone in response to his curt summons, it is in the interest of Comrade Stalin, drunk or preternaturally sober, to accuse her in the crudest possible language of discussing Party matters with Vladimir Ilyich, of telling Vladimir Ilyich what the doctors and the Politburo have forbidden he be told.

In the arms of her mother, Nadezhda Krupskaya groans and weeps and repeats the vulgar abuse.

"Parasite! Syphilitic whore! Continue your defiance, Comrade Krupskaya, and the world will know the name of Vladimir Ilyich's true widow."

Is it the word "widow"? Is it the Inessa Armand taunt? Does Comrade Stalin forget Comrade Krupskaya is the daughter of a spitfire?

In her protest to the Politburo, Nadezhda Krupskaya rails: *This is not my first day in the Party. In the whole of my 30 years I have never been spoken to so coarsely or treated so rudely. What can and cannot be discussed with Ilyich I know better than any doctor or Stalin.*

And then, again: *This is not my first day in the Party.*

Nor would it be her last.

Secrets

"If you do not tell Ilyich, I shall!" her mother threatened.

"No!"

She had overreacted. She should not have screamed and carried on in front of Maria Ilyinichna and her mother. She had become hysterical when she should have stayed calm, contemptuous, indifferent to the threats of Stalin. She had made a mistake; she would not compound that error by telling Ilyich.

"Nadya!"

"No, Mama. I will not upset Ilyich simply because the Georgian has insulted me."

"This insult goes beyond your honor, daughter," her mother said. "Josif Vissarionovich Dzhugashvili must not get away with this. He must be punished, severely and soon."

"Ilyich cannot take on Party squabbles."

"Then tell Lev Davidovich."

"I have protested through Party channels. That is the proper action to take."

"But is it enough?" her mother asked.

"It must be."

"Nadya, listen to your mama. While there is still time, tell Ilyich."

"No," she said again.

For two and a half months, she kept to that pledge, that refusal to involve Ilyich. She wrote letters; she objected; she denounced. On her own she worked to defeat Stalin's designs, block his consolidation of power, thwart his usurpation of the Party.

And failed.

"Only one man in Russia can stop Stalin," her mother said.

"And that man is ill."

"But commands great influence."

Did Ilyich still command great influence? If no one in Moscow had stood up to the General Secretary by now, would mere orders from a sickbed in Gorky stiffen backbones?

"Come, daughter," her mother said. "We will tell him together."

Beside her, Nevsky whimpered.

"The dog is also against it," she stalled.

"We no longer have a choice, Nadya. Comrade Stalin has taken advantage of our silence. He has used it to strengthen his position. We have been helping the enemy. That must cease."

The End

Perhaps I should not have insisted that my daughter tell Ilyich about Comrade Stalin's telephone call. But I believed then and, despite the outcome, continue to believe that it was wrong to keep such a secret from Ilyich. I also believed it to be a secret that, if kept, would hurt my Nadya. She could not save Volodya—no one could. But if she had not tried to save the Party, his legacy, through every means at her disposal, she would not have been able to forgive herself.

Throughout the years, on many occasions, I had seen Ilyich infuriated to the point of near combustion. Never had I seen him as he was after learning of the Georgian's crude treatment of Nadya. His wrath was unparalleled. With his stronger arm he smashed his water glass and overturned the table it had set on. Nevsky bolted from the furor. The dog's howls were no louder than Ilyich's.

"Pack for Moscow. We leave at once."

When the doctors appeared and forbade that journey, Ilyich screamed for Lydia Fotieva.

"Get the swine Stalin on the telephone. We will see this time who is on the receiving end of abuse."

Far too quickly his secretary returned with "profuse apologies." Comrade Stalin could not be reached.

Ilyich denounced, he threatened, he ordered recriminations, but as the day stretched on it became only too obvious that no one outside his sickroom listened to or cared about Vladimir Lenin's upset, orders or ravings.

"Take down what I say, Nadya! Take it down!"

My daughter picked up pen and paper. What Ilyich said, she wrote.

You have been so rude as to summon my wife to the telephone and use bad language. Although she was prepared to forget this, I have no intention of forgetting what has been done against me. And what has been done against my wife, it goes without saying, I consider done against me.

Overnight, Ilyich worsened. His pulse raced. He would take no food. Nadya and I were both with him when, in a moment of cruel clarity, he saw what was coming.

"Oh hell, oh hell," he groaned. "The old illness is back!"

Did the revelation I insisted upon precipitate his third stroke?

Will you think me heartless for declaring the cause immaterial? We had lost; Stalin had won. Death would soon end Volodya's torment; it would be those he left behind, his survivors, who would suffer the victor's punishments.

The third stroke rendered Ilyich speechless. He could not move; he could not blink. Night and day his tortured eyes remained open, staring.

During those last months, my Nadya was terribly, terribly brave. She held Ilyich's hand. She blotted his lips. She changed his sheets.

On January 7, 1924, Nadya asked the guards to cut down a fir tree and invited the children of the village to a party. She had not, in her trials, become religious. Every atheist in Russia decorates a *yolka* in January, as do those of the Russian Orthodox faith.

I supervised the decorations and, along with the guards, wrapped presents for the children. The tree with its lighted candles looked especially lovely, a glittering vision. Nadya got Ilyich dressed and the guards brought him downstairs for the singing. Nevsky chased after the children until they succeeded in tiring even him and then he curled up between Nadya and Ilyich.

During the afternoon of January 21, Ilyich's breathing became labored.

Nadya had been reading at his side.

"Mama, Mama! The doctors! At once!"

They had only to mount the stairs, yet during that briefest of intervals Ilyich's temperature soared.

The force of the convulsions hurled him side to side on the narrow bed.

Nadya held on as best she could.

"Madam Lenin! You will injure yourself!"

And she did. Her bruises took months to heal.

At last the convulsions stopped, and then, too, his breathing. A little before seven in the evening, Vladimir Ilyich Lenin was pronounced dead in Gorky.

My Nadya's bulging eyes remained dry. She did not leave the body laid out on a table, surrounded by pine branches, even to change her clothes.

Once news had spread, the villagers of Gorky formed a line between palm trees and waited for the opportunity to pass Ilyich's corpse and pay their respects.

As still as that corpse, my Nadya sat beside it and beside Nadya, her dog.

I did not urge my daughter to leave her chair. No one, mother included, could have persuaded her to abandon that post. She intended to be with her husband's body for as long as that nearness could be accomplished.

The peasant who had brought Nevsky to us agreed to take him back with a proviso.

"I will keep him for Comrade Krupskaya," he told me. "But he will remain Comrade Krupskaya's dog. And I will remind him, daily, that he does not belong to a peasant. He is the dog of the wife of the great Vladimir Lenin."

We assumed Ilyich would be buried beside his mother, Maria Alexandrovna, in Piter.

That had been his wish.

We did not know Stalin's plans to make a travesty of that wish.

Not then. Not yet.

INTERVIEW WITH HISTORY
Maria Ilyinichna Ulyanova, Part II

"You have returned."

"For the wrap-up slander."

"You accuse *me* of slander? Vladimir Lenin's *sister*!?!"

"Do keep up. The kinship fact is old hat. We've come back for your take on Stalin's reprimand of Nadya Krupskaya."

"He spoke sharply to her and she fell to the floor, rolling and sobbing. It was ridiculous, her behavior. A mountain made of a mole-hill."

"The poison request? Again, your version?"

"Volodya knew he was finished. He asked for cyanide. Nadya Krupskaya hemmed and hawed."

"Which left you, little sister."

"By then the Politburo had voted."

"Against suicide?"

"Against assistance."

"A brother's request, a Politburo order, and you sided with the latter. Interesting."

"Are you deaf?!? The Politburo voted against it!"

"Your statement to the joint plenum in 1926. And we quote: 'In view of the systematic slander on Comrade Stalin by the opposition minority, I feel obliged to say that Vladimir Ilyich Lenin highly valued Stalin. He entrusted him with the most intimate of assignments. He asked, in his illness, only to see Comrade Stalin.'"

"It was *1926*! In 1926 my brother lay in a mausoleum."

"Toadying to save your neck. Understood."

"Why not ask the esteemed widow what she did to save her neck?"

"And succeeded, it would seem, since she saw you in your grave."

"At my funeral, she looked puffy."

"Puffy?"

"Like a puffer fish."

THE WIDOW
LENIN

Insolence

Comrades, working men and women, peasant men and women! I have a great request to make of you: do not raise statues of him, name palaces for him or stage festivals to his memory—all these were to him in life of little significance, even a burden. You wish to honor the name of Vladimir Ilyich? Establish infants' homes, kindergartens, schools, libraries, hospitals. Create a living testament to his ideals.

She had published the appeal, urged this respect.

Stalin had countered with a speech justifying "the deification" to the people: *The pilgrimage of hundreds of thousands of working people here in Russia will be followed by hundreds of millions from all parts of the earth who come to testify Lenin was the leader not only of the Russian proletariat but of all working people of the globe.*

Ilyich's wishes trampled along with her request.

"Nadya, come. Eat. You have done enough glaring for one morning," her mother said.

A Red Square monstrosity, the red marble mausoleum. And inside it, a corpse propped on a red satin pillow. A mummy on permanent display.

It repulsed her. It sickened her.

"But it is not Ilyich," her mother repeatedly reminded. "What Stalin has preserved is not Ilyich."

She knew it was not Ilyich. No more than her mother did she believe that his soul or spirit or consciousness hovered, appalled and enraged by The Revolution's corruption, the cult of Lenin. But the rage he would have felt inflamed her own. Every night in her dreams, stone by stone, she tore apart the mausoleum only to open her eyes and find it perfectly intact. A measure of Stalin's power and her powerlessness.

As much as she now despised the view from their Kremlin apartment, never would she give Stalin the satisfaction of leaving the rooms she had shared with Ilyich.

Never.

Scarcely had they returned with the body from Gorky when Josif Vissarionovich knocked with a relocation offer.

Perhaps the Krupskayas would be more comfortable elsewhere in the Kremlin? In smaller, warmer rooms, spared the buffeting winds of Red Square? In accommodations that did not house so many painful memories?

She did not say: "My memories do not pain me, comrade. The present and future of Russia pain me."

She did not say: "So you imagine you can strip me of my memories as well, Josif Vissarionovich?"

She said: "We are fine where we are. To move would disturb my mother."

"Very prudent, Nadya," her mother complimented. "The moment our last suitcase crossed the threshold Comrade Stalin would make a museum of this space. Ilyich's boots, Ilyich's ink-stained portfolio. Photographs of Lenin and Stalin side by side in Gorky."

Doctored photographs.

In Moscow one could no longer trust photographs. Lev Davidovich's image had disappeared from the archives of The Revolution. Where he had stood beside Ilyich, now stood Stalin—or air.

She had attended the Thirteenth Congress, the congress at which Stalin unveiled "Ilyich in his immortal guise." She had fought to have Ilyich's Last Testament, his denunciation of Stalin, read into the record, but Stalin had again outmaneuvered her.

Vladimir Lenin's Last Testament was based on "misinformation" supplied by Comrade Krupskaya.

Comrade Krupskaya had been under enormous strain in Gorky, caring for Vladimir Ilyich.

Comrade Krupskaya had not been thinking clearly.

She had not given up. Had Stalin forgotten her training in smuggling documents? If she could not get Ilyich's Testament read in the Soviet press, she would see that it was published elsewhere.

The *New York Times* printed the denunciation in full. The capitalists, at least, knew what Ilyich thought of Comrade Stalin.

"The document has been released in the West," her mother said. "You have succeeded. Let history do the rest."

But in Russia, history, too, had been suborned by Comrade Stalin, the revolutionary struggle rewritten and recast. On the anniversary of the October Revolution, in *Pravda*, she read as much as she could stomach before throwing the paper to the floor.

"What is his newest lie?" her mother inquired.

"That Ilyich did not arrive in Piter before the eighth of October. That all so-called Bolsheviks wanted to bring down the Provisional Government."

"He missed his calling, Josif Vissarionovich. He is a fictioneer."

Simbirsk renamed Ulyanovsk, Piter rechristened Leningrad.

Cheap theatrics. Gaudy effects.

"He is exploiting Ilyich's name!" she raged.

The shops now stocked ridiculous children's books featuring "Grandpa Lenin."

At the Education Secretariat, part of her job was to vet such travesties.

"If this one also declares 'Grandpa Lenin says to brush your teeth every day,' I refuse to read it," she informed her assistant—and was reported.

Stalin himself appeared to investigate the defiance.

"Comrade Krupskaya, I understand that this is a matter of some sensitivity. You are childless. The sting of no children now that Vladimir Ilyich is gone haunts you. I understand."

"You forget, Comrade Stalin, my work with the Young Pioneers and the Komsomol. Instead of one child, I have thousands."

Her speeches to the Executive Committee of the Education Commissariat were interrupted, heckled. Arguing in support of polytechnic instruction, she had been jeered, her ideas dismissed without discussion.

But she too could challenge. She too could shout.

"What I think, comrades, I say!"

Her own fiction.

Already she did not say half of what she thought. Tomorrow? Perhaps a quarter. But by tomorrow even a quarter might be sufficient to send her to the Chekists for questioning.

As the Widow Lenin, she enjoyed no special favors. Anyone who had been close to Ilyich, anyone whose memory or conscience contradicted Stalin's version of the present or the past was in danger of preemptive arrest. As in Piter, when Nicholas Romanov ruled, in a Moscow ruled by Stalin whenever she left the apartment she carried prisoner's provisions. Her Moscow bag contained pictures of Ilyich and her mother, the Niagara trinket Zheltishev had given her at the Smolny, a second pair of spectacles, a notebook, a pen. Even to walk the block to her desk at the Education Secretariat, she carried along her prisoner's bag and once on the street hung it from her shoulder, outside her coat.

The Widow Lenin would not go quietly to Lubyanka Prison.

Occasionally she would see someone crossing Red Square who reminded her of Lev Davidovich. Conspiring to create the illusion: the gait, the hurry, the hair. More than once she had been on the verge of marveling: "Fifty years old with such hair!"

But of course the figure in transit was never Lev Davidovich.

Lev Davidovich had spoken out against "the Stalinist course." He had been expelled first from the Central Committee, then the Party and finally from Russia. Opinions, convictions, had become hazardous possessions. Comrades who did not serve Stalin counted as adversaries.

Servant or adversary.

No other classification existed.

"Nadya, breakfast awaits! Join your mother. The bread today is almost fresh."

Her mother looked so frail, so tiny in the wheelchair. The arthritis in her hips and knees made walking impossible, but Yelizaveta Vasilevna's mind remained sharp, her tongue scathing.

And when she lost access to her mother's sharp mind and scathing tongue? When she could no longer rely on Yelizaveta Vasilevna's shrewd assessments? Whose counsel would she then seek? Whose advice would she then trust?

Her mother had begun to neaten the stack of letters that also claimed space on the breakfast table.

"By the time you return, I will have these sorted. Along with the others."

Another full mailbag leaned against the wall.

Hundreds of letters arrived daily from all over Russia, written by workers, literate peasants and old Bolsheviks, many of the envelopes simply addressed: *Babushka Krupskaya, Moscow.* The writers assumed that if their request reached her it would be honored—because she lived in the Kremlin, because she was the widow of Vladimir Ilyich, because in their estimation she remained a person of great influence. She tried not to disappoint them. She tried to answer each letter, to provide assistance and advice. With her mother's help, she tried.

"At least drink your tea," her mother urged. "You have a long day of work ahead."

"There is tea at the Secretariat, Mama. I will have a glass there."

"Do not forget your gloves! It will feel even colder on the street."

"I have my gloves, Mama."

"You will return before dark? You will not cause your old mama to worry?"

"I will return before dark," she promised as if that promise served as guarantee.

"Nadya?"

"Yes, Mama?"

"You will send word if..."

"Yes, Mama. Just as in Piter. I will send word."

Do You Think I Would Have Hesitated?

In my invalid's chair, it was difficult to reach the door, more difficult to open it. To invite Comrade Stalin inside the apartment was the most difficult feat of the three.

"Yelizaveta Vasilevna."

"Comrade Stalin. What brings you to the rooms of the Krupskayas? My daughter is at the Secretariat."

"I have come to speak with you, Yelizaveta Vasilevna."

I had not asked for the assistance but he wheeled me to an area between Nadya's home desk and the dining table. I could not reach either furnishing by stretching.

Had he meant for me to feel marooned in my own residence?

I cannot doubt it.

There are those who will tell you Comrade Stalin's breath was as foul as his politics. This was not true. It smelled sweeter than lilacs.

"Do sit, Comrade Stalin. A woman in a wheelchair does not appreciate a roaming guest."

He did not sit but moved to where I could see him. And then, from Nadya's desk and its photographs of Ilyich, of me, of Inessa, he plucked the last.

"I do not like to criticize Comrade Krupskaya."

"Then refrain," I said.

Blandly he smiled.

"We must—all of us, Yelizaveta Vasilevna—do what is best for the Party."

"You dare suggest my daughter has forgotten the Party?"

"The Party is a collective, not hers to run."

The gall of that statement. The gall!

"Competition displeases you, Comrade Stalin?"

"I come here out of love and affection for Comrade Krupskaya. To enlist your help on behalf of the Party. To save the Party and Comrade Krupskaya much trouble and embarrassment."

You recognize the intricacies of that double and triple threat? The implication that I would be harming my daughter if I did not help the snake?

"My daughter speaks her own mind, Comrade Stalin. It is not for me to interfere with that expression."

Slowly he turned the photograph he held in his hands.

Inessa now gazed at me, not Comrade Stalin.

"I am sorry to hear that you feel that way, Yelizaveta Vasilevna. A comrade who risks the reputation of the Party by insubordination also risks her own."

My pistol lay in the drawer of Nadya's desk.

If I could have reached it, if I could have grabbed it without being hindered, do you think I would have hesitated to use it?

Gladly would I have gone down in history as the assassin of Comrade Stalin. It would have meant cutting short the time that remained with my daughter, but by murdering the scoundrel I would have improved her life immensely.

"My daughter does not need anyone's advice on how best to serve the Party, including her mother's."

He returned the photograph to the desk. He had the presumption to place his thick hand upon the prominent veins of my own. Directly into my face flowed the breeze of his unobjectionable breath. But his eyes had dropped their camouflage of concern and supplication.

I saw what I was meant to see in the eyes of Comrade Stalin.

And then he took his leave.

The Other Nadya

A break in the weather on Sunday, an hour of sunshine that caused the snow to glisten.

"I feel like an outing, Nadya," her mother announced. "Perhaps we could take a turn along the Kremlin's upper path?"

The wheelchair caught on the doorframe. She was jiggling it free when Yelizaveta Vasilevna exclaimed: "The halls are now darker by day than by night. Why do you think this is so, Nadya? Has Stalin decreed we must always live in shadow?"

Quickly she checked the hallway's gloom for shadows with feet, with ears.

"Hush, Mama," she murmured.

If she could not adequately defend herself, how could she hope to defend Yelizaveta Vasilevna? If she considered herself at risk, how much more vulnerable her obstreperous, outspoken mother?

Once they reached open air, her mother insisted they stop and sniff.

"Ah. Breathe deeply, Daughter. Spring is on the way. Soon it will invade even Moscow."

She smelled no conquering spring. She smelled Kremlin sewage.

"Who is that?" her mother demanded, straining forward in the wheelchair, peering at a figure in black.

"You have forgotten the look of the other Nadya?"

"She does not look as she did in Gorky," Yelizaveta Vasilevna observed.

Perfectly true: in Gorky, Comrade Stalin's wife had appeared furtive or sly, sheepish or guilty, but she had not resembled the woman repeatedly bumping her hip against the rough wall as if to ruin on purpose her fine coat. Nadezhda Alliluyeva's spiraling hair was now riddled with gray. Twice she had run away from her husband, in the second instance to Piter. Within days she had been found and returned like chattel to the Kremlin. She was now less wife than hostage.

Skittering in their direction, the hostage seemed to see nothing and no one, but once beside them she pounced.

"Nadezhda Konstantinovna! Tell me! Tell me!"

"Stand back! You are knocking against my mother's knees!"

"Russia's First Lady! How did you bear it?"

She snatched her arm free. She shoved Nadezhda Alliluyeva away from the wheelchair. She might have said: "Russia has no First Lady," but it would have been a waste of instruction. And so to Stalin's hysterical wife she said: "Think more of the people and less of yourself. You might start there."

For a moment the other seemed chastened. Her chin dipped, her shoulders sagged. She again struck the wall with her hip. But then, in another quick change, Nadezhda Alliluyeva recovered her old slyness and spite.

"You should not have spoken to me in that manner, comrade. That was not wise."

"You are blocking our path, hindering our progress. Shall I also report those impertinences, comrade?"

They moved along noisily. The wheelchair needed oiling. She was thinking of wheelchairs, not Comrade Stalin's wife.

"A wiser man would have left Nadezhda Alliluyeva in Piter," her mother observed.

Probably, but what of it?

"Nadezhda Alliluyeva's fate matters less than little," she said.

"I was not thinking of her fate. I was thinking of her husband's. An unhappy woman is a dangerous woman. A mad woman is an unpredictable woman. Nadezhda Alliluyeva is both mad and unhappy."

"Then they are the mad married to the mad," she said with disgust.

"If he continues to force her to stay in Moscow, she may yet kill him," her mother speculated.

"Then let us hope he keeps her close," she said.

"Yes," agreed her mother. "Let us hope."

To Work

She had gotten a late start this morning, indulging her mother by agreeing to a second glass of tea.

The spring her mother predicted and she had doubted was indeed in the offing. Streaks of blue divided and boxed the gray sky. This morning's timid wind could not have knocked over a rock pigeon, much less a comrade as stout as herself. The slippery ice as well as the dirty snow had begun to drip and drain. The pavement was no longer treacherous. At least with regard to pavement for a few months she need not watch every step.

Facing Red Square, she adjusted the strap of her prisoner's bag.

If she were to enter that hideous mausoleum to converse with a corpse, she would say this: "We need another revolution, Ilyich, to depose another tyrant. A Georgian, not a Romanov, this time."

Certainly it would be convenient if Nadezhda Alliluyeva did away with her husband and saved others the trouble. But when had Comrade Stalin's wife ever acted to save others trouble? Nadezhda Alliluyeva's madness was as self-centered as her discontent.

As on every work morning, along the way she encountered comrades, former comrades, who pretended not to know her, who inched past with faces averted, caps pulled over their eyebrows. Long ago she had grown used to snubbing and shunning. Long ago she had learned to set her jaw and proceed.

If she evaded arrest between here and there, at the Education Secretariat she would enter through a side door. In her second-floor office, she would exchange minimal greetings with her disapproving assistant. She would remove her coat and prisoner's bag and hang them on the hook on the wall behind her desk. If too annoyed by the hair in her face, she would haphazardly re-pin it. She would sort through the memos and files that had arrived since yesterday. She would confirm with her assistant which of the projects must be finished within the hour, which within the day. And then she would take up her pen, lean forward and begin work.

Regardless, she would work.

Again at Windows

I would prefer to die in Piter, but preferences count so little in times such as these. I, Vladimir Lenin's mother-in-law, will die, and soon, in Moscow. About my own demise, I have no regrets, but I do not like to think of leaving my Nadya alone in this apartment at the mercy of circumstance and vengeance.

That I do not like.

In Piter, I anxiously awaited her return from the Vyborg; now, from a window overlooking Red Square, with similar trepidation, I watch her leave. Even with the eyes of old age, I can pick out my daughter on the street.

She thinks I do not know about her prisoner's bag. I know about it and, while she sleeps, add to it: a button from her father's jacket, a shard of her childhood plate. As my daughter travels with her copper wedding ring, I travel with mementos of Konstantin and Poland.

Today I see that, after adjusting the bag on her shoulder, she pivots toward the mausoleum she so despises.

Is she communing with Ilyich? Not the Ilyich who lies there, for that husk is the toy of Stalin, no more or less than a Bolshevik doll.

Many on the street refuse to acknowledge they share pavement with my daughter, hastening past as if she were contagious. To watch that slighting again and again galls me but I cannot pretend surprise. The Widow Lenin is not a favorite of the current regime. This is widely known. Comrade Stalin has made it known. He thinks the disrespect will break my Nadya. It hurts her—though she will not say so—but it will not break her. My daughter has endured prison and exile. She has lived through revolutions and civil war. She has survived the loss of Ilyich and the devastating grief of that loss. Once Nadya underestimated Comrade Stalin's strength and resolve; now he underestimates hers.

Up ahead, beyond my daughter's broad back, I am pleased to see one comrade who will not pass my Nadya without greeting her, who will be overjoyed by the chance encounter.

Inessa's child, Varvara.

It is Varvara who looks up first and recognizes her Aunt Krupa. And when she does, she stretches her arm and wildly waves.

The act of running becomes Varvara the woman no more than it did Varvara the child. Not unlike my Nadya, she is rather flat-footed. Just now she resembles a rushing, grinning, flat-footed goose.

As the two embrace, Varvara's nose smacks against Nadya's ear, the prisoner's bag collides with Varvara's satchel.

Hugging, they pitch and teeter.

As she would love a daughter of her own, my Nadya loves Varvara.

You doubt this old woman?

You imagine because Varvara was born of Inessa that Nadya cannot love her as fiercely as she would her own flesh and blood?

A child who sat on the knee of Vladimir Ilyich?

Who grew up hearing the speeches of Vladimir Lenin?

Who has been schooled in the precepts of the Great October Socialist Revolution?

Whose own mother gave her life in service to the people?

Then you do not understand my Nadya. Still you do not understand.

Two Notes for the Historically Curious

*

Yelizaveta Vasilevna Krupskaya died in 1915 in Switzerland. She did not travel home to Russia on the sealed train. She did not live to see her daughter ensconced in the Kremlin, her son-in-law shot, Stalin ascendant, or her daughter reduced to a Party hack.

**

Nadezhda Konstantinovna Krupskaya did in fact have a sly and vicious sense of humor. In the art of withering mockery, she was every bit her mother's and her husband's equal.

Kat Meads is the author of four previous novels and several collections of poetry and short fiction. She last published with Livingston Press writing as Z.K. Burrus. A native of eastern North Carolina, she lives in California and teaches in Oklahoma City University's low-residency MFA program.